6/20

To friends Mac & Kathy
Best Wishes
CCRisenhoover

SATAN'S MARK

C. C. RISENHOOVER

McLennan
HOUSE
WAXAHACHIE

Published by
McLennan House, Inc.
206 South Rogers
Waxahachie, Texas 75165

Library of Congress Cataloging-in-Publication Data

Risenhoover, C. C., 1936–
SATAN'S MARK
I. Title.
ISBN 0–918865–12–3
Library of Congress Catalog Number: 87–60035

Manufactured in the United States of America
First Printing

To Her, Again

CHAPTER ONE

It was cold that winter, much colder than usual. When the sun did make one of its infrequent appearances, it was as if you were seeing it through a pane of frosted glass. The chilling wind was constant, reaching all the way to your bones, whipping your skin and making it feel like a raw, open wound. There was no way to keep your lips from cracking and bleeding. That is, if you were forced to spend any time out-of-doors combating the elements.

For the most part, days were an abnormal gray, pierced by flurries of sleet and snow. Even the snow looked gray. It was as if some mad painter had set out to make the world all one color.

The Hayder house, which occupied the crest of a hill and faced a winding dirt road, looked as though it had been placed there as an act of defiance against the angry land. The road, sculptured from red clay turned frozen and gray, curved sharply to the right of the house past a huge tree. The tree, which looked as though its outstretched limbs were pleading for mercy to the irritated sky, stood just outside a hogwire fence that formed an irregular square around the frame house.

The structure was large, built of rough, unpainted lumber, somewhat like split logs. The weather had colored them gray as the winter sky. A porch of considerable size stretched completely across the front of the house, and through patches of snow, the tin roof showed some discolored spots, which were obviously rust.

An open hallway ran through the center of the house to a back porch. A few feet up from the floor of the back porch was a wide board nailed between two of the posts supporting its roof. It was a crudely-made table that served as a washstand.

On the table was a bucket with a dipper, and there was also a porcelain wash basin. The water in the bucket had turned to ice, freezing the dipper firmly in place. A partially used bar of soap occupied a cracked saucer beside the basin.

Henry Hayder had built this house with his own two hands, and its solidness and roughness was a testimony to the character of the man. He had built the house large to accommodate his growing family, its ceilings high for coolness in the summer, and fireplaces throughout to aid in warding off the chill of winter.

On winter days Henry liked to sit in a rocking chair in front of the living room fireplace, drinking in the music of the fire, watching multi-colored flames lap at the oak wood he had cut during the summer.

It was a time for daydreaming.

For remembering.

Henry was a strong, powerful man, with no smoothness about him, neither in looks nor manners. His leathery looking face was that of one who had spent much of this life outdoors, who was use to the harshness of nature.

Five feet ten inches tall, his muscular body belied his sixty years. Were it not for silver-colored hair, a full head of it, and the wrinkled face, he could have been mistaken for a man in his early forties. As it was, younger women considered him handsome, a fact that did not escape him.

His teeth were firm and straight, though slightly worn with

age, and his dark brown eyes were as uncompromising as tempered steel. The nose was prominent. The mouth suggested humor.

Henry had been a circuit preacher, a sheriff, and now he was a farmer. At least that is what he called himself, though he often told anyone who would listen that he was only a farmer because every man had to be something. Being a farmer, though, probably wasn't the best of trades. It was a time when America didn't seem to need farmers.

The year was 1934, and the nation was locked in the throes of depression.

Again, when Henry could get an audience he would laugh and say he didn't know when the Depression started, the reason being that he had lived in depression from his birth. In truth, however, Henry had never really known want. He was a prudent man, one not given to monetary excesses, so he was quite prepared for the Depression.

For him, in fact, the Depression seemed a million miles away; in places like New York and Chicago. He was aware, of course, that many of his neighbors were having problems, but he attributed their plight to ignorance. They, too, should have prepared.

Henry's smokehouse was filled with hams and bacon, the cellar shelves lined with jars of canned vegetables, fruit and beef. The woods around his house abounded with wild game and the streams in the area were teeming with fish. Those who couldn't make it, Henry reasoned, just weren't trying.

Henry had a lot of something else his neighbors didn't. He had money, all of which he had never entrusted to a bank. He was in an enviable position.

So, anytime a neighbor became desperate, wanted to strike out for the promised land of California, Henry bought their house and land for a few dollars. With all his acquisitions, he would have in better times been considered somewhat of a land baron. At this time, however, most of the people in the area considered his holdings worthless.

But Henry was a dreamer. He could see a better day on the horizon. It was hard for him to comprehend nine million men being out of work, but even if they were, it wouldn't last. Only the year before he had heard President Franklin D. Roosevelt say on a radio broadcast, "This great nation will endure as it has endured, will revive and will prosper. So, first of all let me assert my firm belief that the only thing we have to fear is fear itself."

Henry believed what the President said.

Henry sat in his favorite rocking chair, absorbing the heat from the fireplace, looking out the window at chickens pecking in the yard. He wondered what they could possibly find in the new-fallen snow.

From his vantage point he could also see the carcass of the deer he had killed that morning. It was hanging from the limb of a tree. He would have to skin it soon.

His thoughts rambled, but mostly they centered on that period of time when he had been a preacher. Damn good one, too, he opined. There had been long lonely hours in the saddle, traveling from one small church to the next, never knowing what sort of congregation he would encounter. There was also the bitter cold, the sleet and snow that often froze his clothing to the saddle. And there was the heat of summer, a relentless sun that could drive a man mad.

But in spite of the hardships, there was a good, warm feeling in his bones about being a preacher. He had relished the adoring congregations, the fact they considered him a messenger from God.

Was, too, by god, he thought.

When he was a preacher he felt he was bringing the people something they couldn't buy, a hope for something better. And the poor Arkansas farmers he preached to needed all the hope they could get.

That all ended, though, when he became involved with a deacon's daughter in Little River County. He was thirty-five at the time, had four children, but women were always a problem for him. Still were. He had never had much problem stifling his cursing and drinking, but he just couldn't do without women.

The deacon's daughter was not the first woman he had laid while a preacher. There had been many, but she was the most memorable. And it was the first, the only, time he had been caught.

Funny, looking back on it he could remember it was the girl's mother who first attracted his interest.

If I'd stuck with the mother, I'd probably still be preaching, he thought.

He really hated it, being caught like that. He liked preaching and figured he knew the *Bible* better than most of the preachers with formal educations. At least, he figured he understood the *Good Book* better. Not that he didn't have a good education, it's just that much of it was self-taught. There had never been much opportunity for formal learning.

But by god, he had memorized most of the *New Testament*. There really hadn't been much else to do to pass the time while riding a horse from place to place. Now he regretted knowing so much of the *Bible* and not having a place to show people how much he knew. All because of the deacon's daughter.

It had been a nasty scene. He had taken her to her father's barn for the sole purpose of praying with her, hoping to help her find Christ as her Savior. They had gone with the blessing of her father, whose gullible brain could not imagine a minister taking advantage of a seventeen-year-old child. For some reason Henry could not remember the girl's name, though he had thought of her often through the years.

It could be, he had often reasoned, that she was a servant of the devil, sent to wrest his sacred calling from him.

He remembered that while they were kneeling and praying, his arm around her shoulders, he could not keep his mind off the firmness of her breasts. They were so big, so unlike his wife's. He could not combat the urge to draw her to him, to pull her body close where those breasts were searing his chest like a branding iron.

Even after all these years he could remember it so vividly, their eyes meeting, then their lips. Then they were lying in the sweet-smelling hay, his hands tearing at her undergarmets. After what seemed like an eternity, he had torn away everything that separated him from the whiteness of her thighs. All the while she was tearing at the buttons on his pants, trying to free his penis. His hands helped her until it was free, then he was on top of her, crushing her virginity beneath him.

At least he thought she was a virgin at the time. Over the years he had begun to wonder.

Henry gazed into the fire, the memory of that moment with her so strong that he now had a hardness between his legs. Almost forgotten in the ecstacy of the memory was her father's scream of anguish when he discovered their lust in the barn. Also forgotten was the hard, all-night ride he had made to escape the wrath of angry, God-fearing men. He ran with his heart in his throat, because justice in that part of the country was a rope and a tree. It didn't matter that he was a preacher and had saved many souls from hell.

Henry had ridden all night to reach his home in southwestern Arkansas. There he had loaded his wife, children and all their belongings into a wagon and had escaped to Oklahoma. He had not preached since that time, nor had he attended church. He did, though, consider himself a good Christian and much more learned about God's wishes than those who attended services regularly.

Most of the trauma of that night long ago was all but forgotten. All that remained was the memory of the deacon's daughter's thighs, the sweetness of stolen moment.

Was it worth it?

Well, by god, maybe it was, Henry thought.

He got up from the rocking chair, stretched, and walked to the door leading to the open hallway. From a nail hammered into the door, he removed his heavy coat and put it on. While buttoning it, he walked back to the kitchen where Rachael was busily preparing the evening meal.

Poor, sweet Rachael, Henry thought. It seemed as though she was always preparing a meal, her gaunt, shapeless body stooped over the stove stirring something or other.

"I'm going to walk downtown for a while," he stated.

She didn't speak, merely looked fleetingly at him from her position by the woodburning cookstove, acknowledged his statement with a headshake while continuing to stir something in a pot. They conversed very little. They never had. She knew there was no need to remind him to be home by six for supper. He never had to be called for a meal, always expected her to have it on the table at the same time every day.

Unless a person knew, they would never suspect Rachael of being Henry's wife. They were opposites. She was weak, he was strong. She looked frail, he looked strong. It was difficult to picture her, even in her youth, helping Henry fashion a life from the rough land in which they lived.

But then, Henry could not have tolerated a strong wife. He wanted to dominate a woman, to rule. Rachael was a perfect subject for his lordly manner.

As Henry walked out the door, the cold air slapped the bareness of his face. It was invigorating to him. He was glad that Carl, their son, was using the car. It would be too obvious setting in front of Anise Marie Jones' house.

Horses. He would rather ride a horse anytime than drive a car. There were times when he wished he had never bought the car, that he still had a horse and buggy. Carl was the one that wanted the car, and he had given in to his son's wishes because he didn't want to deny the boy something and have to face Rachael's condemning stare.

She wants Carl to have everything, he thought.

Anise Marie Jones. She was a widow in her forties who, while not being the best stuff Henry had ever had, was available. She had been available to Henry for several years, even when her husband was alive. And for Henry availability was definitely a deciding factor now, a period in his life when he traveled very little.

Rachael, she never wanted sex anymore. How long had it been since he'd had her? Years, he thought.

His pace quickened.

Of course, there were several Choctaw women available, but Henry had a strong dislike for Indians, no matter what their virtues. Besides, he figured the thought of the deacon's daughter would keep him stirred while he was on top of Anise Marie.

That's what always keeps me stirred when I'm with Anise Marie, he thought. A man my age can't be all that damn particular where he dumps his sperm. But Anise Marie is boring. No matter what I do, she's boring.

It was about two o'clock when he arrived at Anise Marie's white frame house. It looked like so many other houses in town, the paint peeling in spots, like everyone had used the same pattern. While knocking to announce his presence, Henry noticed a hole in the screen door.

Well, she doesn't have to worry about flies until summer, he thought.

"I declare," Anise Marie said when she opened the door, "I certainly wasn't expecting to see you today, Henry."

For some reason, he wasn't sure why, her standing there in the open doorway surprised him.

Damn fool, you did knock didn't you? he thought.

She was smiling at him, one hand pushing the door open and the other beckoning him to enter. He greeted her with a nod of the head.

She was a pleasant enough woman, with hair that was dyed coal black, a pudgy nose and a large mouth that was somewhat sensuous. She was fairly tall, five-feet six-inches, and a bit fleshy. Her breasts sagged a bit, but her buttocks were still firm enough that Henry always admired them as she walked away from him. She and her husband had come to Oklahoma from Mississippi, and her voice and manner indicated that she was from the Deep South.

"That screen door has a hole in it," he said. "Remind me and I'll fix it before summer gets here." Helluva a way to start a conversation, he thought, but he never really had much to say to her. To any woman for that matter.

"Don't you go worrying about my screen door," she responded. "Just sit down there on the couch while I get you some coffee."

Henry obeyed and surveyed the room after she had left. It was immaculately clean and well-furnished. It wasn't new to him, because he had been here many times. It's just that he always checked it out, possibly hoping to find something out of place. Over the years, he never had.

Anise Marie wasn't a starving widow. Husband Jake had put aside quite a bit of money before his death, certainly enough for her to live comfortably on. And their son, Edward, probably saw to it that his mother had everything she wanted. He was supposedly making real good money in Oklahoma City.

Ought to be, Henry thought, being college-educated and all.

Henry felt a certain pleasantness at the thought of Edward. There were, after all, a great many folks who whispered that Henry was the boy's real father. He didn't know if it was true or not, but it was possible. He had always been a little afraid that Jake would hear the gossip.

Poor Jake, he thought. Better to hear anything than to be dead.

"The father's always the last to know," he unknowingly spoke half-aloud.

"What's that, Henry?" Anise Marie was back with the coffee.

"Nothing," he responded. "Just talking to myself. I guess it's a sign of senility."

"I doubt that," she said, laughing while handing him the coffee.

They sat beside each other on the couch, neither talking, just sipping the hot liquid. It tasted good. Anise Marie broke the silence, which Henry wished could have continued.

"How's Rachael?"

He knew that she was going to ask, but had hoped that for once she wouldn't. His family had no real place in their conversations.

"She's fine," he replied, not caring to volunteer more information than necessary.

"I didn't see her in church last Sunday."

Church, he thought. She always has to drag the church into our conversations. In a few minutes we're going to be breaking one of the Lord's laws and she's thinking about church.

"I wasn't up to driving her," Henry answered. "Besides, the weather was too damn bad." He wished the hell Anise Marie would have something sensible to talk about, like baseball, if he was going to have to listen to all her crap. Their attempts at conversation always seemed so stilted.

"I really wish you'd start going to church, Henry," she seemingly admonished. There was, however, a plaintiveness in her voice, an almost whining quality that grated on his nerves.

"I didn't come here to be preached to," he said.

What does she know about the *Bible?* he thought. For that matter, what does she know about God? What do any of the hypocritical bastards sitting in the pews every Sunday know? They go to church for no reason or purpose, only because they think it's the thing to do.

"I don't want to make you mad, it's just that all of us are concerned about you," Anise Marie whined.

I should have known, he thought, that I'd have to listen to a lot of her sanctimonious bullshit before getting on top of her.

He was getting pissed off. He wanted to get on with it, to think about a girl in a barn many years in his past, and to somehow imagine that Anise Marie was that girl.

And that's going to take a helluva lot of imagination, he thought.

Anise Marie continued rambling on, talking about the church, his family and town gossip that Henry wasn't a bit interested in. He remained quiet, sulking and thinking, who in the hell really gives a fuck about anyone else? When in the hell is she going to wind down?

"How are the children?" she asked.

Now he was really annoyed. She was hopscotching in her conversation, jumping from one subject to the next. And he also knew that she had only recently discussed the children with Rachael, while they were at church.

"You know how they're doing," he rasped with irritation. "Janie and Ruby are living in California and all their children are fine. Rosie is living in Kansas and all her children are fine. Carl and his wife are living with us right now and they don't have any children."

She seemed hurt by his obvious irritation, but dammit, he wished she wouldn't bring up church and the family just before he screwed her.

It's regular as clockwork, though, he thought. For a little bit of nothing, she could make a stud horse go soft.

Henry had tired of the game, so he pulled Anise Marie to him and began kissing her roughly on the neck, the whiskers of a day-old beard pricking the softness of her skin. His mouth then covered hers, and she responded with the fullness of her body. He didn't particularly enjoy kissing Anise Marie, but thought of it as part of the bullshit necessary to get what he really wanted.

He unbuttoned the top part of her dress and with one hand began rubbing her breasts. The other hand groped inside her panties. Her breathing became heavy and, with her hands, she struggled to unbutton his pants.

"Am I as good to you as I used to be?" she whispered.

"Better," he lied, his mind flooded with the memory of the deacon's daughter. "You're just as good to me as you always were."

"My god, Henry," she exclaimed. "You sure do have a big hard on."

CHAPTER TWO

I T WAS five o'clock when Henry left Anise Marie's house. A light sleet had begun to fall and darkness was shrouding the sky in varying shades of black. As he walked briskly along, Henry pushed his coat collar up around his neck as a fortress against the wet chill of the evening. The ground crust of ice and snow crackled beneath his feet and the cold pierced his body like well-aimed arrows.

But he was in no hurry. He felt as though the cold was cleansing him. The fire was gone from his loins, leaving not one smoldering ember. And he was tired. He recalled some scripture and spoke it aloud into the empty darkness that surrounded him.

"But they that wait upon the Lord shall renew their strength; they shall mount up with wings as eagles; they shall run, and not be weary; and they shall walk and not faint."

He arrived at the creek bridge and started to cross, then changed his mind and went down the embankment and under the bridge. It was dry there.

He removed his clothing and stacked it by one of the pilings supporting the bridge. Then he walked up the creek bank to a deep hole where he often fished. The sleet pelted his nude body until he plunged into the water, letting its darkness cover him like the blackness of a grave.

Henry swam effortlessly, his vigorous strokes parting the current of the water as though it were powerless to his command.

It was very dark now. He could see little except the faint silhouette of the bridge. He swam to the shallow end of the deep hole and began walking out of the water, ignoring the sharp rocks in the creek bed that jabbed at his bare feet.

Beneath the bridge he dried himself with his hands, then dressed. The clothes felt extremely warm on his body. He pushed his hat down on his still wet hair and continued the trek homeward.

Henry swam every day, regardless of the weather. He had taken a swim that morning, breaking the routine of walking his trap line. But for some reason he couldn't fathom, he had again felt the need to be cleansed by a running stream. People should be baptized in running streams, he thought, so their sins can be carried away by the current.

Henry knew nothing of hypothermia, nor could he comprehend such unusual activity making him sick. He had never been sick a day in his life, had never even been examined by a doctor. He thought the illness most persons experienced was in their heads.

He could now see the kerosene lamplight filtering through the windows of the house, the eerie glow like a dying fire. When he arrived at the house, Henry used the edge of the porch to scrape off his boots before going inside.

Rachael had heard him on the porch and was putting supper on the table when he walked into the kitchen.

"We was about to give up on you, Dad," Carl said. "I was gettin' hungry." It was a trite, but normal greeting. It was six o'clock, the time they ate supper every night.

Henry removed his coat and hung it on a peg by the door. He

sat down in one of the straight back chairs at the table, scooted it closer, and nodded a greeting to Carl's wife, Vivian.

"What have you two been doin' today?" he asked.

"Viv and I went huntin'," Carl replied with an almost childlike enthusiasm. "We got seven squirrels and a couple of coons."

"Good. Real good," Henry said, grinning his approval. If Rachael will let the boy alone, not tie him to her apron strings, he'll be alright, he thought. His primary concern was that Carl lacked the aggressiveness that had been so much a part of his own life. So necessary.

"I really didn't think old Rowdy would tree much on a day like this," Henry said, making reference to Carl's dog.

"Best damn dog I ever saw," Carl said, his mouth full of food.

Henry caught Rachael's look of disapproval regarding Carl's language. She had difficulty tolerating the mildest forms of profanity, so Henry was subjected to her condemnatory looks on a daily basis.

He spooned up some venison stew onto his plate from a big bowl, took two biscuits off a platter and placed them beside the plate, then reached into the pickle jar with his fingers and pulled one out.

"I have to admit," Henry said to Carl, "that I wasn't sure that dog was worth the food we was givin' him. Guess I was wrong. Damn wrong."

Rachael looked at her husband with the hurt in her eyes that always seemed to be there. She couldn't understand Henry, how he could have been a preacher, how he could have been so close to the Lord at one time and now be so profane. The *damn* he had uttered had been mild enough, but he was often given to fits of temper and vile language. Rachael feared that her son would try to emulate his father.

She had never understood why Henry had given up preaching and going to church. But she didn't know about the deacon's daughter or the dozens of women Henry had slept with while he was county sheriff. Even when they left Arkansas in such a hurry, she didn't question Henry. It was not her nature to question him, possibly out of fear. She wasn't sure, but she didn't want to risk angering him.

Rachael, thin and wrinkled, kept her white hair pulled back tightly on her head and rolled into a bun. The hair had never been cut, because she had once heard a preacher say that a woman's hair was her glory, that cutting it was a sin.

Her nose was long and thin, but it seemed perfectly at home on her narrow face. It was the sad brown eyes that seemed too large for her face. Her shoulders were slightly bent, and bird-like legs looked too weak to support even her small frame. Maybe she weighed a hundred pounds, but no more than that.

The second of four daughters of a supposedly widowed mother, Rachael had been twenty years old when Henry came into her life. When she was six years old her father had left the family to make his fortune in California, promising that he would send for them when he was settled.

He never did.

The children were told that he had been killed by Indians, or stricken by disease or accident while on the trail. Neighbors, however, were not so kind. They whispered that he had left with a traveling bordello, married the madam, and had become wealthy by operating a large whore house in New Orleans.

Rachael was aware of the rumors as she grew to womanhood, but she never believed such lies about her father. After several years her mother had remarried, but even with a stepfather to help support the family, Rachael knew the meaning of hard times.

She never deceived herself into thinking that Henry had married her for her beauty. She was not plain, though she thought of herself in that way. She was insecure, dependent, and she was convinced that Henry had married her because he was a preacher and wanted a wife he could trust. If that were the case, he had made a good decision.

"Stew's good, Rachael," Henry said, sopping the juice from his plate with part of a biscuit and plopping it into his mouth.

She gave an appreciative nod. His statement about the food was about the closest expression of praise she ever received from him. Henry was one of those people who thought it unnecessary to praise anyone for doing their job well, because . . . well, it was their job and that's the way they were supposed to do it.

"Why don't you fry up some of them squirrels Carl killed tomorrow," he continued. It wasn't a question, more of a command. He didn't even bother to wait for an acknowledgement from Rachael, but without a break in the flow of his conversation asked Carl, "How many coonskins we got now?"

"Those two we got today makes twenty," Carl answered.

"Reckon we can get four bits apiece for them?"

"I reckon so," Carl told his father. "That's how much they paid us for the last batch."

"Carl shot both of the ones we got today in the head," Vivian said.

Henry was glad she had joined in their conversation. He liked talking to her, and looking at her. She was such a damn fine looking woman, and she didn't patronize him. She was the only one in the family who wasn't afraid of him.

"Nobody can doubt Carl's ability with a twenty-two," Henry bragged. "That's cause I taught him to shoot."

"Did you teach him everything he knows how to do?" Vivian teased.

Henry grinned and said, "Not everything. But what I didn't teach him was inherited from me."

Carl was tempted to laugh at the banter between his father and his wife, but before showing any expression he first glanced at his mother to see if she had picked up the sexual overtones of the conversation. If she had, she wasn't letting on. Her head was down and, as usual, she was only pecking at her food.

Carl loved his mother, and it bothered him that there was never any joy in her. She even approached eating as work. It seemed to him that the only real satisfaction she got from life was hearing a hellfire and damnation sermon that assured her that all sinners would burn for eternity.

On the other hand, his father seemed to get so much from life. It was as though he was attacking it, claiming every moment for his own. Carl did fear his father's wrath, but he was satisfied that everyone did. He figured Henry was mean enough to kick the devil in the ass.

"What are you and Carl going to do tonight?" Henry quipped.

"When?" Vivian answered.

"After supper," he answered.

"Well, I don't know," she taunted. "I'm sure as hell not going to let him take me for a walk out in this cold."

"You don't like to walk?" Henry teased.

"When it's this cold, I don't mind walking as far as the bed," she said.

"I don't guess there's much to do in bed except sleep, is there?" he asked.

"You tell me," she said.

"I'm just trying to get information," he said.

"Oh, I'm sure of that, Henry," she said, laughing. "I know you'd never insinuate anything."

"Course not," he replied, grinning.

"You all mind if I join the conversation?" Carl asked.

They all laughed. Except for Rachael.

Henry buttered a biscuit, poured syrup in his plate and sopped it with the bread. The sweetness of the concoction tasted good, as did this peaceful time in the warmth of the kitchen.

By god, he thought, I'm proud of the boy for marrying a piece of stuff like Vivian. I might have done the same thing if the Lord hadn't called me to preach the gospel.

The light from the lamp on the table accentuated Vivian's beauty. She had an olive complexion that blended well with her long auburn hair. Henry liked her luscious mouth and her large hazel eyes, but what attracted him most was her big, succulent tits. He had heard about men spending as much as ten dollars for some New Orleans whores. He figured any whore who could demand that kind of money had to look like Vivian.

Vivian was only five-feet four-inches tall, but Henry thought every inch was in the proper proportion, that the good Lord had created a masterpiece when he made her.

When Carl first brought Vivian home, and Henry learned that her mother was a widow in her early forties, he became excited about meeting his son's mother-in-law. When he did meet her, he was disappointed. She was a big, rawboned woman, as tall as Henry, and with none of Vivian's delicate features. Henry's dream of a possible intimate friendship with Vivian's mother, whom he had imagined looked like his daughter-in-law, quickly dissolved.

Damn it, Henry thought, it's just not right for a father to lust after his son's woman, but when she swishes her pretty little ass around the house, I just can't help myself. He chuckled to himself while thinking, incest is a game the whole family can play. He hoped Carl was man enough to handle Vivian. He knew damn well that he was man enough to handle her, even at his age.

At six feet, Carl was a good two inches taller than his father, but he never thought of himself as being bigger. In fact, he always thought of Henry as being much bigger. It was, perhaps, because he had seen Henry whip bigger men, some as much as fifty to seventy pounds heavier. He had never seen a situation where his father was not dominant.

Carl had inherited his mother's nose and his father's strong chin and mouth. His hair, which was combed straight back, was black. The hair possibly made his brown eyes look darker, that and a swarthy complexion. Though some might not think of him as muscular, the muscles he did have had the look of sinewy fiber.

Carl was the last of five children born to Henry and Rachael, the only living son. His brother, named after his father, had answered the call to arms in World War One and had died in battle. Rachael had never really recovered from the death of her eldest.

"When are you and Carl going to get me a grandson?" Henry asked Vivian.

"We're working on it," she said, laughing. "We're really working hard on it."

Vivian's response caused Carl to blush.

"Good night to work on it," Henry replied. He expected Rachael to show disapproval of the conversation, to allow her eyes to relay disgust. But she remained expressionless.

"I'd better get the dishes done," she said, her only contribution to the supper conversation. Her lack of response frustrated Henry.

It's like she's dead, just going through the motions of being alive, he thought.

"I'll help with the dishes," Vivian volunteered.

While the women were washing and drying the dishes, Henry went to the cupboard and took down the checkers and checker-board. He sat down, pulled his chair close to the table, then motioned for Carl to take the red checkers. Henry always chose the blacks.

Carl didn't like playing checkers with his father, because he rarely ever won. They played three games while the women were doing their chores. Henry won all three.

After Rachael removed her apron, signaling that the work in the kitchen was done, the four of them moved to the living room. While Henry stoked the logs in the fireplace, Carl pulled a small handmade table out from the wall and placed it close to the warmth of the fire. Henry took a box of dominos from the fireplace mantle while Carl was putting three straight back wooden chairs around the table. The scene was one that was repeated on a nightly basis, ritualistic in its sameness.

Henry, Carl and Vivian began playing dominos and making small talk while Rachael worked at piecing a quilt stretched on a frame hanging from the ceiling.

"We got a letter from Janie today," Vivian said, speaking of the Hayders oldest daughter.

Studying his dominos, Henry responded matter-of-factly, "How are they doing?"

"They're fine."

Henry had not seen his daughter or her children for five years. He did not care if he ever saw her husband, whom he considered a dumb ass. Part of his disdain for Verdo, Janie's husband, was that he acted somewhat feminine, certainly not with the kind of masculinity Henry would have chosen for his daughter. He figured Janie only married the man so she could rule the roost. Janie may look like her mother, he continued in thought, but there's such a difference in the two. Janie is strong-willed and dominating, not the way a woman ought to be.

"Put me down fifteen," Henry said to Vivian as he placed a

domino against the already irregular line on the table. "I don't care if I never see that bastard husband of hers again," he verbalized as an afterthought. "Never could understand what Janie saw in the stupid sonofabitch. Course I never figured him to be man enough to be a logger."

He watched for Rachael's disapproving look. It came quickly enough, but she didn't speak.

By god, Henry thought, she's as predictable as day and night. He wished that just once she would quit her quilting and play dominos with them. We've got quilts out the ass, he thought. Never will get around to using them all.

"Been quite a while since we heard from Ruby and Rosie," Vivian said, nervously, making reference to two of Henry's other daughters and trying to get him off the subject of Verdo. Vivian liked her mother-in-law and didn't want her hurt by Henry's sharp tongue, but her attempt to ease the situation failed.

"That's because they don't need any money right now," he reasoned aloud. "They'll write as soon as they need something. Never fails." He talked calmly enough, but his words reeked of sarcasm.

"The girls didn't do too well in their marrying," he continued, seemingly thinking aloud. "Ruby married that goddam Jack Rebb, and there ain't a decent Rebb in the whole county. When I was sheriff I kept his daddy's ass in jail most of the time.

"But Rosie, she really takes the cake, marrying that goddam Catholic. There's got to be something wrong with a man that falls for all that shit the Catholic Church dishes out. I can't understand people that will take their orders from some asshole from a foreign country. There's no man that's going to tell me what to do. God's the only one that can tell Henry Hayder what to do."

Rachael remained passive throughout his softly-spoken tirade. He wished she would speak up, be angry, fight with him. She just sat there, though, obviously trying not to show any emotion.

Rachael continued to work on the quilt a while, primarily because she didn't want Carl or Vivian to think that Henry's words were chasing her from the room. It was hard to listen to his profanity, which she thought was increasing with each passing day.

After a few minutes, punctuated only by the click of dominos on the table and trite conversation regarding the game, Rachael put away her needle and thread and said goodnight. A chorus of *good night* followed her as she left the room.

Henry listened to her footsteps in the hallway, then heard her open and close the door to their bedroom. "Shake up the dominos, Carl," Henry ordered. "I'll be back in a minute."

He went out the living room door and down the hallway to the back porch. He stood on the edge of the porch and pissed into the night, then went down the steps and walked to the barn. There was still a mist-like sleet that peppered his face, but he paid no attention to it. He was too intent on his mission. It was dark in the barn, but he had no problem finding the reason for his visit.

When he returned to the living room, Henry put a gallon jar of muscadine wine on the table. Vivian brought glasses from the kitchen, and the three of them sat there drinking and playing dominos.

Henry did not drink in front of Rachael. It seemed a contradiction, even hypocrisy, to Vivian and Carl that he didn't attempt to curb his profanity but did keep his drinking a secret from her. They were sure Rachael knew, but they were not about to suggest that he be open about it.

Mother must have seen him go in saloons hundreds of times, Carl thought. Still, Henry's ways were Henry's ways, and no one was going to change him.

"Understand the Gazette's for sale," Henry said, peering at his dominos.

"Well, it's not much of a newspaper," Carl responded.

"Always wanted to own a newspaper," Henry said. "Only problem with the Gazette is that asshole who owns it."

"Are you thinking about buying it?" Vivian asked.

"The thought crossed my mind," he replied.

"Dad, you don't know anything about newspapering," Carl said.

"You might be surprised what I know, Carl," he said. "I know how to run a business and I know what's news."

"Maybe so, Dad," Carl half-argued, "but the way things are now isn't the best time to be buying anything, the Depression and all. Be almost impossible to get advertisers for a newspaper."

"Son, I wish you had a little more foresight than you do," Henry said. "There couldn't be a better time for buying something than now."

"Henry, Carl and I have talked about all the land you've been buying," Vivian said, "and I have to admit that we've wondered why you're doing it. With times as hard as they are, it seems that you'd want to hold on to your money."

"What you and Carl forget," Henry semi-scolded, "is that things aren't going to stay the way they are. The land I'm buying for a little bit of nothing today is going to be worth a lot in the future. It's going to be worth a whole lot more than all the money I got now. This country's going to revive, and the people who had the foresight to take advantage of this opportunity are going to be the ones that get rich."

"You're already rich, Henry," Vivian teased.

"Compared to some, I am," Henry admitted. "But what I'm talking about is big money. Power, too. I might not live to see it, but my children and grandchildren will benefit from what I'm doing now."

"C'mon, Dad, you'll outlive us all," Carl said.

"I sure as hell will, or die trying," Henry laughed.

"Well, are you going to buy the Gazette?" Vivian asked.

"I'm thinking about it," Henry said.

"If you're going to have all this money from land, why do you want a newspaper?" Carl asked.

"Money's one thing," Henry responded, "and power is something else. You have a newspaper and you have power."

Vivian and Carl looked at each other. They didn't know what he meant, but neither wanted to pursue the matter.

"Fifteen," Henry said putting a domino on the table. "If you two don't get in the game, I'm going to have to look for some better competition."

What Henry had bought, or planned to buy, was no longer a topic of conversation. There was smalltalk, drinking wine and playing dominos for another hour.

"Bedtime," Carl yawned at the completion of the game, which Henry won, as was nearly always the case.

"You have something to go to bed for," Henry said. "I guess I'll stay up for a while. Why don't the two of you work on getting me a grandson?"

"We'll try, Henry. You can bet we'll try," Vivian laughed. "And it's sure a good night for trying."

They laughed together, then Carl and Vivian went to their bedroom, leaving Henry in a rocking chair in front of the fire.

The wine had warmed him inwardly, mellowed his thoughts, and the flames from the fire sent flickering shadows chasing across the room, causing memories of many such nights. He sat there drinking wine, peering into the fire, not moving the rocking chair.

He was in a reflective mood, his mind skipping from one thing to another. And as he had so many other times in the past, he questioned the meaning of life, especially his life. He wondered if other people ever did the same.

Of course they do, he thought. Except for Rachael. I don't think Rachael ever questions anything.

There is some reason I'm here, he thought. God has some great plan for my life. The mystery that was the plan eluded him, kept passing too quickly through his mind. There's something. There has to be something.

Then, as he continued sipping wine, Henry wished he could be more affectionate toward Rachael. As he remembered it, he had always wanted to be more affectionate toward her.

But my god, he thought, even when we were first married she was unresponsive. She never liked making love, always thought there was no purpose to it except to have a child. That's why I had to have other women.

Henry again wished Rachael would play dominos with them instead of constantly quilting, but he knew she wouldn't. She thinks all games are evil, of the devil. She thinks it's nothing but idleness. But, by god, what's wrong with being idle once in a while. Nothing, absolutely nothing.

Henry's emotions ran rampant during times of meditation, run-

ning the gamut from anger and frustration to sympathy and melancholy. He wondered why he had made the remarks about his
daughters and their husbands earlier that evening, then reasoned
it was for Rachael's benefit. Maybe it was so she would leave
allowing him to get the wine.

Her eyes are always so damn condemning, he thought. She
doesn't approve of anything I do anymore. And she sure wouldn't
approve of me drinking this wine. Hell, even the Bible says there's
nothing wrong with a little wine. Jesus drank wine. So did the
Apostles. Damn it, I'm just going to drink it in front of her from
now on.

But he knew he wouldn't. Henry's thoughts raced to Janie and
her children, and to her sonofabitch husband. The bastard's certainly misnamed, he thought. Verdo's last name was Smart.

Two of his daughters and their families had moved to California
five years earlier, and he wondered if he would ever see them
or his grandchildren again. Of course you will, you stupid old
fucker, he thought. They'll all be back here soon enough, trying
to pick your pocket.

Henry hadn't seen his children all that much after they married,
because their husbands were made very much aware of his animos-
ity toward them. They planned their visits to the Hayder house
at times when they knew Henry would be gone. The sons-in-
laws were reluctant to have their children around him, because
Henry was not adverse to heaping verbal abuse on the fathers in
front of the children.

Henry was sheriff during the time all his daughters married,
and there was never any doubt about his opposition to their mates.
Janie had married when she was seventeen, Ruby at eighteen
and Rosie at sixteen.

Rachael was so damned scared they'd be old maids, he thought.
If I could have been around the house more, I'd have run all
those bastards off. Henry wasn't sure whether he loved his daughters, but he damn sure wanted a say about what they did with
their lives, being his children and all.

Rosie had married Arlo Shipley and had given birth to six children, four boys and two girls. They had moved to Kansas nine

years earlier and Henry had seen them once since then, in October of 1931.

Raise a child in the way she ought to go, he thought, and she up and marries a goddam Catholic. Got about as much use for Catholics as I got for Niggers and Indians.

Raising his eyes from the fire, he looked at a picture of his dead son that was hanging on the wall. It was barely visible by the flickering firelight.

Now only Carl is left, he thought, and Rachael doesn't want to let him be a man. His eyelids were heavy. Weariness gripped his body like a steadily tightening vise. Before going to bed, though, there were things to do.

First, he went to the kitchen and rinsed out his glass. Then he took the empty jar back to the barn, noting that the sleet had intensified. Have to make some more wine when the grapes get ripe, he thought. That will be on a warmer day.

After getting back to the porch, he stood on its edge and pissed for a long time. He really didn't mind the cold.

In the dark of the bedroom he noted that Rachael was fast asleep, her frail body barely sinking down into the feather mattress. Only her head was visible above the several quilts she was using for cover.

She's always been cold natured, he thought, but then, so are most of the women I've known. He removed his clothes and got into bed and, though there was no heat in the room, shoved all the quilts off him except one.

He lay there for a while wondering why women were colder natured than men. By god, he thought, when a man starts trying to figure out women, he's damn near senile.

Then he slept.

CHAPTER THREE

Spring painted the Kiamichi Mountains in varying shades of green. Wild flowers burst forth from their graves in the earth, and rattlesnakes crawled from their lairs to greet the warmth of the sun. Pine trees spewed powdery pollen all over the land as the harsh blasts of winter's winds were replaced by warm gentle breezes.

This new birth that came to a land that had been buried by winter found Vivian four months pregnant. Carrying the child, she was even more beautiful than she had been as a bride. And the prospect of a grandson filled Henry with an eager anticipation that he hadn't felt in years.

By god, he thought, at last we'll have another Hayder around here. Not a damn Smart, Rebb or Shipley, but a Hayder. Dammit, a man's lineage is important. Abraham begat Issac; and Issac begat Jacob; and Jacob begat Judas and his brethren. What else did a man have to be remembered by except by his children and grandchildren, sons and grandsons that carried his name?

In Henry's thought processes, it never occurred to him that the child Vivian was carrying might not be a boy. "It is, by god, a boy," he would say angrily to anyone who suggested it might be otherwise. "It won't be long before young Henry will be fishing, hunting and trapping with me."

If Carl or Vivian objected to Henry prematurely naming the child after himself, they certainly didn't say so. They were seemingly pleased that he was so interested and excited about the birth of the baby.

Henry laughed and joked with Vivian, as always, but he was also very protective of her; objecting to her working in the garden, doing housework, or even going fishing with Carl and himself.

"I'm fine, Henry, quit worrying about me," Vivian would insist.

"There's no point overdoing it," he would say. "You have to be careful."

There were times when Henry's concern for Vivian amused Rachael, and on other occasions it caused reflective anger. *He was never all that concerned when I was with child,* she thought.

It was on a fishing trip, one that Henry didn't want Vivian to go on, that his concern for her became even more pronounced.

They had driven the Ford up in the mountains for a day of fishing in Ouachita Creek. Their destination was a stretch of the creek about a quarter mile from where the road ended. It was not a difficult walk, but Henry fretted that it might be too much for Vivian in her condition.

They walked the rocky trail to the fishing spot that, for as far back as Henry could remember, had been called the *Blue Hole*. It was a long, deep stretch of water with shallows at both ends. The current in the middle section of the hole was as lazy as a hot summer day, but at both ends the water hurried over the rocky creekbed.

Their fishing tackle consisted of cane poles with line, hooks and bobbers. Their bait was a bucket filled with crawfish that Carl and Henry had seined the day before, and a smaller bucket filled with earthworms they had dug.

"Henry, put a worm on my hook," Vivian demanded.

"Since when has it got to the point that you can't bait your own hook?" he asked.

"Since I got pregnant," she said.

"Hell of an excuse," he countered, but he already had the hook on her line in his hand and was stringing on a worm that wiggled wildly at the bite of the barb.

"I'm going to use crawdads," Carl said, "and try to catch some bass."

They sat there fishing, exchanging pleasantries, feeling the warmth of the sunlight filtering through tall oaks, and listening to a choir of birds greeting the new day. It was the best of times.

Henry watched the bobber on his line move slowly with the lazy current, stop in the swirl of a small eddy, then go out of sight. He jerked up on his pole and felt the pressure caused by the weight of the fish at the end of his line. The fish made a few quick runs before he lifted it from the water.

"Goggleye," he matter-of-factly stated. Grasping the fish with one hand, he removed the hook from its mouth with the thumb and index finger of the other hand. Then he pushed the sharp metal point of a homemade stringer through the lower part of the fish's mouth, ran the point through a loop at the other end, and staked the fish out in the water.

"That's a nice fish, Dad," Carl acknowledged.

"You're just lucky," Vivian teased. "I'll still catch more fish than you before the day's over."

He laughed and retorted, "Daughter-in-law, the day's not going to last that long. I can't recall anyone ever beating me at fishing."

"That's because you've never had to fish against me," she challenged.

"You start catching too many," Henry threatened, "and I'll quit baiting your hook."

"Got one," Carl yelled, then battled a two-pound bass to the water's edge where he could grab its lower lip with his fingers.

"Dammit, when am I going to catch one?" Vivian pouted.

"Watch it now, Viv," Henry chided. "Remember that you were going to show me how to catch'em."

"I will, too," she replied indignantly. "I sure as hell will." While Vivian was very competitive, the truth was that she really didn't care whether she caught fish or not.

By ten o'clock Henry had caught seven goggleye, two channel catfish and a bass. Carl had caught three nice bass, but Vivian had caught nothing. She faked pouting about the situation, enjoying the attention of her husband and Henry.

By the time they broke for lunch she had caught four perch, but the men had continued to catch fish at a rate that made overtaking them improbable. On a grassy knoll shaded by a large whiteoak tree, they ate the lunch of biscuits and fried ham that Rachael had prepared for them, drinking in the mountain air as if it were a rare tonic. It was, indeed, a good day to be alive.

CHAPTER FOUR

SINCE EARLY that morning Rachael had been working in the garden, stopping only long enough, on occasion, to get a dipper full of cool well water to quench her thirst. Before daylight she had fixed breakfast for Henry, Carl and Vivian. Then she had sat at the table reading the *Bible* by lamplight until the day broke.

The mornings were still chilly, so she bundled up before feeding the chickens and livestock. After milking the cow, she transferred the white liquid into lidded buckets and lowered them into the well with a rope. The well water kept the milk cold. After that she started working in the garden, hoeing and doing some weeding by hand.

She was worried about Rosie. For two days she had been trying to summon up the nerve to talk to Henry about their younger daughter's plight. Things were not going well for the Shipleys and, in a letter from Rosie tucked in her apron pocket, their daughter had indicated the family might move back to Oklahoma. It was a possibility Rachael prayed for every day.

But there was more in the letter. Rosie had also asked about the possibility of borrowing two hundred dollars from her parents. If Rachael had been allowed access to money, she would have honored the request immediately. However, she never had any money, except that which Henry provided for specific purposes. Though she accepted without complaint Henry's contention that women had no business handling money, on these occasions when her children had needs and she was helpless in providing for them, she felt resentment toward him. It was a feeling she fought, because she thought of such feelings as being un-Christian.

Rachael knew that mention of the loan request would set Henry off, that he would call Arlo every name in the devil's vocabulary. He would, however, send the money. Maybe he would send it because he couldn't stand the thought of Rosie or his grandchildren doing without, or maybe he would send it to make Arlo realize that he was a failure and couldn't provide for his family. Rachael had difficulty reading Henry's motivation. She never knew why he really did things.

Rosie had borrowed two hundred dollars from Henry the previous year. Her request then had sent Henry into a tirade against his son-in-law.

"Why doesn't the sonofabitch ask for himself?" he had raged. "Why does he make his wife do his dirty work for him? I'll tell you why. It's because he's not a man. He's just a goddam snake in the grass. I had to loan him money to get him to Kansas, and now I'm supposed to loan him more to keep him there. Loan, hell. There's no loan to this. It'll be a cold day in hell before the bastard ever pays me back. It's probably worth the money, though, to keep the sonofabitch out of the state."

It was after three days of ranting and raving, cursing the ground that Arlo Shipley walked on, that he had sent the money.

Maybe, if they don't get the money, Rachael thought, they will come home. I'm getting old and tired, and when I die I want my children and grandchildren around me.

Rachael wondered how she could word a letter to Rosie, telling her that she would talk to Henry about the loan, but that they should use the money to come home on. She would have to be very careful. If Henry even suspected such a stipulation on her part, he would throw a fit.

CHAPTER
FIVE

I T WAS about four o'clock when the rattlesnake crawled from its den. The snake was hungry and full of venom. It slithered along until it came to a trail, then positioned itself by the path, waiting with deadly anticipation for some small prey.

"Better turn your head, Viv," Henry said. "I'm going to take my swim."

"I doubt that I'll see anything that I haven't seen before," she laughed.

"You might see more of it," he replied.

"My god, Dad, what you won't say," Carl laughed, shaking his head in mock disbelief.

"Well, goddam it," Henry responded, beginning to peel off his clothes, "there's no reason for false modesty among friends."

"Whoa," Vivian commanded. "I'm not quite as bold as I make out to be. Besides, I'm still fishing. You go on downstream to do your swimming."

Henry grunted consent, then walked to the other end of the *Blue Hole* to take his swim, like he intended doing all along.

It was about five o'clock when they decided to head for home. The sun was still hovering above the treetops, but the spring chill of the mountain air pricked at bare skin like pine needles.

They walked down the trail, Henry leading, Vivian behind him and Carl bringing up the rear. They were about halfway to the car when the nerve-shattering rattle resounded like a chorus of thunder.

Vivian saw the snake just before it struck at her. A scream stuck in her throat and she thought a thousand sledgehammers were pounding at her heart, but she was in motion. She was running, stumbling down the hill. Then she fell.

She heard Henry curse and, looking back up the trail from her position on the ground, she could see him beating the snake with a stick. Carl was kneeling beside her, his eyes filled with concern.

"Are you okay, honey?"

"I think so." Carl helped her to her feet. Except for the sting of a skinned elbow and knee, she felt okay.

Henry was on his knees now, pounding the snake's head with a rock, angrily quoting from the *Bible*.

"In that day the Lord with his sore and great and strong sword shall punish Leviathan, the piercing serpent, even Leviathan that crooked serpent; and he shall slay the dragon that is in the sea." He wasn't sure what the scripture meant, but he had memorized it years before, and it did seem appropriate for the time.

Getting up from his knees, Henry hurried down the trail to where Carl and Vivian were standing.

"You okay, Viv?"

She nodded her head, choking back the tears. Carl put an arm around her and pulled her close. She sobbed then, softly, fear still making her heart race uncontrollably.

"God, we were lucky," Henry said. "It's a good thing Viv was carrying her fishing pole the way she was, because that's what the snake struck." She had been using the pole like a cane, supporting herself as she walked down the trail.

"And for god's sake," Henry continued, "let's not mention what happened to Rachael. If we let on that Viv got scared by a snake, she'll think for sure that it will mark the baby."

His statement was so funny to Vivian that her sobbing turned to semi-laughter. And later, as the car was bouncing along the mountain road, Carl driving, Vivian questioned Henry as to what he meant by saying that Rachael might think the baby would be marked.

"Who knows?" he answered. "It's just an old wives tale, but you know how Rachael gets religion and superstition mixed up. She's heard for years that anything that scares a pregnant woman can mark the baby. I don't know how in the hell a pregnant woman being scared can mark an unborn child, but I don't want to argue with her about it."

They all laughed at that, the part about him not wanting to argue.

"C'mon, Carl," Henry said, "let's get on to the house. We've got to eat supper and get these fish cleaned."

CHAPTER
SIX

I T WAS raining, big drops spattering on the dry ground and sending up little curls of dust. Henry liked sitting on the porch, especially during a shower. It was during such times that he was most reflective.

He leaned back in his rocking chair, sucking the fresh smell of the rain into his lungs. His mind was like a spinning wheel, never stopping for long on any one thing.

For years I've searched for the meaning of life, my life, he thought, and I don't know that I've ever really found it. I'm tired, a tired old man looking for something, and I have no idea what I'm looking for.

Feeling the wrinkles on the back of his neck with a hand, he felt sadness at the thought of his body decaying. Everyone and everything has to decay and die, though, he thought. Why have I always figured I was different? I wonder if I even believe in God, or is He like so many other things I've tried to believe in.

He tried to think about God for a while, but his mind skipped to his childhood, to his mother and father. It startled him to realize that he couldn't remember what either of them looked like. You should be able to remember your mother and father, he thought. But I wonder if any of my children will remember me? Or will my face decay in their memories as my body decays in the earth?

Henry was not immune to self-pity, or to contradictory thoughts. He felt a sadness about dying, but no fear. There was actually an anticipation. He wanted to know what was beyond life on earth, if anything. It would be an adventure into the unknown, and that excited him. He had the heart of an explorer and adventurer, and he refused to be fearful of anything life or death held for him.

If there is a God and judgment . . . he broke the thought. He tried to concentrate on a more pleasant subject, but his mind was out of control. It would not obey him.

Judgment.

What about the women he had laid, the men he had killed, and the money he had stolen?

Thinking about the women was pleasant enough, but it was also a bit frightening. There had been so many. Their names, their faces, all ran together in his mind; a kaleidoscope of flesh. There had been several while he was in the ministry, even more after he left it. He wondered why he had entered the ministry in the first place, then reasoned that God had called him. If He called me, then He must exist, Henry thought.

The faces of the Claxton brothers, Rush and Roth, began playing tricks with his mind. He would just as soon not be able to remember their faces. Theirs or the Choctaw's.

On a hot summer day in 1923, the two drunken brothers, armed with shotguns, had robbed the bank in broad daylight. Everyone knew the brothers, but in their drunken stupor they didn't even bother to cover their faces. Henry, who was sheriff at the time, knew their father well. He often played checkers with Bob Claxton.

The boys had robbed the bank at noon, while Henry was in bed with Frances Mickelberry. He had her husband Floyd in jail for being drunk and disorderly. Henry's deputy, also the jailer, had no problem locating his boss.

Some of the townspeople wanted to organize a posse, but Henry quieted the idea. "It's my job," he had told them, "and besides, they're just kids. A posse might scare them into doing something foolish." He could still picture Bob in the crowd, his face showing the anguish, pain and shame for what his sons had done.

The boys had headed into the Kiamichis on horseback, into an area impossible to reach by car. Henry knew the Kiamichis like he knew the backs of his hands. He stopped by his home, saddled his horse and picked up a bedroll. Rachael packed some food, which he placed in his saddlebags with two boxes of shotgun shells. He preferred his double-barrel shotgun to a rifle, though he carried both.

On his way to the mountains he stopped by Jake Moody's cabin and hired him on as a tracker, promising to pay the Choctaw a dollar a day for his services. Henry wondered about Jake Moody, where he'd gotten his white man's name.

Jake had no problem picking up the trail of the Claxtons. They were amateurs who knew nothing about covering a trail. Henry remembered what he thought at the time, that he really didn't need Jake. He had also thought about how scared the young robbers must be.

They caught up with the Claxtons on the morning of the third day, before the two boys had broken camp.

"Okay boys, that's it," Henry said, stepping from behind a tree. "Don't try anything." It was close range and he had them covered with the shotgun. Jake was backing him up.

"My god, don't shoot, sheriff," Roth had said. "We give up."

Henry remembered them both being ashen-faced and scared, Roth shaking with fright and Rush whimpering. And he remembered seeing the sack of money beside their bedrolls.

"Don't shoot, sheriff," Roth repeated.

He did shoot, though. He remembered Roth's pleading eyes, how his face disintegrated as he caught the full force of the shotgun blast. He remembered that Rush stopped crying and stared in disbelief, how he seemed to want to run, but he took the second blast from the shotgun before he could even turn.

And Jake Moody, he just stood there in paralyzed fright. Henry had plenty of time to reload the shotgun, point it at the Indian and pull the trigger. He had brought all three bodies back to town, wrapped in their blankets and tied to their saddles.

"After they killed the Indian and opened up on me, there was nothing else I could do," he told the grief-stricken parents. He remembered the scene well, Bob with his arms around his sobbing wife, having difficulty choking back his own tears.

"I didn't want it to be this way, Bob," Henry had said. "I wanted to bring them back alive."

Bob said he understood, but Henry recalled they never played checkers together again. A couple of years later Bob's heart played out, and his wife moved away.

Henry's explanation about the money was that "They must have buried it somewhere in the mountains before we found them." He did organize a posse to search for the missing money, but they gave up after a week. Through the years some people continued to search for it, though now it was mostly just kids hoping to find buried treasure.

There were, of course, some who suspected Henry of taking the money, but no one was brave enough to accuse him.

Almost fifty thousand dollars, he thought. Now Rachael wants me to send another two hundred dollars to Rosie and that worthless husband of hers. If they only knew what I had to go through to get my money.

He had been careful with the money, not changing his lifestyle because of it, never spending so much that he would come under suspicion. He had used some of the money to make investments near Oklahoma City and Dallas, mostly in land. He had always felt compelled to laundry the money before using it.

The Claxton boys were not the only lawbreakers to fall before Henry's shotgun during the time he was sheriff, but they were the only ones he felt any sorrow about. God will forgive me for the rest, he reasoned, because most of them was real outlaws, Niggers and Indians. I do feel bad about old Jake, though. He was a good Choctaw as Indians go, one of the few I ever enjoyed hunting and fishing with. But my god, the Lord put the temptation of the money in front of me, and He must have known it would be too much for me.

Henry was never adverse to blaming God for his mistakes or decisions.

He wondered what Anise Marie was doing on this rainy afternoon, whether she would like for him to screw her. He answered the question himself. Of course, she would. She's probably frittering around the house now, doing a whole lot of nothing.

Dammit, if I'm going to think about a piece of tail, I ought to be thinking about somebody's a helluva lot better than Anise Marie. Rachael kept crowding into his mind, and he tried to remember the last time he had been on top of her. It had been so long that he could not remember.

It was difficult for him to think of Rachael sexually. He could vaguely remember how frightened she had been on their wedding night, and always he remembered her lack of reaction to his love-making.

I always wanted to be able to get along just sleeping with her, he lied to himself, but her sexual appetite just wasn't strong. Not strong, hell. It was non-existent.

His mind then wandered to a river slough, a place where he was fishing. He was wading, a stringer of fish tied to his belt, and a water moccasin was following him, trying to get his fish. He thrashed at the snake with his fishing pole, but it would not go away. Finally, he cut the stringer from his belt, giving the fish to the snake. But the snake and the fish continued to follow him.

He was daydreaming now, almost asleep. The rain and gentle movement of the rocking chair sang him a lullaby. The image of the snake was now replaced by the blurred vision of a child. He kept trying to see through the fog-like blur, thinking the child could be Henry Junior, or his unborn grandchild. But the more he tried to see, the more the shape of the child melted away. Don't go, he wanted to cry aloud, but no sound came from his throat. The face disappeared. He tried to bring it back, but he had lost control of his thoughts.

His mind now pictured a winter scene in the Kiamichi Mountains, a big buck staring at him. He saw himself raising a gun and drawing a bead on the deer, but then the child was there in his gunsights and the deer was gone. He tried to put the gun down, but he had already pulled the trigger.

My god, no, he cried. Suddenly everything was black and then light again. He could see the batwing doors of a saloon, a hitching post between him and the entry. It looked familiar.

Suddenly, the doors crashed open with a violent flurry as two men, grappling with each other, pitched headlong into the dusty street. One had a knife and he was shoving it at the other with maniacal desperation. Beads of sweat stood out on the faces of both men as they struggled. The weaponless one, already bleeding from knife wounds to an arm and his face, held doggedly to the wrist of the arm and hand holding the cold steel.

A crowd had gathered and he remembered a voice asking, "Aren't you going to stop them, sheriff?"

"Let the fuckin' Indians kill each other," he said. "Town would be a lot better off if they all killed each other."

He watched, fascinated, as the two Choctaws rolled in the dust, both like wild animals. Finally, the weaponless one lost his hold and the knife plunged into his chest. He heaved, spat blood, and then lay still on the street.

"Okay, you bastard you," Henry said to the victor, "let's go to jail."

The Indian, hearing the voice behind him, swung around in a puzzled crouch, the bloody knife still in his hand. Henry watched the slug from his pistol catch the man in the chest and knock him backward. He could see the faces of the men, women and children who had watched the fight, their gasps of horror at what had happened.

"Self defense," he muttered.

He tried to shake his mind of killing, to think of placid lakes, gentle flowing streams, fish frying in a pan over an open campfire. Instead, his mind had him playing checkers with Bob Claxton. The checkerboard was on two coffins, the Claxton boys coffins.

He tried to end the game, but it was endless. And all the time they were playing he had to hold the coffin lids down, because Roth and Rush were trying to get out. A maddening sobbing was coming from inside both coffins.

He struggled to hold the lids down, to concentrate on the game. He kept waiting for Bob to make a move, but then he looked at his eyes. They were blank. Bob couldn't make a move because he was dead, just like his sons.

A wetness hitting him in the face broke the spell. The wind had changed directions and was blowing rain onto the porch. He continued to sit there a moment, letting the raindrops wash his face. He wanted a cup of coffee. He would go to the kitchen and have Rachael make him some coffee.

"Fuck it," he said aloud. "Fuck it all."

CHAPTER SEVEN

Bethel was making very little progress toward becoming a modern city. The sidewalks were still made of rough boards and the streets were unpaved. Hitching posts ran the length of Main Street, and the town's two saloons still had batwing doors. Most of the town's buildings were constructed of unpainted lumber, though a few of the newer additions were built of native stone. It was as if the town wanted to cling to the past, was reluctant about moving into the twentieth century.

Henry hated the place.

It was not the buildings or sidewalks or unpaved streets that he hated, but rather the obvious pride most of the town's leaders had in stifling progress. Henry equated the town's leadership with the smell of the public outhouse at the end of Main Street. To him, they were all shitheads.

Bethel was always a beehive of activity on Saturdays. People from throughout the area came to town to buy groceries, and to sit in their cars, pickups and wagons gawking at other people walking up and down the sidewalks.

The Hayders usually arrived in town about mid-morning, which enabled Henry to get a good parking spot on Main Street. He didn't really care to go to town on Saturdays, nor did he give a damn where he parked. He went, though, because Rachael wanted to go, and he always found a good parking spot on Main Street where she could sit in the car and watch all the people go by. She especially liked for Henry to park in front of the drug store.

Gives her a chance to see who's sick and buying medicine, he grumbled to himself. That way she can have something to talk about with her church cronies.

Sitting in the car, watching people mill up and down the street, talking to neighbors who chanced by, was Rachael's only social outlet other than church. All her conversations generally centered around the church, primarily in regard to the preacher and his topic of the previous Sunday. But there was also gossip about the marital and financial problems of neighbors, which included much shaking of heads and mock sadness about the woes of others.

The gossip and looking would go on until late afternoon, then the Hayders would buy their groceries and go home. In the summer, however, there were often baseball games at two o'clock, so Henry would have Rachael and the groceries home by one-thirty, which, though she didn't say anything, didn't please her at all.

Carl being the ace pitcher for the town baseball team was no small delight to Henry, who fancied himself to be the most knowledgeable man in the county about the sport. His fanciful knowledge was based on watching and reading about the game, not on having participated.

Though not a man of formal education, Henry was a avid reader. He was one of the few people in Bethel to read *The Daily Oklahoman* thoroughly every day, and he often contributed an article to the town's weekly newspaper. If anything, his constant reading of all types of books, and his professed knowledge of so many things, made him less than comfortable to be around for most of the townspeople.

In truth, it was Carl's considerable skill in pitching a baseball that enabled him to get a job at the lumber company. Though the baseball team carried the town's name on its uniforms, it was actually the sawmill that sponsored the club.

But hard as jobs were to come by at the time, Rachael would have preferred that Carl not be a ballplayer. She feared for his soul, because most of the team's games were played on Sundays.

He shouldn't play on Sunday because it's the Lord's Day, she thought, though she never voiced her objections aloud for fear of Henry's rage.

Henry wished he could see a baseball game every day, and he would have preferred games that would last all day on Saturdays. He hated Saturdays without ball games, the sitting in the car staring at people, which he felt obligated to do because of Rachael. However, his obligation seldom lasted more than five minutes. It just seemed longer to Henry.

He would usually stay in the car long enough to shock one of Rachael's friends with his language, then he would wander over to one of the saloons. Either of the saloons was a good place for conversation, for listening to music and for dancing, not to mention the enticement of cold glasses of beer. He figured a few cold ones in the morning would warm him up for some serious afternoon drinking.

Carl and Vivian usually accompanied Henry to the saloon, which caused Rachael a great deal of mental anguish. She always acted ignorant regarding their whereabouts, but she also knew about the wine that Henry kept in the barn. Her primary fear was Henry's influence on Carl, and it also upset her that Vivian would go into a saloon.

She wanted to like Vivian, but it was hard for her to share her only son's affection. She felt that Vivian was robbing her of that.

Rachael often wondered about Vivian, what she was thinking, what she was planning. She was relatively sure that Vivian was pressuring Carl to move out of the Hayder house, to get a place of their own. She even suspected Vivian of trying to talk Carl into moving away from Bethel.

Thinking about Carl moving out of the house where he was

born caused pains in Rachael's chest. She could not stand the thought, and she tried to think of a way to negate Vivian's influence over him.

Her thoughts were interrupted by a voice saying, "Well, Rachael, it's so nice to see you."

"My goodness, Anise Marie," Rachael replied, "sit down here in the car and talk to me a spell."

Anise Marie opened the car door and squeezed into the driver's seat saying, "Tell me all you've been doing this week."

"There's sure not much to tell," Rachael said. "I've just been working in the garden and cooking."

"Are you getting any work out of Henry?" she questioned, laughing.

"You know Henry," Rachael replied. "He does pretty much what he wants to. He's always buying somebody's land, but he doesn't show much interest in farming it." Rachael liked Anise Marie and knew nothing of her relationship with Henry.

"I don't guess there's any need working when you don't have to," Anise Marie responded.

"I'm just not built that way," Rachael said. "There's just too much work to be done, and the good Lord put us here to be busy, not idle."

"I know what you mean," Anise Marie confirmed. "When I don't spend my day doing housework and working in the yard, I feel guilty about it."

"If you'll remember, the preacher said last Sunday that an idle mind is the devil's workshop," Rachael recalled.

"Wasn't that a wonderful sermon," Anise Marie stated.

"It certainly was," Rachael agreed. "I wish every sinner in Bethel could have heard it."

"I'm afraid that's a wish you'll never see fulfilled, Rachael."

Rachael nodded and sadly lamented, "I know, I know."

The two women sat quietly for a few moments before Anise Marie broke the silence with, "How's Vivian getting along, carrying the baby and all."

"She seems to be doing fine," Rachael said. "I think it's going to be an easy delivery."

"I tell you, mine was easy," Anise Marie replied.

"None of mine were easy," Rachael said.

"Which one was the hardest?"

"I don't recall," Rachael answered.

"Where's Henry, Carl and Vivian?" the younger woman asked.

"I don't know," Rachael lied.

Three beers and Henry became philosopher, historian, wit and political analyst, all rolled into one.

"You boys can all vote for Roosevelt if you like," he said, "but I'm going to give some serious thought to voting for that feller Long from Louisiana."

"I heared he was for the Niggers," Dan Slocum said, "and that he called the Klu Klux Klan a bunch of sonofabitches."

Henry looked incredulously at the short, balding man. "Well, Dan, you sure as hell heard wrong," he chided. "And there isn't a bigger Nigger loving sonofabitch in this country than Roosevelt. He's a damn New York yankee, and by god, I've seen pictures of his wife and if she's not half-Nigger, I've never seen one."

"Now don't go off half-cocked, Henry," Fred Bascom warned. "Roosevelt's our President and I know damn well he can't be married to no part Nigger."

"I'll wear my boots full of piss for a year if you can prove she's not half-Nigger," Henry retorted. "Problem with you, Fred, is that if somebody's a Democrat, you'd eat a yard of their shit."

"You're gettin' off the subject as always," Dan said. "What about this fella Long sayin' what he did about the Klan? He sounds like a Nigger lover to me."

"Long didn't call members of the Klan sonofabitches," Henry informed. "It was the Imperial Wizard of the Klan that he called a sonofabitch, and that's because the bastard was planning to come to Louisiana to campaign against him."

"Well, there's got to be some reason the head of the Klan would come to Louisiana to campaign against Long," the thin faced Fred said. He moved a wad of chewing tobacco around in his mouth, aimed a squirt of tobacco juice toward a spittoon a few feet away and missed.

"Maybe the head of the Klan's a Democrat," Henry said, angrily.

"I can tell you that Huey Long's not working for Niggers or Nigger votes. He's working for poor folks, folks like you and me. You know what his slogan is? It's every man a king."

"Since when have you been poor folks, Henry?" Fred asked. "For somebody who's so all-fired poor, you always seem to have money to buy up every piece of land you can find. What are you goin' to do with all that land anyway?"

Henry didn't like Fred. He didn't like his looks and he didn't like the fact that he was a Democrat. Fred was thin as Rachael, but what was most distasteful about him was greasy-gray hair and droopy eyes.

"It's none of your fuckin' business why I'm buying land," he said.

Dan interrupted, "I don't know, Henry. I think Roosevelt's doin' a pretty good job."

"Are you goin' to vote for the bastard?" Henry asked.

"I reckon I will, Henry," Dan said. "I'm sure as hell not votin' for no Republican, and I'm not sure this Long feller is any better than a Republican."

"Dammit, Dan, sometimes your ignorance is amazing," Henry said sarcastically. "You're like a lot of other stupid bastards who think the Republicans are responsible for the Depression."

"Well, we sure as hell had a Republican President when this damn Depression started," Fred replied.

Henry shook his head slowly with disbelief and cursed under his breath, obviously disgusted with the reasoning of his companions. He swigged beer from his glass, then motioned for Eli Barstow to join them at the table. "You want to play some dominos with us, Eli?"

"Sure, Henry, be glad to," Eli replied. A gaunt looking man with a two-day growth of beard, he had been standing at the bar drinking alone.

Dan began shuffling the dominos. Neither he nor Fred said anything more about politics for, while they would argue with Henry on occasion, they knew it would be the subject of conversation again only if Henry chose to make it so.

Carl and Vivian were sitting at a nearby table drinking beer and talking, both amused at Henry's political tirade.

"That Henry," Vivian laughed. "He could argue the horns off a billy goat."

Carl chuckled and said, "You're right, and I can guarantee you the argument's not over. Dad will begin to wonder if he had the last word. Tell you what, though. If Dan and Fred had been for Huey Long and against Roosevelt, Dad might have taken the other side. He'd damn near rather argue than eat."

"I really like your father, Carl," Vivian said. "He's so full of life."

After a sip of beer Carl replied, "He likes you, too, Viv. And you're right about him being full of life. He's never been short-changed on living."

"Your mother doesn't like me much, though, does she?" Vivian asked.

"Why do you say that?"

"Just little things."

"Like what?" he asked.

"The way she looks at me," Vivian responded, "and she seems to be so reluctant to talk to me."

"She doesn't talk to anyone all that much," he defended. "I think you're being overly sensitive."

"Am I?"

"I think so. I've never heard her say a bad word about you, and I've never seen her look at you in a bad way, either. Hell, she talks to you as much as she does to me and Dad."

"The difference, Carl, is that I'm around her all day. She has a lot more opportunity to talk to me than she does to you and your Dad."

"Are you trying to start something, Viv?"

"No, I'm not," she testily replied.

With obvious exasperation Carl asked, "What do you want me to say, that my mother hates my wife?"

"There's nothing to say, and I don't think she hates me. Dammit, Carl, it's just that living with your parents is getting on my nerves.

I just want a place of our own, a place where we can have some privacy."

"I'd like to move out, but we can't afford it now," he responded.

"When will we be able to afford it, Carl? Will we ever be able to afford it?"

"Dammit, Viv, don't start nagging," he said with controlled rage. "You're getting damn close to pissing me off. I'm not getting rich at the sawmill and we do have a baby on the way."

"I know, I know," she replied with resignation. "I just hope that when our baby's a man, he can stand on his own two feet."

"What in the hell do you mean by that?" he demanded.

"Nothing."

"You don't say shit like that without meaning something, Viv."

"Let's just drop it, Carl."

"No, dammit. I want to know what you meant by that fucking statement."

"C'mon, Carl," she half-teased, the other part of her a bit angry. "Don't be so defensive. People will think you're the one who's pregnant. I'm supposed to be irrational at this time in my life." He was not, however, amused by her semi-attempt at humor.

"You're a real smart-ass, Viv. A real smart-ass."

They sat quietly then, gazing at their half-filled glasses of beer. Their world was the sound of clicking dominos at nearby tables, the mumbling voices of other people involved in conversation.

Vivian pondered the men playing dominos with Henry. Eli was a strange looking man, the bone structure of his face so pronounced that he looked emaciated. She was sure that underneath the obviously dirty plaid shirt and overalls, the man's entire body was as wasted away as his face. The ears were too large for his thin face, and they were accentuated by the dirty felt hat he always wore. He was, she supposed, a farmer, and she couldn't help but wonder about the appearance of his wife, whom she had never seen.

And Dan Slocum, he reminded her of a friendly pig. He's a real porker, she thought, and he could pass for a pig if his nose were bigger. As it was, the man had flared nostrils and a wide flattened nose, oversized lips and beady eyes. And his pinkish-red hair was greasy and plastered down on his head. A pig, she continued thinking, a definite pig. I wonder what sort of sow his wife is. A smile tugged at the corner of her lips as she envisioned Slocum making love to a pig.

And what about Fred Bascom, he with the tobacco-stained teeth, the weak chin and mouth, and yellowish skin color that reminded her of baby shit. She smiled mentally, thinking of Bascom as six feet of skinny diarrhea clinging to bones constructed of constipated shit.

My god, what kind of mind do I have? she wondered.

Whatever kind of mind she had, it saw her father-in-law differently than it envisioned other men. Vivian liked Henry's strength, the resoluteness that seemingly made him tower above other men she had known. And while she did not admit it even to herself, she possessed many of Henry's characteristics. She was mentally stronger than her husband, much stronger than most of the women with whom she came in contact.

I wish Carl could be more like Henry, she thought, knowing it was impossible. She thought she loved Carl, but she could have loved a man like Henry more. That bothered her, that she had settled for less than what she really wanted. Then she wondered what it would be like to make love to Henry.

Carl interrupted her thought processes with, "I'm sorry, Viv."

She smiled, put her hands on his and said, "No, I'm the one who should be sorry. I guess I'm getting bitchy, the baby and all, you know."

"You're right, though," Carl admitted. "We should get a place of our own."

She knew he didn't mean it, that he was being patronizing. She hated it, him for his attitude. But she responded, "We'll have all that in time."

Their conversation was interrupted by Henry's booming voice, "I'll tell you what Huey Long will do, by god. He'll see that all poor men get a chance for a decent living and education. If you bastards don't want that for yourselves and your families, you sonofabitches are even crazier than I thought."

Carl laughed and surmised, "The political talk must have started again."

Henry stomped over to where Carl and Vivian were sitting and said, "Let's go. These stupid bastards are going to mess around and make me mad."

Vivian wanted to laugh. Henry could be so childish. But, instead, she and Carl obediently followed him out the batwing doors.

His face flushed with anger, Henry looked down Bethel's dusty street in disgust. Bethel, holy place of God, he thought.

He was referring to the Book of Judges, that passage about the people going to Bethel to ask counsel of God when Israel had no king. There's no damn similarity between the Bethel in the *Bible* and this Bethel, he reminded himself.

For some reason he remembered the Second Book of Kings, how Elijah visited Bethel and the sons of the prophets lived there. I'm the only prophet here, he thought. It amused him to think of himself in such a context.

His mood changed with his thought, The people here just depress the hell out of me. He wished Rachael were not waiting in the car, because he wanted to visit Anise Marie. It's been almost a week since I've had any, he thought. Can't remember ever going that long before, even when I was riding the circuit.

"What do you want to do now, Dad?" Carl asked.

"Hell, let's get the groceries and go home," he said. He figured to go by Anise Marie's after depositing Rachael at home.

Rachael didn't like leaving town early. It was only one o'clock and there was no ball game.

CHAPTER EIGHT

H ENRY PARTICULARLY liked to read about the St. Louis Cardinals, his favorite team. He had never seen the Cardinals play, though it was listed among the things he wanted to do before he died. Because he had been born in Pennsylvania, he also had a passing interest in the Philadelphia Athletics. He always rooted for the Athletics when they were playing the New York Yankees, a team he hated with a passion.

Had it not been for the children, he often thought, I might have moved to St. Louis after I got the money. I could have gone to all the Cardinals' games then. At such times he regretted having children, but such sorrow turned to pride when people around Bethel started calling Carl the best pitcher in Oklahoma.

Bethel was a hotbed of baseball interest. People turned out in large numbers to see the team play, in spite of warnings from the clergy about impending doom if the team did not stop playing on Sundays.

The lumber company, extremely careful in its hiring practices, attempted to field the finest semi-pro team in the state.

The people needed a winner and the team was definitely a winner, seldom losing, especially on its home field. Such an enviable record was, in part, due to the fact that Bethel did, indeed, have a fine baseball team. Another reason could have been that, at home, the team enjoyed excellent preferential umpiring. To suggest, however, that such preferential umpiring was anything less than honest could be detrimental to one's health. One outsider who made such a suggestion had his nose rubbed in moist cow shit by some of the more rowdy drunken fans.

Local fans were drafted to umpire games and, admittedly while some were not all that familiar with the rules, siding with the home team in spite of protests from the opposition earned them the respect of their peers. Honorable men who tried to umpire impartially were so chided by their neighbors that they never tried again.

Home-grown umpires did not require Bethel pitchers to come as close to the strike zone as was mandatory for opposing pitchers. And close calls on the bases always seemed to favor Bethel.

But what the opposition faced in terms of umpiring at Bethel, the local team faced on the road. It was something the ballplayers learned to live with and anticipate. It was important for every town to field a winner. Other than a winning baseball team, there was little else to take pride in. Jobs were scarce and life was little more than existing from day-to-day.

The players received no money for displaying their skill, only a job if they were lucky. So, there was nothing resembling a paid or impartial umpire.

With Carl pitching, however, Bethel didn't lose often even when they played away from home. He had all the tools; a fastball that was a natural sinker, a quick-breaking curve, and unbelievable control. He rarely walked a batter and his strikeout total was staggering, almost two per inning.

"Who you think's going to win today, Henry?" The questioner was a smiling Zack Beatty, owner of one of the town's three barber shops. Henry always figured that was too many barber shops for a town the size of Bethel, and he often wished Zack would mash some of the more obvious blackheads from his oversized nose.

"Carl's pitching," Henry said, "so that ought to tell you who's going to win." Zack had joined Henry where he had been standing watching Carl warmup, along the hogwire fence running parallel to the left field foul line.

"Who's umpiring?" Henry asked.

"Dwayne Darby's umpiring," was the reply.

"Well, we goddam sure better win or that little bastard had better leave town," Henry warned. He was rarely soft-spoken, and certainly didn't deviate on this occasion, so his profanity resounded in the ears of blushing, indignent women nearby. They turned to their husbands, only to find their spouses looking off and acting as though they did not hear Henry. No man in Bethel was willing to call Henry down for the way he acted or the way he spoke.

The rough board stands behind home plate and down the first and third base lines were filled with fans. Cars and wagons lined the fences stretching down the left and right field lines. Since there was little else to do on Sunday afternoons, there was always a crowd for baseball games. But this game was more special than most. It was against Broken Bow, Bethel's most-hated rival. Broken Bow had already beaten Bethel once two weeks earlier at Broken Bow, but Carl wasn't pitching that game.

"What do you think about the Cardinals being in fifth place?" Zack asked. Henry wished Zack wouldn't fuck with him. He just wanted to watch Carl warm up.

"It's early," Henry responded. "They'll be in the thick of it before long."

"I don't know," Zack said, leaning his short, thin frame against a fence post. "The Giants and Dodgers are awful strong this year."

Dammit, Henry thought, I wish the weazel-eyed little sonofabitch would leave me alone.

"Zack, if you knew a damn thing about baseball, you'd know that the Cubs are the only real competition the Cardinals have this year."

The obvious sarcasm of Henry's response rolled off Zack like water off a duck's back because he, like everyone else in town, knew that anytime you talked to Henry you stood the chance of being ridiculed.

"Detroit's in sixth place in the American League, too," Zack continued. "Don't look like they're going to win it again either."

"Goddamit, Zack, everything you're telling me is something I already know. If you had any sense, if you'd do just a little thinking, you'd know that the Tigers have played just fourteen games and the Cardinals have played thirteen. The last time I checked, teams in the American and National Leagues each had to play one hundred fifty-four games. It's too early for your asshole evaluations."

"Yeah," the persistent Zack said, "but I just don't believe Paul and Dizzy Dean can win forty-nine games between them like they did last year."

"That's something I'm willing to admit I don't know," Henry said, "but I'm willing to bet you that the Tigers and Cardinals play in the World Series just like they did last year."

Big-nosed sonofabitch, he thought. I probably ought to pity him because he's so stupid.

"Carl's going to have his hands full with these Broken Bow boys," Zack opined.

"He can handle them," Henry countered.

"I don't know," Zack fretted. "That big-assed Indian catcher can hit the ball a mile, and that sonofabitch they got pitching can really throw a fastball."

"That's right, Zack, you don't know, but I do," Henry matter-of-factly stated. "Their pitcher does have a good fastball, but he doesn't have a curve. Our boys will get him."

"I wish I was as sure as you, Henry. I bet that feller over there four bits that we'd win."

"Who the hell is he?" Henry asked, looking in the direction where Zack was pointing.

"Some feller from Broken Bow," Zack said.

"Well, I'll sure as hell take some of his money," Henry stated, confidently.

He walked to where the man was standing by the fence, sizing him up enroute. The man was medium height, with slicked back black hair, a checkered shirt and baggy trousers. He was wearing the kind of pointed-toe shoes that Henry was sure were worn by New Orleans pimps.

"Understand you're trying to give some of your money away," Henry said.

The man laughed, stuck out a hand and said, "Name's Bob Marks. I'm from Broken Bow."

Henry ignored the man's offer of a handshake and said, "Don't apologize, we all have to be from some place."

The man laughed again, this time a bit uneasily.

"My name's Henry Hayder, and I'll take two dollars of your money."

"You're on," Marks said.

"Play ball."

Dwayne's holler was more like a whine. He was a gawky, tow-headed youngster, clad in overalls, a blue denim shirt and what looked to be oversized brogans. A flunky at Ellers Grocery Store, he was a comic-like figure with his straw-colored hair sticking out from the straps holding the mask on his face. But he was the home plate umpire and, as such, represented authority. It was the most authority he had ever experienced, though he had once been left in the store for a couple minutes on his own.

Carl stood on the pitcher's mound, his shoulders slumped forward, waiting for the sign from the catcher. The heavy-set, squatty hitter fidgited nervously in the batter's box, swinging his bat over the plate in a rhythmic ritual. The fans buzzed quietly as Carl began his windup, then the ball was exploding out of his hand and into the catcher's mitt.

"Strike one," Dwayne yelled. The crowd roared its approval.

Dwayne had no problem calling the pitch because the batter did swing at it. In fact, he had no problem calling the next eight pitches. All three hitters struckout swinging.

For seven innings neither team could score, but in the eighth Bethel pushed across a run. All Carl had to do was stop Broken Bow in the ninth. With the hometown fans screaming their appreciation, he did just that, striking out the side.

Carl had struckout seventeen, walked none and had given up

just one hit. Fans passed the hat for him and the mayor presented him with the take, nine dollars and seventy-one cents.

Henry couldn't have been prouder. He would once again write a letter to the Cardinals, telling them about the exploits of his son.

CHAPTER NINE

T HAT SEPTEMBER the unmerciful pounding of the sun worked like a hammer and chisel on the granite-like crust of the earth, leaving winding cracks that resembled miniature earthquakes. The flow of creeks and rivers was slowed to a trickle, and stock ponds shriveled to little more than mud and mire.

Fish that had inhabited ponds and creeks now lay bloating and rotting in the mud, a stench to the nostrils but a delight to the water snakes that congregated in the last small recesses of putrid liquid.

Once green gardens that had yielded vegetables were now parched and brown. Any vegetables that had not already been harvested were cooked by the sun, and the remnants of once proud plants and fruit trees were so dry their leaves crackled with the slightest breeze.

But there were all too few breezes, and those that came were like a blast from an oven.

Heat rose from the ground like vapor from a teapot, causing distant objects to look distorted through eyes irritated by baked dust that swirled up from the ground. That dust seemed to hang in the air, burning your nostrils as though you were breathing a suffocating gas.

And when you walked, the heat seeping from the earth penetrating your shoes like thousands of tiny stabbing needles. Your sweat mixed with dust to clog the pores of your skin, making it seem as though dirt was replacing blood.

Nights were almost as hot as days, making sleep a fitful but necessary discomfort. And it was during the night that the cockroaches came from their hiding places, swarming like a great black army of armored vehicles. Undisciplined in their battle plan, the invaders scurried from place to place in search of food.

The roaches were, perhaps, as irritated by the heat as were the people. But unlike the people, the heat did not slow them to the point of collapsing. If anything, their speed and maneuverability intensified, meaning that very few of them fell to the tired feet of the enemy.

And while roaches claimed the night, flies became the occupying force of the day. It was as if Satan himself had loosened the bowels of hell on this part of the earth.

Meals were miserable because of the incessant buzzing of the flies, their all too often successful attempts to land on the food, or on the mouths and faces of the humans they held captive. There was no escape from what was happening, no place to hide.

The people began to think that hell could be no worse than the heat that kept them sleepless and filthy, or the devilish flies and roaches that often caused them to turn their food to vomit.

Punishment from God? Henry wondered.

Satan's work? Fuck the devil, he thought.

To some extent, Henry found the torment of the drought refreshing. He figured it would weed out the weak, purge the land of those who shouldn't be there in the first place. There were times when, lost in thought, he would laugh inwardly at the plight of his neighbors. It's time the fuckers learned to suffer, he thought. They're like the flies and roaches, no purpose. All they do is eat and fuck.

There was, of course, prayer. Much prayer.

The preachers looked to the heavens and prayed for rain. The people prayed, too. They wanted to believe, if only for the sake of their own sanity.

Henry thought the devil was probably sitting inside the fire of the sun laughing at them, pouring the rays of hell on them. You might bring them to their knees, he thought, but not me, you sonofabitch.

The preachers stood behind their pulpits sweating, yelling and gesturing less than they did in more pleasant weather, admonishing the people to "remember Job's affliction."

"What the fuck's that got to do with anything?" Henry kept saying to anyone who would listen.

On the eighth of the month, the St. Louis Cardinals beat the Boston Braves eight to five. The victory moved them two and one-half games in front of the Chicago Cubs. It was Paul Dean's seventeenth victory of the season.

On that same day, the Detroit Tigers held a ten game lead over the New York Yankees in the American League.

Possibly of lesser significance, it was also the day Vivian went into labor.

By four o'clock that afternoon the contractions were regular enough that Rachael sent word to Carl at the mill. Carl, fearful that his peers might consider him overly concerned, worked until the normal five o'clock quitting time. He then dropped by the saloon to have a beer with friends before going home.

Vivian lay on a feather mattress in the bedroom allotted to she and Carl. It was the only sanctuary they had, because the Hayder house was now also home to the Shipleys. Their presence there was, supposedly, temporary. They were planning to stay only until Arlo found work.

However, the planned brief stay had now stretched into the third month, and Arlo had made little effort to find another job. He was quite content to sit on the front porch in a rocking chair, explaining to anyone who would listen why he had failed at farming in Kansas. The failure was, of course, not his fault. The elements had been against him.

Vivian was in great pain. Beads of perspiration were popping

out on her forehead, then exploding like small balloons that had
been stuck with pins. Sweat trickled down the back of her neck
like rivulets, causing the sheet beneath her to be wet and sticky.
She continually rolled her body from side to side in a rocking
motion, moaned and bit her lip again and again until it was bloody.

Rachael knew the pains of childbirth, not only from having children of her own, but also from having helped deliver a number
of babies when medical help was not available.

Professional medical help had not been available when she delivered and even now there was only one doctor in town. The nearest
hospital was more than fifty miles away.

At this particular point in time, Rachael felt closer to her daughter-in-law than she ever had before. Vivian's pain had become a
bond between them, so she stood by the bedside wiping perspiration from the young woman's face and neck with a washcloth periodically dipped in a pan of cool water taken from the well. And
she wished the doctor would hurry.

Rosie had assumed a stance of helplessness at the bedside. She
stood with arms folded, watching her mother minister to Vivian's
needs and wondering why she felt such resentment toward her
sister-in-law. Was it envy of Vivian's beauty, or was it because of
the attention her mother was giving Carl's wife?

Be sensible, she thought. She's in pain. Mother's helping her
because she's in pain. She'd do the same for anyone.

That much Rosie was sure of, that Rachael would have aided a
neighbor as readily as she would Vivian. It was Rachael's way.
But Henry's infatuation with Vivian was another matter, one that
angered her. It's as if she is carrying his child, Rosie thought.
The resentment was intense because she believed Henry was doing
more for Carl and Vivian than for her family. Had Rosie known
about a recent conversation between Vivian and Henry, she would
have had even more cause to resent her sister-in-law.

"Henry, if the baby is a boy . . ." Vivian had begun.

He interrupted, "Of course it's going to be a boy." He would
not accept the child being a grand-daughter, not even the possibility.

"I think you're right, Henry, about the child being a boy. That's
why I think it's important that we talk."

"About what?" he wanted to know.

"Well," she continued, "your grandson is going to be carrying the Hayder name, and unless I have another child he will be the only one. I want you to promise me he won't be just another grandchild lost in the shuffle."

"You know better than that, Viv."

"I just want to be sure," she said. "He is going to be a special child . . . I feel it . . . and I want your word that he will be treated special."

"Why are you saying all this, Viv?" Henry asked.

Vivian knew how to appeal to Henry's ego, and the question gave her the opening she needed. "I want my child to be like you, Henry. I want him to be strong mentally and physically."

Henry knew there was a special chemistry between them, and her statement was verification of it. And though he hated to think in terms of a man being weaker than a woman, he knew his daughter-in-law was stronger than his son.

"I'm flattered, Viv," he responded, "but what are you asking me to do?"

"I guess I'm asking you to see to it that he receives his just birthright," she said. She knew her request would play games with Henry's active mind, trigger positive responses, because of his Biblical knowledge. She knew he liked to think of himself as some strong *Bible* character, and that the thought of being able to administer a birthright would appeal to his inflated ego.

She was right.

Mentally, Henry was already envisioning a strong bond with his grandson, so Vivian's request intensified his thought processes. The boy would take up the mantle, finish the work he had begun. He would make the Hayder name the most respected and the most feared in the county. Henry liked the idea.

Vivian spoke further to him of her respect for his intelligence, strength, courage and accomplishments. She spoke to him as no woman ever had before and, in so doing, assured her lineage control over the older man's land, money and anything else of material worth that he possessed.

Though only in her early twenties, Vivian had already become tired of suppressing her intelligence to appease Carl. In her discussion with Henry, she had not only opened the door of opportunity for her child but for herself as well. Henry, whether he would openly admit it our not, had discovered under his roof an intellect equal to, possibly superior, to his own. He would from that point on refer to Vivian as a woman with great common sense. And while he might never overcome his sexual desire for her, he would no longer see her as just another piece of flesh to appease his longing.

Vivian did not expect Henry to change his attitude toward all women because of her, nor did she expect her son's attitude to be any different than that of his grandfather. Like Henry, she thought of most women as being good for cooking, washing dishes, sewing, housework and as sperm depositories for men.

But she knew she was different.

Rosie possessed none of Vivian's confidence or shrewdness. She was the epitome of Henry's definition, unspoken though it was, of a woman. And there was no way that she could ever compete mentally with Vivian.

Only thirty-two, Rosie looked much older. What little beauty she might have possessed had been left on a barren Kansas farm. She had features somewhat like Rachael's, though she was forty to fifty pounds heavier. But for all practical purposes she was nondescript, so much a part of nothing that she was rarely noticed.

Childbirth had been easy for her. She had the kind of body that lent itself to easy birth. Of course, there had been some pain, even with the sixth child. She often regretted having six children, thinking that giving birth to so many had sapped the strength from her body. She wasn't sure whether Arlo wanted so many children because of his love for her, his religious convictions, or because he felt it made him more of a man. She suspected the latter, because Arlo was always trying to prove his manhood.

Rosie did love all her children, and she loved Arlo, though there were times when she shamefully felt that she could have married better. She suspicioned that Rachael knew about her feelings, but she prayed her father never would. She had married Arlo against Henry's wishes and, come hell or high water, she never wanted her father to have any inkling that she thought it might be a mistake. He would have reveled in such an admission from her.

The pain continued for Vivian. She was biting her lip, groaning, writhing in agony. She could hear Rachael talking to her, asking if there was anything she could do, but the voice seemed to be coming from some disjointed dream. Still, she shook her head negatively at Rachael's questioning, shut her eyes tightly against the pain, and mentally cursed what was happening inside her body. At that moment she hated Carl for doing this to her, and she hated the beast inside her that was trying to tear her apart.

Carl was now home, but the doctor still had not come. Carl took refuge on the porch with Arlo and Henry, not wanting to see Vivian suffer, and certainly not wanting to witness the birth of the child. Thanks to several beers, his talk was boisterous. But his thoughts were that what was going on in the bedroom was a woman's work, or a doctor's.

Rachael wasn't worried about having to deliver the baby herself. God knows, it won't be the first time, she thought, and I've got Rosie to help me. Thought of any of the men helping never entered her mind.

By now the sun had become a red ball of fire in the west, its rays filtering through the large oak trees and streaking the porch with varying shades of light. The oppressive heat remained, causing the tin roof to give off sounds like it might be breaking under the strain of the sun.

Arlo, peering through squinty eyes at Henry, said, "I don't think she'll have any trouble with the baby, do you?"

Henry refused to answer, just continued rocking steadily in his chair and looking off into the distance. His mind did not want to acknowledge that Arlo even existed.

Carl was both amused and uncomfortable at his father's attitude toward Arlo, which is why he answered, "Well, Arlo, she's pretty strong, but she's had more problems than we expected."

Arlo smiled with satisfaction that Carl had not ignored him and responded, "Rosie never had any trouble having any of our kids."

Henry glimpsed Arlo's smile, though he seemed to be totally disinterested in the exchange between his son and son-in-law.

He spat a wad of saliva into the dusty yard and thought, how in the fuck would you know, you sonofabitch.

Henry hated Arlo's appearance, thinking he looked like an idiot. And though the man was certainly not handsome or strong-looking, he didn't look that much different than thousands of other men. You might say that he was, like his wife, nondescript.

Arlo was a slightly built, with a weak chin that was accentuated by a pock marked face. His hair, reddish with streaks of gray, was combed straight back, further emphasizing a receding hairline. And he probably did use far too much hair oil.

Arlo was not oblivious to Henry's hatred, though he tried to hide the fact. His own hatred and resentment toward his father-in-law was intense, but he did need Henry's help. And as long as he needed that help, his hatred would remain submerged. Of course, he could not predict when he would be free of the need for Henry's help. He could not remember a time during his married life when he did not need his father-in-law's help.

Carl and Arlo continued making small talk, Henry ignoring it, until Arlo made the mistake of asking a question that hung in the heavy air like the stench of a dead dog that had laid in the sun for a week.

"Reckon Rachael's goin' to fix any supper?" he asked. Arlo knew he had made a mistake by the time the final word exited his mouth. Henry had always said Arlo let his mouth overload his ass.

Henry was out of his rocking chair, verbally lashing at the man like a rattlesnake, "You damn sonofabitch. Vivian's in there suffering and all you can think about is your fuckin' gut. I've a good mind to kick your balls off, you bastard."

Carl stepped between them, fearing that his father would do exactly what he was saying. But Henry, teeth clenched in anger, turned and stalked down the hallway toward the back porch. Arlo's muttered apology was wasted on angry, unhearing ears.

Jerking a towel from a nail in the wall above the wash basin, Henry went to the well and drew a bucket of water, which he poured over his head. The cool liquid soaked his hair and tickled his face and the back of his neck. He repeated the process a couple of times, then vigorously dried his hair with the towel.

The cool water made his head feel better, but he was still a raging inferno inside.

It's just like a bastard who's contributing nothing to be all in a sweat about supper, he thought. He was hungry himself, but certain things were more important than having supper on time. Vivian was more important.

He gripped the wooden side of the well until his sunburned knuckles whitened because of the pressure. He was boiling inside and wanted to calm himself before going back to the front porch. There was no reason to go back, except that it was his porch and no lazy-assed sonofabitch Catholic was going to keep him off his own porch.

There were times when Henry was actually afraid of himself. He feared the hatred that boiled over inside him, knowing that he was capable of killing under certain circumstances. He had, of course, killed a number of times before, but never in anger. The men who had fallen to his gun when he was sheriff were either no-goods who had done wrong, or they were men who died because of his calculating mind. He was not beyond killing in order to benefit his position.

He walked back to the front porch and sat down in the rocker, his face still flushed. Arlo didn't say a word. His bearing was that of a whipped hound. Had he possessed enough courage to speak, it could have been nothing more than a whimper. He sat on the edge of the porch with shoulders drooped forward and eyes downcast.

I wish the sonofabitch would get mad and cuss me, Henry thought. I wish he would say just anything so I could knock the hell out of him.

Henry had no doubts about his ability to beat Arlo to a bloody pulp. His mind-set was such that he was incapable of comprehending anyone might be stronger than himself.

Henry's vanity about his strength was well-known and, while most people considered it just vanity, no one dared challenge him. Even the most ignorant of men could see the violence in his eyes. And his body was obviously as hard as a rock. The daily swimming kept it that way.

Arlo certainly was not interested in a physical encounter with his father-in-law. He dreamed, though, of a day when Henry would be old and helpless, when he, Arlo, would be in control. He often imagined himself in control of a great many men, perhaps as a foreman at the sawmill. He would have been quite content, though, to just have some control over Henry.

The problem was that Henry acted younger than he did, and was definitely stronger and more aggressive. Arlo frowned at the thought of Henry outliving him and, in his mind, he envisioned the old man looking down at his dead face and grinning with delight. Arlo shuddered at the thought, but he couldn't get it out of his mind.

Rachael and Rosie had, of course, heard Henry's outburst against Arlo. It was pretty easy to hear him roar when he was angry.

Rachael, busy applying a cool cloth to Vivian's forehead, seemed unmindful of Henry's tirade, so Rosie volunteered, "I think I'll go fix supper for the men."

Rachael nodded approval and said, "I have some greens cooking on the stove, and you can warm up the leftovers from noon."

Roaches scurried from Rosie's footsteps as she entered the kitchen. The fire in the cookstove made the room unbearably hot.

She stirred the turnip greens that were already overcooked, and watched a piece of salt pork dance on top of greenish liquid that bubbled rhythmically. She boiled slices of salt pork, then fried them, and made a pan of cornbread. Pinto beans left from noon were warmed. The meal was ready.

After calling the men to supper, Rosie suggested that they fill their plates and eat on the porch, since the kitchen was so hot. They followed her suggestion, washing down the meal with cool glasses of milk taken from buckets hanging in the well. Henry and Carl ate with their usual hardiness, but Arlo picked at his food.

Rachael declined supper in spite of Rosie's insistence. Her mother's reluctance to eat properly, her thinness of body, was a source of constant concern to Rosie. She ate in the kitchen alone, feeling guilty that she had not prepared supper at the proper time.

With a little forethought, she reasoned, I could have prevented the conflict between Arlo and my father.

The conflicts between the two were inevitable, though Arlo was never a willing participant. Rosie, anxious to keep as much peace in the family as possible, had worked hard through the years to keep her father and Arlo separated. That was now impossible.

They had, with the help of the money Henry had sent, gotten back to Oklahoma by the skin of their teeth. She always hated asking her father for money, but Arlo had been insistent. He was always saying Henry had more than he knew what to do with, but she had never seen much evidence to support Arlo's claim.

Henry had sent them considerable money over the years, and like a dutiful wife she had turned it over to Arlo. He liked to have money in his pocket so he could brag and buy beer for his friends. Arlo had wasted all the money Henry had sent to them. He had never put any of it to good use, nor had he been generous with his family.

Now they had absolutely no money, Arlo didn't have a job or prospects for one, and they had to depend on her parents. There was no one else they could turn to for help, because Arlo's folks were dead. But Rosie knew that even if they had been alive, they couldn't have helped. So she was home again, and she hated it.

She also knew that the longer they stayed with Henry, the less respect she would have for Arlo. What little respect she had was close to total disintegration. Still, she knew that she could never leave her husband. She was like her mother in that respect, for better or worse. She just wished the children did not have to see their father suffer humiliation at the hands of their grandfather.

Thinking about the children, she decided to keep the rest of the supper warming on the stove, though she was sure that they had stuffed themselves in town and would not be hungry. That afternoon Henry had given each of the children two dollars and told them to go to town and have a good time.

Henry had demonstrated his generosity in front of Arlo, who had never given any of them more than a dime. Rosie resented it, the way Henry lorded it over Arlo. And twelve dollars, she thought, that's a fortune to us. The kids will waste it all.

The six children arrived about thirty minutes later, and Rosie's evaluation proved correct. They had spent all their money and they weren't hungry.

The Shipley children, like their parents, were nondescript. They were dressed in a hodge-podge of handed-down homemade clothing, much of which Rosie had made. They gave every indication of being poverty-stricken, which angered Henry.

I've given them enough money that they could dress the children properly, he thought. He could have taken them to town and bought them a decent wardrobe, but that didn't enter his mind. He figured seeing that the children were dressed properly was Rosie's job, but he also figured Arlo had never given her the money to do it properly.

Thanks to Rosie, the six children were not ingrates. They showed appreciation for both grandparents and, for the most part, were well-mannered. Though none of the six would have registered above average on an intelligence test, they did know their bread and butter was not coming from their father. And they were more than willing to appeal to their grandfather's inflated ego.

Shortly after their arrival home, they received a report on their aunt's condition, then the boys joined the men on the porch and challenged Henry to a game of checkers. He played a game against each of them, winning all four easily. He was, and considered himself to be, somewhat of an expert in checkers.

Rosie once asked him why he never let his grandchildren win.

"Let, hell," he responded. "You don't let somebody win anything. They either win or they don't. You let people win at one thing and they expect you to let them win at something else. That's the problem with this country today, the reason people are out of work. They want someone to give them something. I don't want my grandchildren to expect something for nothing. I don't want them to be like your husband. So, if they win from me they're really going to win. I'm not going to give them something for nothing."

Rosie never brought the subject up again.

"Cardinals won today," Mark volunteered. He was a husky boy, clearly Henry's favorite of the Shipley children, and he shared his grandfather's interest in baseball.

Looking up from the checkerboard, Henry asked, "Dizzy pitch today?" Because of Vivian, he hadn't been keeping up with the scores or pitching rotation for a few days.

"No, Paul pitched," Mark continued. "Beat the Cubs eight to five. They got twelve hits off him, but he beat'em."

"Seems to me that's Paul's seventeenth win of the season," Henry said, "and Dizzy's already won twenty-four. You know, those two might even win forty-nine between them, like they did last year."

Henry liked talking baseball with his grandsons. He liked to demonstrate his knowledge of the game, but the thing he liked most was Arlo's objection to his sons interest in baseball. Arlo called it a waste of time.

If anybody knows anything about wasting time, it's him, Henry thought. He's an expert at wasting time.

They continued chatting about baseball in general while playing checkers, about the Pirates great shortstop Arky Vaughn hitting over four hundred; about whether the Braves Wally Berger, who had thirty-one homers, could catch Hank Greenberg, who had thirty-four; and about Carl Hubbell, who already had twenty victories. How many more would he have had if he had been pitching for the Cardinals? The checkers and baseball talk cooled Henry's anger.

Maybe next year, he thought, the Cardinals will want Carl to pitch for them. It was a dream he had for himself as much as for Carl.

But even with all the baseball talk and checker games, Henry could not forget the fact that Vivian was about to give birth, a child he was sure that would be a boy. And Vivian's recent talk with him had not gone unheeded. He had a present for the child that he had not told anyone about. He had bought the local newspaper for his grandson, and he planned to present the deed to Carl and Vivian as soon as the child was born.

Of course, it will be a few years before he can run the newspaper, Henry thought. I'll have to direct things for a time. But when he gets grown, he can be a newspaper man and a baseball player.

Unknown to family members, Henry had made several recent purchases, one of which was the local bank. He could loosen up

and spend some money now, because oil had been discovered
on some of his land near Oklahoma City. It was something else
he hadn't told the family.

By nine o'clock Arlo and his sons said goodnight and went to
bed. Arlo's bedtime edict didn't set well with the boys, who preferred to stay up a bit longer with their grandfather. Arlo insisted,
however, that they needed their rest, more to prove his authority
than any real concern about how long they slept.

Any other time, Henry might have argued, asking Arlo why
he or the boys needed rest since they didn't work. But this night
was different. He had even lost interest in belittling the man.

"Carl, I got a jar of muscadine wine cooling in the well," Henry
said. "Go get it for us, and bring a couple of glasses from the
kitchen."

Carl obeyed, and as Henry poured them both a glass of wine
he said, "I wish to hell the doctor would get here."

Henry checked his watch. It was nine-thirty. At that exact time,
a time when Vivian was suffering her most severe pains, in Baton
Rouge, Louisiana, Dr. Carl A. Weiss shot Senator Huey P. Long.

The doctor arrived at eleven o'clock. He examined Vivian and
shook his head negatively moments later when Carl asked him
how she was doing. The doctor made periodic checks on her,
but let Rachael and Rosie stay in the hot room applying cool cloths
to her face. He spent most of his time with Carl and Henry,
helping drink the cool wine. By two o'clock that morning the
threesome had consumed three gallons.

At ten minutes after four that morning, Carl Henry Hayder
was born. It was at the same time that Senator Long died of his
wounds.

It was a couple of days later that Henry was reading about the
senator's death. He felt strange when he noted that his grandson
was born at the same time Senator Long died.

Better keep this to myself, not mention it to Rachael, he thought.
She'll think it's some kind of sign.

CHAPTER TEN

CARL HENRY Hayder grew in stature and wisdom. And, if not in favor with God, certainly in favor with his grandfather.

There was reason.

Henry spent a great deal of time with the boy, teaching him many of the things he had learned. He taught his grandson the intricacies of hunting and fishing, and he taught him to love and appreciate nature. But more important, Henry taught the youth his basic philosophies, his attitude toward people and life in general. Almost from the day he was born, Carl Henry was being molded into a mirror image of his grandfather.

During this period things changed dramatically for the entire Hayder family. Both the newspaper and bank were doing extremely well for the times. Not that either business would have had to prosper, because Henry was receiving substantial sums from his oil-rich lands.

The newspaper's prosperity was based on what some businessmen quietly referred to as blackmail. If a merchant wanted to do business with Henry's bank, he advertised in Henry's newspaper. Henry didn't consider it blackmail, merely good business.

Henry had finally achieved the basis for power, and for almost complete control of the town. He had money, plenty of it, and a newspaper that gave him the last word on every issue. The money gave him all the power he really needed, and he wielded that power casually, like a king who had been given the right through birth.

Still, though, Henry refused to be pretentious. He could have built what would have been considered a mansion in Bethel, but he refused to leave the old house. It held too many memories to be abandoned.

The Shipley family had finally moved out. Or had been kicked out, depending on interpretation. Henry had given Arlo an ultimatum, and Rosie goaded her husband into getting a job at the sawmill. That job was made available to him only because Henry owned the bank. The sawmill also depended on Henry's bank.

Arlo had envisioned himself having an important job at the bank, but Rosie eventually convinced him that until he proved himself at the sawmill there was no chance. So Arlo went to the sawmill to prove himself, and with his first check he rented a house in town for his family.

Though Arlo could not be described as bright, he figured his marriage to Rosie assured him a windfall at Henry's death. The old man's death was something he prayed for daily.

But Arlo was not the only one who smelled the pie. The Rebbs and Smarts had returned to Bethel to make sure they wouldn't be cut out of their piece.

Their return made Rachael happy, because she now had all her children and grandchildren near. But Henry considered their return, along with that of Arlo's, as a gathering of buzzards.

About his sons-in-law, he thought, it will be a cold day in hell before they get anything for me. My grandchildren I'll take care of, but not those bastards.

Sons-in-law Verdo and Jack quickly realized Henry wasn't about to give them work at any of his operations, so they, like Arlo, took jobs at the sawmill. And like Arlo, they were both confident their time would come.

The switch in ownership at the bank and newspaper went smoothly. Henry retained the employees at both operations, even bought their loyalty by giving all of them a raise. He left no doubt, though, that in terms of decision-making and authority, he called the shots.

He made Carl vice president of the bank and general manager of the newspaper, fearing even as he did it that his son lacked leadership qualities. The move angered his daughters and sons-in-law, which in Henry's opinion made it worthwhile, even if it was wrong.

It soon became apparent, however, that Carl was not meant to wear a suit and tie. He was miserable in his new positions. He was incapable of grasping even the most elementary business methods, and could never be trusted to make logical decisions in regard to money. Carl was more atune to working at the sawmill, drinking beer with his pals, and undertaking nothing more mentally demanding than reading a western novel. While he might not admit it to himself, subconsciously Carl wanted to be told what to do. He hated responsibility.

Carl's unhappiness with the responsibilities imposed on him by his father were so obvious that Henry suggested he return to the sawmill. Carl was more than happy to oblige.

But then Henry made a move that further alienated his daughters and sons-in-law, and even infuriated Carl. Henry made Vivian vice president of the bank and general manager of the newspaper.

To name a woman to such positions of responsibility was unheard of, and such a young woman at that. In town the move was greeted with whispers of incest, and Carl took considerable ribbing on the job about his wife taking his jobs. Because he was already unsure of himself, Carl's fragile ego was shattered by his father's decision. And Vivian's willingness to take on the responsibilities caused strife between them.

Henry, as was generally the case, knew exactly what he was doing. He realized Vivian was smarter than any of his daughters or sons-in-law, that she had a mental toughness his son did not possess. She was also completely trustworthy. He knew her sole motivation was to provide a future for Carl Henry.

Bank and newspaper employees were, of course, also incensed about having a woman for a boss. Some even talked of quitting, but there was really no place for them to go. Henry considered their plight humorous.

Vivian turned out to be a prototype of the perfect business-woman. Employees at both the bank and newspaper quickly came to respect her sound judgment and fairness. They did fear her, because beneath an exterior of friendly persuasion they sensed a Henry-like toughness.

Regular and business customers who came to the bank thinking they could manipulate a woman vice president soon became wiser for their efforts. Vivian, like Henry, knew how to wield power.

For example, if a merchant came to the bank wanting a loan, Vivian insisted on loaning him more money than he requested. She then insisted that the extra money be used for newspaper advertising, and an advertising contract with the paper would be signed at the same time the merchant was signing his loan agreement with the bank. Those who refused to advertise usually didn't qualify for loans. And when it came to collateral to secure a loan, she always insisted on tying in everything the applicant owned.

"I'm sure you're going to pay the loan back," she would tell an applicant, "so what difference does it make how much of your property you pledge against it?"

An applicant did not want the banker to think he might renege on the obligation, so he normally went along with Vivian's abnormal collateral requests. She was actually better at squeezing collateral from an applicant than Henry, which is why some of her foreclosures made the Hayders all that much richer.

Vivian so completely controlled both businesses after a time, that Henry was content to step aside and spend more time with his grandchild. Spending time with the boy, next to screwing, was what he enjoyed most.

At night, Young Henry would always join his grandfather on the back porch for the purpose of taking a leak before going to bed. Henry always urged the boy to piss for distance. That's why, during the day, Carl Henry would stand on the porch and try to piss on one of the chickens pecking in the yard.

And when he was at the saloon, Henry would often boast that his grandchild could piss further than most grown men. In Bethel, being able to piss long distances earned a man the accolades of his friends. After all, life was pretty simple in that corner of the world. There was little else to do except drink beer, piss, screw, hunt and fish. About the only other entertainment were baseball games in the summer and high school football games in the winter.

Summers also brought out a continual stream of evangelists, all doing their best to call the right-thinking people of Bethel back to God. During that period preachers were suffering hard times, because offerings were small. So they preached more for less.

Rachael loved summers, and the outdoor revival meetings.

It was at one of these outdoor revival meetings that Arlo Shipley was saved from the evils of Catholicism. He became a Methodist.

Henry's reaction to Arlo's conversion was as expected. Simply put, "We don't want that sonofabitch in the Methodist Church. It's enough to make me quit being a Methodist."

For all practical purposes, Henry's last contact with Methodism was years before when he was a preacher, but on occasion he liked to consider himself a patriarch of God.

"By god, I might just join the Baptist Church," he threatened, a warning that sent the good Baptists of Bethel to their knees in prayer entreating God to keep Henry a Methodist.

Arlo's professed conversion could have in part been due to despondency for what he termed bad luck over the years, something he had been indoctrinated to think might be a direct result of his Catholicism. Or subconsciously, he might have been trying to slip into Henry's good graces, proving himself worthy of the Hayder fortune. He might have figured his conversion wouldn't do Rosie any harm in Henry's will, if indeed the old man had a will.

And there is the possibility Arlo would not have been converted were it not for the liquid courage he consumed before going to the revival meeting. He had drunk a quart of muscadine wine prior to agreeing to accompany Rosie to the revival.

In Arlo's tortured mind, battered by Protestant fervor in a town that didn't even have a Catholic Church, he probably reasoned that conversion would do him no harm, if Arlo was capable of reason.

Regardless, Arlo's new-found spirituality did nothing to soften Henry's antagonism toward him. If anything, Henry was angry because he no longer had a Catholic to badger.

Henry might have been even more incensed were it not for a greater worry. A schism had developed between Carl and Vivian, primarily because she could do the work he couldn't, and now he spent most of his free time drinking. Henry wasn't opposed to a beer now and then, but he never wanted it to get to a point where alcohol controlled him or his son.

CHAPTER ELEVEN

HENRY WAS in bed with Anise Marie on his sixty-fifth birthday, complaining about Arlo and his newfound religion. He had just finished screwing Anise Marie, his first piece in almost two weeks. She was rubbing his balls with her left hand. He wished she would quit. When he was finished, he was finished. Besides, her rubbing his balls didn't cause the sensation it once did.

He began wondering about how much longer he would be able to get a hard on. Right now, he thought, I can get one on every day, but how long can a man go? He thought about his last piece, or pieces to be exact. Prior to Anise Marie, he had earlier screwed all three of the Chaney sisters.

"What are you smiling about, Henry?" Anise Marie's questions always came at inappropriate times.

"Just thinking about young Henry," he lied. "The boy's a real cutter."

She snuggled closer to him, still fiddling with his balls. "You

79

sure think the world of that child, don't you?" She expected an
obvious answer to her obvious question, so Henry obliged. All
their talk was trival, extremely boring to Henry. "Let's see now,
how old is he, Henry?" She knew the answer to that question
too, but he went ahead and told her that his grandson was four.

"Well, he certainly is big for his age," she rattled on. "Why, I
saw him the other day at the store with Vivian and he looked
every bit of six."

The mention of his daughter-in-law caused a tingle in Henry's
loins. He pictured her in his mind; the full, firm teats, the beautifully shaped butt and legs. God knew what He was doing when
He made a woman like Vivian, he thought. Vivian seemed to get
more beautiful with each passing day, and Henry couldn't help
but wish that it was her beside him. He tried to dismiss the
thought, because even he felt it was wrong to want his son's wife.
But it was impossible to get her out of his mind.

"Well, I'll declare," Anise Marie exulted. Henry's penis was
hard, standing up as straight as a flag pole.

My god, he thought. He would have to screw her again, no
matter how distasteful it was to him. He started to roll over on
top of her, but she stopped him.

"Let me get on top of you this time, Henry. You just lay still."
She placed his penis between her legs and began to move with a
slow, deliberate rhythm. It was pleasant enough, as long as he
continued thinking about Vivian. After a while he quit thinking
about her, though, and started thinking about the Chaney sisters.
They were all in their late forties, or early fifties. He wasn't sure.
Practically every able-bodied man in town had laid one, or all of
them, but not all of them in the same day.

The Chaney sisters were whores, of course, who normally
charged two bucks a screw. But since Henry had visited their
house at mid-day, and since business was very slow on a weekday,
he had bargained with all three to go to bed with him for only
two dollars.

Anise Marie squealed with delight as he exploded inside her.
Then, resting her sagging tits on his chest she squeezed him tightly
and said, "I wish you would come by more often, Henry. You
know there's no one else. I'm always here waiting for you."

Her sentimentality sickened him. "You have to remember that I'm getting on in years, Anise Marie. I'm just not up to it." He rarely used age as an excuse for anything, but with her he made an exception.

"We don't have to go to bed, Henry. We can just talk. I always enjoy just talking to you."

"I like talking to you, too," he lied, "but if I hang out here too much people will start talking. I don't mind them talking about me, but I don't want them talking about you."

His professed respect for her status in the community caused tears to swell up in Anise Marie's eyes. She was a very emotional woman. "You're so sweet, Henry. I guess that's why I've always loved you."

Henry had no difficulty lying about most things, but telling Anise Marie that he loved her was a falsehood that always stuck in his throat. He just couldn't get it out. "You know how I feel about you," he acknowledged, "but it seems like circumstances have always kept me from doing what I wanted to do. Of course, there was the age thing, too."

Using the backside of a hand to wipe away the tears, she told him the age difference was never a problem. They made small talk for a while, then with false sadness in his voice he said, "I've got to go now. They're having a little birthday get-together for me at the house."

She nodded understandingly. "I'm glad you came to see me on your birthday, Henry."

"I wouldn't have wanted to be with anybody else," he lied.

Henry didn't go home. Instead, he went to the saloon. It was only four o'clock, two hours until supper and three hours until the party. He wasn't really keen on the idea of a party, but Vivian had insisted, and she had Young Henry backing her up.

Zack Beatty was standing alone at the bar, talking to the bartender, Casey Gause. Henry squinted after stepping from the sunlight into the dimly lit saloon, and didn't see Zack right away. By the time he did, it was too late. Zack waved for Henry to join him.

"Want a cool one?" Casey asked. He was a large man with heavy jowls and thin brownish-gray hair. Henry nodded affirmatively and wondered if there was any such thing as a thin bartender. He'd never seen one.

"Well, how's the top pisser in this part of the country?" Zack asked with a grin. Even in the dim light, Henry could see his yellowed teeth.

"You talking about me or Young Henry?"

"Young Henry, of course. Man gets your age and mine, he's not gonna have enough lead in his pencil to piss very far."

"Talk for yourself," Henry replied. "I can still piss as straight and as far as any man in this county."

"I'm sure not challenging you," Zack responded, wiping beer foam from his upper lip with the back of a hand, "but Henry, you just can't be the kind of stud you were twenty-five years ago."

"Why can't I?" Henry challenged. The way some men of his own age talked made Henry wonder if his own sex drive was not something unique. Guzzling the last of the beer from his glass, Henry motioned for a refill and said, "I'm going to tell you something, Zack, that you can believe or not. It makes no difference to me. But today I had three different women in the space of about two hours. Does that sound like the lead is gone from my pencil?"

Zack flashed that grin Henry couldn't stand and feigned disbelief. "C'mon now, Henry. Don't feed me that kind of bullshit."

"It's no bullshit, Zack. If you don't believe me, ask the Chaney sisters."

"Are you telling me that you laid all of them in one day?"

"Not in a day, Zack, in two hours."

"Hell, Henry, you might have paid them to lie for you."

"Have you ever known me to pay for something I didn't get, Zack."

"Well, Henry, I've never knowed you to pay for any pussy. You've had free stuff all over town for years."

Casey put in his two bits worth. "Zack, maybe you ought to go ask the sisters to give you the same treatment they gave Henry."

"Do you believe him, Casey?"

"Of course. I don't have any reason not to, and I never call a customer a liar."

Henry raised his glass and, before draining it, said, "By god, Casey, I'll drink to an honest man and a diplomat." He knew Zack wouldn't understand the word *diplomat*. Casey either, for that matter.

"Dammit, Henry, the older you get, the worse you get," Zack said. "If that grandson turns out to be anything like you, he'll go through every pair of drawers in town." Zack spoke with some envy and Casey laughed.

"Well, he's just liable to be worse than me," Henry confided. "The little booger already gets a pretty good hard on."

"By god, Henry, I don't think anything's sacred to you," Casey said.

"That's not true, Casey. When it comes right down to it, I'm a pretty religious man, even though I do have a few faults, women being one of them. Another is that I say pretty much what I damn please."

No one in Bethel knew Henry had once been a preacher. Rachael and the children had been warned to say nothing about it.

"I have to admit," he continued, "that I haven't been active in the church for some time, but I'll bet you I know as much scripture as any of the preachers in this town."

Zack shook his head in a form of amazement. "Dammit, that's what Casey was talking about. You don't give a shit for nothing. You'll bet on anything and say anything. You'll talk nasty about your grandson and bet on the *Bible*. Damn if you ain't something, Henry."

"Now hold on, Zack," Henry admonished. "I figure what I said about Young Henry was a compliment. There's nothing wrong with getting a hard on, but maybe you wouldn't know about that."

Casey joined with Henry in laughing at the innuendo.

Zack scowled and tried to laugh off the insinuation with a brag. "You ought to ask those two Choctaw women that I laid last week whether I can get a hard on."

"Choctaw women," Henry semi-yelled. "Choctaw women. By god, I'd just as soon play with myself as stick it in some filthy squaw. That the best you can do, Zack?"

"Dammit, Henry. I happen to know you've laid a few Indian women yourself," Zack responded.

Finishing his beer and motioning for another, Henry said, "Do you now, Zack? Have you ever seen me with a Choctaw woman?"

"Naw, I ain't seen you, but everybody in town says you'll fuck anything with two legs, so as many Choctaws as there are around, it just don't make sense that you ain't laid some of them." Though agitated, Zack seemed pleased with his reasoning powers.

Henry, his elbows on the roughly hewn wooden bar, peered at himself and Zack in the dirty, cloudy looking mirror that stretched along the wall behind Casey's back. "Have you ever laid a Nigger, Zack?"

"What?" Zack was surprised by Henry's question, so much so that he forgot about his earlier logic pertaining to Henry and Choctaw women.

"Have you ever laid a Nigger?" Henry repeated.

"No," Zack replied, shaking his head. "Why do you ask something like that? I know there's got to be some reason."

"Well, have you ever heard the old saying that fucking a Nigger can change your luck? You've heard that, haven't you?"

Zack hadn't heard it, but he didn't want to appear ignorant. "Yeah, I've heard it, plenty of times. What about it?"

"Well, Zack," Henry said, "you've always figured I was pretty lucky, haven't you? You know, not being hurt all that much by the Depression. Having good health and enough money to live comfortably on."

Zack nodded agreement that he considered Henry lucky.

"Things weren't always that way, Zack. There was a time when most of my luck was plumb bad. You got time to listen to this story?" Henry asked.

"Sure," Zack responded. Casey was also paying close attention. Both thought they might learn something of Henry's past, which had always been somewhat of a mystery.

Henry took a long swig from his glass before continuing. "I guess I was about eighteen at the time. Maybe nineteen, I'm not real sure. Anyway, we were living in Pennsylvania at the time. Like most farm folks, we didn't have much. My parents had a couple of cows, a pretty good piece of land for farming, even a few chickens. We always had plenty to eat, but we sure didn't have any money, so the clothes on our backs were hard to come by.

"My daddy was a good man, worked real hard, but he didn't seem to be getting anywhere. You know what it's like. Just like a lot of other folks we were just getting by.

"But one year things got worse. Pour me another beer, Casey. Like I was saying, it was a bad year. The crops failed, the cows went dry, and the old chickens wouldn't even lay. The coons, possums, squirrels and deer seemed to have disappeared into thin air. And it was impossible to catch a fish. I tell you, we were in bad straits, not even knowing where our next meal was coming from. My daddy was doing the best he could, but it just wasn't enough.

"Well, ever since I had been a little shit I'd heard the old saying that fucking a Nigger would change your luck. I guess you fellers can understand that we needed a change of luck real bad, so I decided to find myself a Nigger and do what I could for my family.

"I have to admit that I had already been eyeing a little Nigger bitch that lived down the road a piece. I guess she was about fifteen at the time, and she had one of the finest little asses you've ever seen. When she walked it twitched in such a way that you knew she wasn't wearing anything under her dress.

"I don't care if she was a Nigger, a man could see her and get a hard on even if he was plowing in hundred degree weather. She had big tits that stuck out as firm and straight as a bird dog on point. I don't care how old she was, she was some woman.

"Well, I coaxed her into our barn one day and laid it on the line. I told her about our bad luck and what I was proposing to do about it. I told her that if she would go along with it, I'd buy her a big bag of candy down at the store. As soon as my luck changed, of course.

"Well, fellers, she confessed that she had been eyeing me just like I was eyeing her, and that she was hoping that I would be the first to stick it in her. In spite of what you may have heard, Nigger gals are pretty particular about who lays them first. And there's even a sort of special blessing that goes along with the luck if you happen to be fortunate enough to get a virgin.

"Well, we climbed up in the barn loft and laid in the hay and, just as I suspected, she didn't have any drawers on under her dress. To be so young, she really knew how to stir me up. I sucked on her tits until they were as white as snow, then I stuck it to her.

"Let me warn you that the hair around a Niggers hole is a lot like barbed wire, so you may get a few cuts. But damn, it's worth it.

"I don't know how long we stayed in that loft. I had her ten, maybe even fifteen times. When you're fucking for luck you don't keep count. Besides, a Nigger woman can get you up a lot more times than a white woman. Boys, I'm going to be completely honest with you. It was so damn good that I had serious thoughts about marrying the girl." Henry paused, letting his statement soak in, watching the dismay registered on the faces of the two men. Then he continued.

"When I started thinking about marrying her, I had second thoughts. It just wouldn't have been right. If the Lord had meant for Niggers and whites to be married, He would have made them the same color. I decided there wasn't any point trying to change your luck if you were going to break one of God's laws.

"Anyway, our luck started changing almost immediately. We started catching some fish, the hens started laying and the cows started giving milk again. It was like a miracle, but the best was yet to come.

"After the little Nigger gal and I had finished in the loft one day, I decided to go fishing. I was digging for fish bait when I found a can full of money. From then on things got better and better for us. And I have to give credit where credit is due, to that little Nigger gal.

"What all this is leading up to, though, is Zack talking about me laying a Choctaw woman. I never have done that, and with good reason. You see, that little Nigger gal told me that if I ever laid an Indian woman the good luck spell would wear off."

Henry finished his beer.

"Damn if that ain't some story," Zack opined. He and Casey had been listening with rapt attention.

Henry's eyes clouded with seriousness. "Maybe the worse sin I ever committed," he acknowledged, "was not buying that little Nigger gal the sack of candy I promised her. I'm sure the Lord will punish me for that." With those final guilt-laden words, he turned and walked out of the saloon, waving farewell to Zack and Casey, both of whom had been hypnotized by the story.

"Do you think that old bastard's telling the truth?" Zack asked.

"I don't rightly know," Casey replied. "Henry's a hard one to figure out."

Meanwhile, Henry shuffled along the road toward home, home to the birthday party he didn't want. It was a nice day, though, just cool enough to be pleasant. And he was happy about the lie that he had just told Zack and Casey. He started thinking about what he had enjoyed most, the lie or laying Anise Marie twice.

The lie, he thought, chuckling aloud. God, it's good to be alive.

CHAPTER TWELVE

CARL HENRY was eight when his father went to war. Many of the folks around Bethel said going to war might be the best thing for him, since it would take his mind off the Cardinals not signing him, and off his problems with Vivian.

Cardinal scouts had watched Carl until the summer of thirty-nine, a year in which he developed arm trouble. His fast ball just lost its zing, forcing him to develop a knuckler. And though he continued to be a big winner for the Bethel team, scouts said his knuckler just wasn't big league caliber.

Being turned down by the Cardinals was the worst thing that ever happened to Carl. Maybe even worse than Vivian becoming such a successful businesswoman. That's why, folks said, he started drinking so heavily and running around on his wife.

Henry put a stop to the running around, though. He let Carl know in no uncertain terms that he wouldn't tolerate a man cheating on his wife. If Carl knew anything about the old man's woman chasing habits, he didn't let on.

The year Carl went off to fight Hitler's forces, Young Henry bagged his first deer.

It was one of those gray, wintry dawns that breaks slowly in the mountains. A deathlike silence hung over the land, broken only by the soft breathing of Henry and his grandson.

From their vantage point on the hillside, the two hunters could survey the gulley below without being detected. Henry had checked the area a few days earlier and had found signs of a big buck. He had planned carefully for the moment, because it was important to him that the boy not fail. Young Henry was armed with a twelve gauge double barrel shotgun. He was using a fallen tree as a brace. It was the same shotgun with which his grandfather had taught him to shoot squirrels and blackbirds.

The boy whispered, "I see one, grandpa." Henry scanned the brush until he saw the animal. He was pleased that the boy's keen eyes had detected the deer before he did.

"Easy boy, that's an old doe. Let's wait for a buck."

They continued to wait, giving the old man a chance to study his grandson. Young Henry was a muscular boy, tall for his age. He had his mother's dark eyes. His hair, which had been almost as white as cotton, was beginning to turn as gold as a lion Henry had once seen in a picture. Remnants of a summer tan remained, with freckles chasing each other across the bridge of his nose and onto his cheeks.

"There he is." Henry wasn't sure whether he had whispered the words, or just thought them. It didn't matter, because the boy had also spotted the buck, which was very close and unaware of danger.

Young Henry's heart pounded as he took aim at the animal, its proud horns heaped in a beautiful symmetry. It was suddenly hard to breathe. There was an imaginary obstruction in his throat. The old man touched him lightly on the back to lend encouragement.

The buck raised his eyes then, and seemed to be staring directly into the boy's eyes.

"Shoot! Shoot!" Henry's voice resounded through the woods. Startled by the outcry, Young Henry pulled the trigger. The deer leaped as though it had been frightened by Henry's voice, but then it staggered and fell.

There was a feeling of exultation that swelled in the boy's chest, but then he shuddered, sickened by the death of such a graceful animal.

"By god, boy, you got him. You sure as hell got him." His grandfather's obvious delight made Carl Henry momentarily forget his shame. They walked then to where the deer had fallen, and Henry took out his knife and handed it to the boy.

"Butcher him, Young Henry, just like I taught you. You've watched me do it enough times to know how." The boy began field dressing the deer, often glancing at his grandfather to make sure he was doing it properly. He was very close to vomiting, but the pride written across his grandfather's weathered face made him hang on.

Finally, it was finished. The old man reached inside the animal and bloodied his hand. Then he rubbed some of the blood on the face of his grandson. It was the deer slayers ritual.

"Now," said Henry, "you are a man."

On that day the boy learned that in a hard and unforgiving land, a man is measured by his ability to administer pain, blood and death.

CHAPTER THIRTEEN

CARL HAD no difficulty adjusting to army life. For the better part of his life he had been told exactly what to do, so it was merely a matter of different people telling him. As far as Carl was concerned, his company sergeant represented the same type authority as his boss at the lumber company, or for that matter, his father, mother and wife.

Though he had no real complaint with the army, he did complain because it was expected. He was big on doing what was expected.

So, he complained about the long marches, the food and the officers. The truth was that the marches didn't bother him, and he liked the food. He had less difficulty complaining about the officers, since they represented something akin to the owner of the lumber company. He would have been lost without the direction of some authority.

Carl was assigned to the Forty-fifth Division, which had been federalized fifteen months before Pearl Harbor. After basic train-

ing he joined the main force at Camp Patrick Henry, Virginia
for amphibious landings practice, and to stage for the invasion of
Sicily. He received his first stripe soon after arriving in Virginia.
He was a model soldier. He did what he was told to do.

For Carl, the next best thing to chow call was mail call. Vivian
wrote faithfully, one or two letters a week. The letters were filled
with information about Carl Henry, his parents, and the few events
taking place in Bethel. She always mentioned missing him and
loving him. He felt a little guilty when he read those words, because he liked the army so much.

There were really only two times Carl thought much about
Vivian, one being when he received a letter and the other when
he was screwing a nineteen-year-old girl who lived near the base.
Her name was Shirley, and anytime Carl could get a pass to town
he got in her pants.

You might say Carl and Shirley were going steady. She didn't
date anyone else, and had been screwed only once before meeting
Carl. That had been a bad experience for her. She contended
that the guy had forcibly raped her.

Carl met Shirley at church. He wasn't particularly religious,
but the church sent a bus to the base to pick up soldiers interested
in attending services. And Carl figured a man going to war ought
to be religious, especially since he had been told the war was for
the purpose of preserving Christianity.

He met Shirley at an after-church fellowship, complete with
cookies and punch. He didn't see much point in telling her that
he was married.

"Can I get you some more punch?" Carl asked. "You're not
with anyone, are you?"

"No, I'm by myself," she replied, shyly. She had noticed Carl
almost immediately, liking the way his eyes admired her figure.
And he was ruggedly good-looking.

"I'm Carl Hayder," he said, taking a closer look at the firmness
of her breasts, which were attempting to pop the buttons off her
blouse. He liked the small waist, the just right hips.

She was about five feet four inches tall, with blonde hair and
beautiful blue eyes. Her skin was fair, susceptible to blemishes

and sunlight, and her nose was small and upturned. Short hair accentuated high cheekbones, and her larger than average lips drooped slightly at the corners. The face was pretty, but it was her shapely figure that first attracted a man's attention.

"I'm Shirley Seales," she nervously said, her voice giving away the unsureness she felt about being approached by an older man. Carl, of course, didn't look all that old. He might have even passed for twenty-one, but it was his poise and confidence, not his looks, that made her know he was older. With the exception of Vivian, he was that way around women; confident, sure of himself. He wasn't that way around men. Maybe confidence with women was one of the few traits he inherited from his father.

"Don't be nervous," he assured in an almost whisper. "I'm not trying anything with you. I'm just a lonesome guy from Oklahoma who would like to talk to a beautiful girl for a few minutes. If I'm bothering you, I'll go."

"Oh, no, you're not bothering me," she quickly responded. "I'd like to talk to you."

"Well," he grinned, "what do you want to talk about?" They laughed then, the ice broken.

That's the way it had been at first, him talking to her a lot and acting as though screwing her was the last thing on his mind. Their first kisses were light, sweet and tender, but those soon gave way to passionate embraces.

They had been out a half dozen times before Shirley invited Carl to her room. The room was on the second floor of a modest hotel, furnished only with the essentials. But it was all a girl working at the phone company could afford.

There had been a certain awkwardness initially, but passionate embraces soon resulted in Carl pushing her down on the bed and placing a hand underneath her dress and between her legs. He was soon fingering her, kissing her. She responded, mildly protesting his hand, but writhing on the bed and groaning with pleasure. The only sounds in the room were those of their heavy breathing and the squeak of the bedsprings.

She protested mildly as he removed her brassiere and began sucking her tits. As he removed more of her clothing, even the mildest form of protest disappeared. He began to turn his body then, kissing her all over her nudeness, until his tongue was between her legs.

Shirley groaned with pleasure, reached for and grasped his cock in her hand. She adjusted her body until she could get his penis in her mouth.

How soon, Carl thought, even the virgins learn. Moments later, he was on top of her, forcing his cock into the small opening between her legs. She was tight, very tight. She was grunting with a delighted pain, and Carl couldn't remember a piece of pussy ever being so good.

That was the first time. Later, all her inhibitions dissolved, she would say, "God, how I love your cock in me." Then she would almost shriek, "Fuck me, fuck me." Sheltered as she had been, the very word *fuck* created an intense excitement within her.

Carl, sensing how excited she became at vile language, would say, "I love to fuck you. I love to stick my dick in your cunt."

At first they didn't spend entire weekends in bed. Shirley would insist on going to church, saying "I found you in church and that's why it is important to me. Only God could have brought us together like this." Carl would agree, of course, but they were soon missing church regularly in favor of more time in bed together. That really didn't bother Carl, because he didn't give God that much credit for helping him get in Shirley's pants.

Because it never occurred to her that she and Carl might not get married, Shirley had dismissed any idea that their sleeping together might be sinful. And though he had never actually proposed marriage, the way he made love to her convinced her that he could not do without her. Marriage, thought Shirley, was only a matter of time. It would definitely happen before he shipped out. She would see to it.

At work she would often daydream, imagining herself as the dutiful wife while Carl was overseas, saving money for a house where they would have children and live happily ever after. They would first purchase a good bed, one that didn't squeak so much.

Typical conversations were "Do you love me, Carl?"

"What kind of a question is that? You know I do."

"You don't tell me very often."

"Hell, Shirley, I try to show you. Do you think I could make love to you the way I do and not love you?"

"No, it's just that a woman likes to be told sometimes."

"Okay, I love you. Does that make you feel better?"

"No, because I forced you into saying it."

"So what? It doesn't take away the fact that I love you."

"I know, Carl. I guess I'm just worried about your leaving and all. I wish we were married, settled down somewhere, and didn't have to worry about this war. I just want you and to have your babies."

"That's what I want, too, darling," he would lie, "but it's just not fair to leave you here tied to me while I'm off somewhere maybe getting killed."

Soldiers rarely talk about dying unless it suits their purpose. Carl was no exception.

"Please don't talk about dying, Carl. You're not going to get killed. You can't."

"I wish I was as sure as you are."

"Besides, it doesn't matter. There will never be anyone else for me. I just want you. I could never be with another man."

Shirley meant it, but Carl didn't really believe her. He had screwed too many women whose husbands had been out of town for a day or two. He always thought that if conditions were right, there was no such thing as a completely faithful woman.

"Baby, this war will be over in no time, and I'll be back here to get you. That's the time to talk about marriage, babies, and all that stuff. Besides," he would tease, "you might find someone you like better when I'm gone."

"You know that's not true," she pouted. "I don't know why you say things like that, things that hurt me."

"I'm sorry, baby." Carl wanted to believe her, because he felt that he might actually be in love with Shirley. Or maybe it's just her ass, he would think. It was really hard to know the difference. One of his real fears of involvement with Shirley was that Henry might come looking for him, and he still feared the old man.

Shirley was a good pouter, considering she probably didn't get
her way all that often as a child. She was the oldest of six daughters
born to Seth and Rubilee Madison. Carl couldn't remember the
name of the small town in Virginia where her family lived.

Shirley's father was a tobacco grower, but he wouldn't let his
daughters smoke. Shirley said her father considered smoking unla-
dylike. He had been a good teacher, because she refused to even
take a drag off Carl's cigarette, though he teasingly offered her a
smoke everytime they got together.

"It's really nice lying here in bed listening to the radio and
watching you," he said. He wasn't lying. He did enjoy watching
her wander around the room in just her panties. And he knew a
few well chosen words would get her mind off marriage, at least
temporarily, and on screwing.

When conversation went awry with Shirley, Carl believed in
doing what he did best, and if he could believe what a number
of women had told him, he did know how to screw. The big
problem, he thought, as his cock searched for the opening between
Shirley's legs, is that every woman I screw wants to marry me.
And all I want is a good piece of ass.

As they moved rhythmically together, Shirley put the marriage
conversation out of her mind. It felt good having Carl inside her,
and there was plenty of time to talk about marriage later.

Carl enjoyed his weekend passes, but he was usually ready to
get back to soldiering by the time he reported back to base on
Sunday evening. As his friend, Julius Harding, put it, Carl always
looks "fucked out."

Julius was the typical Oklahoma farm boy, thin from a life that
demanded much more than it returned. He was almost six feet
tall, but weighed only about one hundred forty-five pounds. He
had gained at least ten of that in the army. His black hair was
slicked straight back, which made his thin face look even narrower.

Julius would tell anyone who would listen that Carl needed to
get back to the ease of fifty-mile marches, digging trenches, and
running the obstacle course, just so he could be rested for the
coming weekend. Many of the men in his outfit knew Carl was

banging Shirley regularly, and they knew he was married. But most figured infidelity was just part of being a soldier.

Carl's close friends, married and single, envied his relationship with Shirley. There just weren't enough women available, except for the usual camp followers you could dump your sperm in for two bucks a throw. Most of the soldiers did just that, though they resented having to pay for a piece of ass.

Melvin Vann put it as succinctly as anyone could when he said, "By god, by the time I got to Mabel her cunt was so wet and sloppy that she didn't even know that I was in her. Those of us with the little peckers ought to get to go first."

Jody Emmons, a man with absolutely no sense of humor, disagreed. "It's first come, first serve, Vann."

"How do you spell that, Emmons? C-U-M or C-O-M-E?"

"Anyway you want to spell it, you little fucker. I just think the first man that lays down two dollars ought to get the first lay with Mabel." Jody just didn't understand kidding, He wasn't overly bright, and when he got serious, he could be mean.

Jody was a huge man, six feet six inches tall, with heavy jowls and a face that looked like it had been clean-shaven. The eyes were dark and deep-set, the head thick, the chin square. He weighed close to two hundred fifty pounds, but it was all muscle.

Melvin, on the other hand, was an exact opposite. He claimed to be five feet six inches tall, but no one believed him. And though a real peewee compared to Jody, he would not back down to anyone. He was constantly getting in fights and, though he normally always lost, he never quit.

"Take it easy, Emmons," Melvin chided, "not all of us are hung like you." That brought some good-natured laughter, but not from Jody.

"Just what do you mean by that, you little sonofabitch?"

Carl, realizing the banter had gone far enough, interceded. "Easy, Jody. Melvin's just complimenting you on having a bigger pecker than the rest of us."

"Oh," he responded, surprised and pleased. He even tried to join in the laughter, but it was forced. He was thick upstairs, but with the savvy of a cornered killer. No one in the outfit liked

Jody, but most of them wouldn't mind having him nearby in battle.
There had been some talk that Jody had killed a couple of men
with his bare hands, that a judge had actually sentenced him to
the army.

"I reckon we'll be pulling out soon," Terry Parker injected,
changing the subject to something that was constantly on their
minds.

"Shit, I don't think we'll ever go," retorted Harry Graham,
tossing the remains of a cigarette in a butt can. "Somebody else
is going to whip the fucking German before we can get a crack
at them."

"Dream on, Harry. You better wish your fucking ass that somebody whips them for us." The speaker was Darby Waldron, a
former English professor at the University of Oklahoma, who had
exchanged his doctorate for private's pay.

For the most part the outfit was made up of small town, good
old boys, none of whom had any financial or political clout. Most
of them had been working at menial jobs at the time they were
called up, and the future held very little promise for them. But
Darby was different. They respected Darby because he could have
been an officer. He had chosen to be one of them. He was always
reminding them, however, that his reasons for being a private
were not noble.

"I'm going to write a book about the war," he would say, "and
wars are fought by privates, not officers."

Darby continued his discourse on the war by saying, "Whether
you guys realize it or not, this war is a long way from being over.
We'll eventually whip the Germans, because we can produce war
materials faster than they can, and we've got the resources. But
they have the best trained army in the world, and they will make
us pay for every inch of ground we take from them. It may take
two years to win this war, or it may take five. A lot depends on
the kind of fuckups we have at the top."

"You talking about Roosevelt?" Harry asked. There was a rumor
floating around that a soldier could be shot for knocking the com-
mander-in-chief.

"Hell yes, I'm talking about Roosevelt, and Eisenhower, and

any of the fucking generals who decide when, where and how we fight the Germans. To them we're just a bunch of pawns on a chessboard, and they'll move us around at their whim, play with our lives anyway they like. It's just a game to them, but its life and death to us poor sonofabitches in the trenches." Darby enjoyed barracks oratory, and as far as most of the dogfaces were concerned, he was their spokesman. With the exception of Eskridge Scallan, a tall, thin twenty-year-old whose father was a career army man.

"Darby, I ain't believing that the President thinks no more of me than a checker. He's concerned about every one of us, about every drop of American blood spilled on foreign soil."

"The trouble with you, Eskridge, is that you believe everything you hear on the radio," Darby lectured. "The President and the generals don't give a shit about poor dogfaces. They just want to stick us in a hole somewhere and make us point our rifles in the right direction. After they get through playing with us, they'll probably sit down and have a drink with Hitler."

Unintimidated, Eskridge replied, "Sometimes, you talk just like a Communist."

"Hold on just a minute," Darby retorted. "Whether you realize it or not, we're fighting with the Communists, not against them. They're our allies. Besides, Eskridge, what is a Communist? Do you know?"

"Hell yes, I know," Eskridge said, "but it wouldn't do any good to tell you. You don't listen to nobody."

What the hell is a Communist, Carl thought, but he said, "I'd rather be fighting the Germans than the Japs. Those slant-eyed folks are just downright scary."

"I'm with you," Darby agreed. "The damn Japs just don't have any respect for life. People who think it's honorable to die give me the jitters. On the other hand, I'd say the average German soldier is just as scared of dying as the average American GI."

"Do you think we'll have to fight the Japs?" Carl asked.

"Not this division," Darby replied. "Unless, of course, we clean up the Germans before the Japs surrender, and that's not likely. Nope, this division will be fighting the Italians and Germans in

Sicily within a few weeks. The Italians won't be a problem, but the Germans will."

"How soon do you think we'll ship out?" Jody asked.

"Within two weeks," Darby answered.

It was exactly two weeks later that the Forty-fifth Division shipped out. Carl had seen Shirley once before leaving, and she had vowed to wait for him and to write every day.

Though not an avid letter writer, Carl wrote love letters to Shirley and Vivian the night before they boarded the troop ship.

Carl's outfit was billeted three feet below the waterline of the vessel, the entire ship crammed to capacity below deck. There was promenade space on deck that was roped off and placarded *Officers Country*. The injustice of the situation caused Darby to launch one of his famous tirades. The troops were forced to spend all their time below deck, except when they were bucking a chow line.

"Officers' Country," Darby would say, his voice thick with sarcasm. "We're crammed in this hole for the express purpose of getting our asses shot off so those bastards can advance another rank, and they don't have the decency to treat us like anything more than a pile of shit."

"There's not enough showers for half of us to clean up once a week," Harry opined. "All you guys smell like a pile of shit to me."

"Thank god that a man thinks his own shit smells okay," Melvin complained. "I've been sweating like a stuck pig for days. I wonder where the hell we are?" Unknown to the GIs, the convoy had taken the sunny route, toward the Azores, which meant the ship soaked up sun throughout the day.

Days were spent in endless poker games, and in trying to get a meal. A soldier who wanted to eat three meals a day was usually on his feet for at least fourteen hours a day, the chow lines slow, long and continuous.

"I intend to get my fucking three meals a day, even if they're so bad I have to throw them overboard," said Darby. "The army owes me three meals a day, and by god, I'll get mine. What pisses me is that the officers sit down and have their meals served to them, and we have to stand in line like pathetic orphans, holding our little tin plates. And all we get is slop."

"C'mon, Darby, the food's not all that bad," opined Jack. "It's hell to get it, but it's pretty good."

Darby snorted, "Maybe you've never had any decent chow, Jack, but I have, and this stuff we're getting isn't fit for hogs." Then he would launch into a dissertation about the fine restaurants where he had eaten, places in New York, San Francisco and McAlester, Oklahoma.

Some of the men felt Darby was putting them on about fine restaurants in McAlester, but Darby swore there were at least two places there that would rank with the finest in New York or San Francisco. So descriptive was he of the delicacies in these restaurants, and how they tasted, that the men would be drooling, anxious to get in the chow line. However, what the army considered both nutritious and delicious, soon had them agreeing with Darby.

It became so hot in the hole that there were no places on their bodies that were not covered with sweat, causing Carl to quip during a poker game, "Dammit, Melvin, when I was pitching I was accused of throwing a spitball, but you just threw me a spit-card."

Melvin grinned. "That's a damn good card. It doesn't take long to mark 'em when you've got a little sweat on your hands. Take a good smell of that card, Carl. I marked it with the sweat from my balls. It smells heavenly."

"Heavenly, hell," Jack retorted. "You could be our secret weapon, you little bastard. One smell of you and every German within ten miles will pass out. When in the hell was the last time you took a shower?"

"The little bastard hasn't taken a shower since we've been at sea," Jody volunteered, "and that's been twelve days."

Melvin, an idiotic grin on his face, responded with, "I'm afraid you guys will laugh at my little dick."

"Bullshit," Jack said. "This little bastard took off all his clothes and ran up and down the counter of a cafe in Abilene, Texas."

Some of the men hadn't heard the story, so they pressed Jack for more details.

Disgustedly, Jack continued. "He was drunk, of course, and all of you know how crazy the little bastard is when he has a little whiskey. He kept asking the waitress for a piece, and she told him to go fuck himself. He told her he couldn't do that with his clothes on, so he just flat-ass took them off. It's a wonder he wasn't put in the stockade, and me with him. The MPs blamed me for letting him get out of hand. Can you imagine the stir a little bastard like him caused in a town full of Baptists and Camp-bellites?"

"Shit, Jack, it wasn't all that bad," said Melvin.

"The hell it wasn't," Jack concluded.

Days later the convoy anchored at Arzew, near Oran on the Algerian coast. The troops were allowed to go ashore to get their land legs back, a welcome relief from the cramped, stinking conditions in which they had been living. Rumors were flying that the enemy was on the run everywhere. Some of the more gung-ho types were saying that they hoped the Forty-Fifth would get a piece of the action before the armistice.

"Stupid sonofabitches," Darby commented.

Well educated, but a bigot, he also had some choice words for the French and Arabs who inhabited Arzew. "The fuckin' French are as sour as Virginians, and these Arabs are nothing more than a bunch of sand Niggers."

There were, of course, the usual stories about the Arabs murdering American soldiers for their boots, cutting the balls off their victims and stuffing them into their mouths.

On July 9, 1943, a gale force storm was brewing, tossing the invasion force up and down on the violent sea. Carl was sicker than he had ever been in his entire life, partly from fear and partly as a result of the churning water. And he began to pray more seriously than he ever had before.

His thoughts were like a continuous film, tracing moments in his life over and over, with memories of Vivian and Shirley jumping in and out of his mind, the letter received months before telling about Carl Henry's first deer. There were also memories of his mother and father, competing with the machine gun like exercises shooting through his mind.

Soldiers all around him were doubled over in convulsions, the floor slippery with bile. He had already vomited until there was nothing left but a dry retching. But he continued to do that. He was struck by the fact that Darby seemed unaffected by it all, standing to his left and reading a book, the former professor was oblivious to everything around him.

"Dammit, Darby, how do you do it?" Carl asked.

"Do what?" he responded.

"Not throw up."

"It's simply a matter of concentration, or you might call it disassociation," Darby replied. "You see, right now I'm imagining that I'm sitting in my living room in Norman, sipping a beer, and reading this book."

About that time, the ship lurched and seemed to nosedive, sending Darby onto the floor and into the bile. He clawed himself back to a standing position, looked in disbelief at the vomit on his clothing, and threw up. He was no longer disassociated.

On July 10, they invaded Sicily.

In the early morning hours they climbed down the nets into landing crafts that were rising and falling in the choppy sea. The battleships were belching fire, smoke and unbelievable noise at the still unseen enemy.

As Carl emerged from a landing craft and ran onto the beach, he could hear tons of projectiles tearing through the sky overhead. His ears acclimated to the sounds so that he had no difficulty hearing the commands of his sergeant. Time became meaningless as he moved forward on command, fired at the still obscure enemy, and groveled along in the sand.

They moved forward then, inland. Someone said the beach was secure. He didn't know or care. It was like a dream, a dream where you walk toward death, sure that it's right there in front of you. He was hypnotized by the faces of dead soldiers all around him, their glassy eyes staring and empty, their bodies containing gaping holes rimmed with blood. He moved forward in a trance-like state, to afraid to know or understand fear, doing what he had been trained to do.

A man with a different uniform rose from the sand in front of him, his hands raised in surrender, but Carl saw his attempt too late. He fired and watched the strickened face of the man disappear. All around him he could see others surrendering then, and he wanted to shout with the elation of victory.

Darby, however, brought his elation to ruin by saying, "Fucking Italians are surrendering by the droves. The Germans won't be so easy."

He was right. The Germans demanded blood and death for every inch of ground they surrendered. The day seemed as though it would never end, but then night came. They dug in to hold what they had fought so hard to gain, alerted to reports that German paratroopers would come during the night.

Carl ate his rations without really tasting, listened to the big shells as they passed overhead, and watched orange glows as they made impact with the earth. It was like a technicolor dream, reality far removed from the dirt and ghost-like men waiting to kill other ghost-like men.

"It's worse than I thought it would be," Darby confided. "I don't guess I've ever been so scared in my entire life. Did you kill anyone today, Carl?"

"I don't know," he lied, the echo of his statement bouncing off the walls of his mind like it was a great canyon.

"I killed my share of the mother fuckers," Jody claimed, "and I'm going to get a helluva lot more of them tomorrow."

"I do not," Darby said disgustedly, "find any pleasure in killing men, even those who are trying to kill me. These Italians and Germans shooting at us are as much pawns of politicians as we are. It's hard to swallow, letting a chosen few decide where and how so many are to die."

"All I know," Carl replied, "is that I'm sick of seeing Oklahoma boys die beside me, their guts spattered all over creation. I feel helpless as hell, all those bullets flying around me, and the big stuff trying to creep up on me all the time. All those speeches about saving democracy ain't worth a damn when you're rooting in the dirt, trying to get lower than a German bullet."

"It's the way it's always been," Darby surmised. "GIs' don't have much time for all the high sounding praises about glory, honor and country. The foot soldier is busy getting his ass shot off, and the generals sit around in comfortable quarters drinking scotch and plotting strategy. I've read all the books about the glory of fighting and dying for your country. They're enjoyable, even make you proud, if you happen to be sitting in front of the stove on a winter day. But if you're on the front, it's a helluva different story."

Julius said, "This outfit fought like hell today. We didn't give an inch, just kept pushing on."

"By god, I'm proud of that," Darby replied. "You never know how men are going to act in battle, but today I didn't see one man in the Forty-Fifth turn tail and run."

"I saw one guy break," Jack said, "but dammit, the kid wasn't more than seventeen or eighteen years old. Some of the boys turned him back in the right direction. I have to admit that the thought of turning tail and running sure as hell entered my mind."

Carl confessed, "I was scared enough to run, guess most of us were, but this is a damn disciplined outfit."

"Can you believe that fucking Jody?" Julius asked, pointing to where the big man was fast asleep.

"No nerves at all, that bastard," Jack replied enviously.

"We'd better all get some sleep," Darby suggested.

"How?" Melvin wanted to know, "I don't mind saying that I can't sleep. I've been scared shitless all day, and I'm still scared."

Darby comforted with "We all are, Melvin. We all are."

The planes came at midnight, their throbbing drone echoing across the sky. It was, they thought, the dreaded German paratroopers. Navy guns lit up the sky, quickly joined by U.S. Army firepower. Planes fell, and chutists by the hundreds died in their harness before reaching the ground.

"Stop shooting!" voices began shouting above the din of gunfire. "They're our guys."

They were. The American paratroopers were supposed to drop

at Gela to aid the First Division, but a navigator had sent the planes to the wrong place.

The gray dawn brought a harsh grimness to the scene as paratroopers began picking up their dead comrades, killed by American firepower.

Disgustedly, through clenched teeth, Darby asked, "Dammit, doesn't anybody know what they're doing?"

They didn't have long to ponder the situation, because their sergeant came by and said, "Okay, assholes, you've been resting long enough. Let's move up to where the fighting is."

As the division fought on, the dogfaces lost track of time, the only measurement of real importance being the loss of friends. Fighting eastward along the north coast, the Germans fought a ferocious rear guard action while evacuating the bulk of their troops across the Strait of Messina and into Italy. It was during this fighting that Darby was killed.

Carl had very little time to mourn Darby, only to reflect on the tremendous human waste that war brought. Most of his friends were dead now—Melvin, Jack, Jody—replaced by new faces, men he preferred not knowing, because they, too, might be dead tomorrow. It was only the constant fighting, the movement of the Division, that kept him from breaking. He had already decided that his own death was only a matter of time.

Three days after Darby's death, Carl's company took the brunt of a small German counter offensive. During the fighting, he felt a sudden searing pain in his chest. Pressing his hand to the point of the pain, he pulled it back, looked at it, and saw that it was covered with blood. It was all he remembered.

CHAPTER
FOURTEEN

CARL HAD been in the army two months when Vivian moved out of the Hayder house. It was a move she had been contemplating for a long time. Rachael was upset about the move, but did not express her displeasure.

Henry would have preferred that his daughter-in-law and grandson continue living with them, but he could also understand Vivian's desire to have a place of her own. And really, the move would not affect in any way his relationship with Carl Henry. On the other hand, if the boy continued living at the Hayder house, Rachael might influence him in such a way as to cause weakness.

Like Henry, Vivian was convinced that at least some of Carl's problems stemmed from his mother's influence. That influence, she felt, was what made her husband weak and indecisive. When Carl returned from the war, if she could keep him away from Rachael, Vivian thought he might then take control of his life.

Surely, being in the army has helped him, she thought.

Though Vivian was aware of Henry's sexual escapades, she never thought of her father-in-law as being a bad influence on her husband. In fact, she empathized with Henry, never even mentally blamed him for running around on Rachael. She, instead, blamed Rachael for Henry's carousing.

With her job and new household chores, time passed swiftly for Vivian. She planted a small garden in back of the house and, for Carl Henry's benefit and with his help, built a small chicken yard.

She took great pleasure in her son, especially in how seriously he took his role as man of the house.

Still, he took time to be a child. When his friends visited, they would charge around the house shooting imaginery Germans and Japs with their stickguns. Or they would build small forts from tobacco sacks filled with sand, and they would use cardboard soldiers to man their defenses.

As Vivian watched her son play war with his friends, she often thought of Carl, whose war was real. She both longed for and feared her husband's return. The fear was that he might not have changed, and she wasn't sure she could continue living with him if he was the same. She knew that she could not respect him until he threw off his shackles of self-pity.

Bethel had given its share of young men to the war effort, with some notable exceptions. The Keyser boys, Kevin and Kurt, were passed over by the draft board though there was nothing physically wrong with them. They had been exempted from the draft because their father, who owned the sawmill, insisted they were essential to its operation. And while the boys were rarely seen at the mill, no one on the draft board was going to argue with old man Keyser. He controlled the draft board because most of its members worked for him.

So Kevin and Kurt spent most of their time trying to screw the wives of the men who were in the military. They weren't all that successful. While they might not have been classified ugly, they were well-fed to the point of being pudgy. Henry referred to them as porkers.

Vivian was at the newspaper office working on the books when

the telegram about Carl being wounded in action arrived. She
read it several times, emotions of fear and anxiety churning within
her. She didn't cry, though there was a great reservoir of tears
in the pit of her stomach.

She felt compelled to control her emotions. There were things
she had to do, decisions she had to make.

The first thing was to tell Henry and Rachael. She could tell
Carl Henry later, or should he be told? Of course, he had to be
told. Everyone in town would know about it, and they would be
talking. She didn't want him to hear about his father's wound
from another child. Where was Carl Henry? Then she remembered
he was with his grandfather. She thought they had said something
about going fishing. Clutching the telegram in her hand, Vivian
left the office, got in her car, and drove to the Hayder house.

The old man and his grandson had a good string of panfish
before noon, but the boy wanted to continue fishing into the afternoon. The boy's decision pleased Henry, because it meant that
young Henry enjoyed his company. The old man had never tried
to please anyone more than he tried to please the boy.

About noon they swam in a deep hole in the creek, downstream
from where they were fishing. The sun was hot, and the cool
creek water was refreshing. They returned to their fishing spot
after the swim and found that a two-pound channel catfish was
making the end of young Henry's pole dance up and down. He
had stuck the pole in the bank of the creek, and had baited his
hook with a crawfish before going swimming. Watching his grandson's excitement over the fish was more exciting to Henry than
catching a fish himself.

They sat side-by-side, their backs against the trunk of a huge
oak that had chosen to grow in just the right spot on the edge of
the creek bank. They held their fishing poles loosely, soaked up
the shade of the tree, and watched their bobbers dance in the
gentle current of the creek. It was peaceful.

"I guess you really miss your daddy, don't you, boy?"

Carl Henry nodded affirmatively and said, "He'll be back soon.
Mama said it wouldn't be long until the Germans give up."

"I hope she's right. It seems a damn shame to have a bunch of American boys killed for Roosevelt and the Jews."

"What are Jews, Grandpa?"

"That's a damn good question, boy. The Jews were God's chosen people. Fact is, Jesus was a Jew. But the Jews had a big hand in killing Jesus, and unless I miss my guess, that's when God rejected them. It's kind of funny about Jews. It's sort of a religion, I guess, but nobody calls us Methodists excepting to identify our faith. My grandparents were Germans, but my mother and dad were born in this country, so they were Americans just like I'm an American. A Jew can be born in this country, and he still claims to be a Jew, because his folks are Jewish. A German is from Germany, an Englishman is from England, and a Frenchman if from France. A damn Jew can be from anywhere, because he hasn't got a country. I can't answer your questions as to what a Jew is, but I can tell you to be damn careful in dealing with them. They'll skin you and make you pay them for doing it.

"There's lots of folks you have to be careful about, boy. There's Jews, and Indians, and Niggers. Now, I think God put us here to deal with the Niggers and Indians. My daddy had to fight to free the Niggers, and he didn't like it one bit. Can't say as I blame him, seeing as I haven't seen a Nigger worth killing in my entire life. You can hire a Nigger to do a job of work, and it takes more work on your part getting him to work than it would if you'd done it yourself. Indians are the same way. They think the government owes them a living. This country would be a lot better off without Niggers and Indians, especially nasty-assed Choctaws.

"I know you have to go to school with Choctaw kids, boy, but listen to your old grandpa and stay away from them. I'm just thankful to God that you don't have to go to school with Niggers. You'll have to do that if that old bitch, Mrs. Roosevelt, gets her way."

Carl Henry always listened intently to his grandfather, and the old man's remarks about Indians and Niggers was not new to him. The old man had indoctrinated him thoroughly with a hatred for black, red and yellow people. He had heard many times that Communism, which he was unable to comprehend, was the mark of the beast, and that Stalin was a disciple of the devil. Most of these discourses had taken place when he was with his grandfather in downtown Bethel, when Henry was talking with some of his old cronies.

Carl Henry was not sure what the mark of the beast was except that it had something to do with the *Bible*. He picked up quite a bit of information about the *Bible* from his grandfather, along with a comprehensive vocabulary of profanity. When they weren't fishing on summer days, the boy and his grandfather would spend a great deal of time in the saloon, the old man drinking beer and espousing his philosophy, Carl Henry drinking cokes and listening to the conversation around him. Occasionally, the old man would give him a sip of beer, all the time warning him that he should never smoke or drink.

"The teacher has been trying to make us call Niggers Negroes," the boy said, "but I ain't going to do it. I'm going to call them Niggers just like you do, grandpa.

Henry laughed. "Good for you, boy. Good for you."

As the shadows of the afternoon lengthened, Henry told the boy about catching huge turtles from the Red River, and about catfish weighing as much as a hundred pounds each. The boy was intrigued by his grandfather's stories, especially when he told about catching a turtle large enough for a grown man to ride.

Then the old man changed the subject and said, "I'll tell you something, boy. There's money in law. Get yourself a good education and get into law."

The boy wasn't sure what his grandfather made reference to, but he filed the information in his mind.

The old man continued, "A man with an education can do pretty well what he wants to do in this world. Yep, education is the important thing. You ought to try to play big league baseball, but you ought to have a good education to fall back on."

To the boy, it seemed that Henry was often just talking to himself. He knew of his grandfather's obsession with baseball, because he insisted on Carl Henry having a baseball glove on his hand from the time he was able to toddle, and nothing pleased the old man more than to know that Carl Henry was playing baseball with his friends.

"Another thing, boy," Henry said, while looking contemplatively across the creek at a bluejay twittering in a tree, "A man's got to watch getting mixed up with women. A woman can ruin a man's future, mess up his mind."

The boy listened intently, because women were a mystery to him. Though he couldn't understand why, seeing a pretty woman's nylon-clad legs caused his pisser, as his grandfather called it, to get hard and straight. It felt good, especially when he touched it. It got hard mostly when he saw pretty women in the movies, but sometimes it got stiff when he was watching his mother. His grandfather's admonition about women was worth heeding, because just watching them did strange things to the body, especially to his pisser.

The boy liked the word piss much more than pee-pee, which is what his mother called it. Piss sounded so much more appropriate, just as shit sounded so much better than do-do.

Half-listening to his grandfather telling him what he should do in life, the boy's mind wandered to some of the words he had heard that were not used by his mother. Fuck. What does that mean? Should he ask his mother? He'd better not, because he suspected it was a filthy word. Pussy. He'd better not ask his mother about that word either. Shit. Damn. Sonofabitch. Goddam. He's sure better not let his mother hear him say goddam, or she'd burn up his bottom.

He remembered reading in the restroom at school, *Sue Ann sucks dicks*. He knew that dick and pisser were the same thing, but he couldn't understand a girl being linked to sucks and dicks. He knew it was probably nasty and that he should dismiss it from his mind.

"Have you heard the new evangelist in town, Grandpa?" He knew the old man hadn't, but after thinking about what he thought were evil things, he felt compelled to get religion into the conversation.

Henry shook his head and said, "Has your mother been taking you to hear that holy rolling quack?"

"Yeah, almost every night," he replied. Vivian had often been taken with spells of religion, most of which lasted for a brief period of time. However, since Carl's induction into the army, she had been fairly active in church. Since she liked her religion hot and heavy, she was a Pentecostal. Henry disapproved of so much emotionalism in religion. It was one of the few things about Vivian that he found distasteful.

Carl Henry told his grandfather about going to the outdoor revival meeting, how hot it was, and how the cardboard fans provided by the funeral home just weren't sufficient. No matter how hard and fast you waved them in front of your face, it was still just too hot.

"They have a foot washing every night, Grandpa. What does that mean?"

Henry shook his head in disgust and said, "Not a damn thing, boy. Not a damn thing. If there's anything you've got to be careful about it's people that are so *godalmighty* religious. Those Pentecostal preachers will holler, shout and jump up and down, but they never say a damn thing. You'll find that's true of most preachers, though. A man that wants to find God has to look for God himself. These preachers will just confuse you to the point where you won't know what in the hell to do, or what direction to go in. Study the *Bible* for yourself, boy, then you'll know what to do."

"Mama's been talking about being baptized with the Holy Ghost."

"Don't tell your mama I said so, but that's all a crock of shit. Those damn Pentecosts think that if they get people worked up enough, they'll give them all their money. Has your mama been giving much money to the preacher?"

The boy pondered the question and said, "I don't know. I usually sit with some of the other kids. I think she might give them a dollar once in a while."

"That ain't too bad, but it's a damn site more than they deserve. Boy, the most useless things on earth are Pentecostal preachers and Catholic priests."

"I don't know any Catholics," the boy said.

"That stupid-assed Uncle Arlo of yours is a Catholic," Henry said.

Carl Henry replied, "I thought he went to the Methodist Church."

Henry snorted. "Well, he does, but he sure as hell ain't a Meth-

odist. Claims to have been converted, but I ain't ever seen a
Catholic converted to being a Methodist."

"Weren't you a Methodist preacher one time, Grandpa?"

"Where in the hell did you hear that?"

"I don't know, maybe from Grandma."

"It figures. Women never know when to keep their mouths
shut. The truth is that I did a little preaching at one time. Probably
knew more *Bible* than any man in this part of the country, which
is why I'm a Methodist."

"You don't go to church now, though, do you?"

"Well, not now," he said. "That preacher down at the Methodist
Church knows so damn little about the Scripture that I can't stand
listening to him. Listen to him and we'll have Niggers sitting in
the same pews with white folks. Now, anybody that knows God's
Word at all knows that's not right."

It was hard for the boy to keep his mind on one subject on
such a lazy day. "Do you know we haven't had a bite in a long
time, Grandpa?"

"You don't have to tell me. I think the fish have up and left
this hole, or they're all asleep."

"I'm ready to go home when you are. I'm getting hungry."

Henry nodded and said, "I'm with you, boy. We'll clean some
of these fish and see if Grandma won't cook them for supper.
Maybe your mama will eat with us."

"I hope so." They began walking toward the house, which was
only a couple of miles from their fishing hole. The old man, carrying
the fish, still had a lively step, and it was difficult for the boy to
keep up with him. As they approached the house, Henry saw
Vivian and Rachael standing on the porch, looking in their direction. He sensed something was wrong, and immediately thought
of Carl. As he drew closer he could see that the women had
been crying. The boy seemed oblivious to this as he began telling
his mother about the fishing trip. She hugged him and told him
she would prefer to hear about it later.

Then she told Henry and her son about Carl being wounded.

CHAPTER FIFTEEN

Vivian RECEIVED a letter from Carl two weeks after the telegram arrived. He told her his wound was not serious and that he expected to be returned to active duty within a couple of months. The German bullet had caught Carl in the side, but it was a clean wound. The letter was cheery, expressing love for Vivian and his desire to be home with his family.

Shirley, who was now pregnant, received a similar letter. Carl was not the father, despite her statements to him concerning eternal love and faithfulness. He had been gone only a week when Shirley met a young captain at church. The captain was very attentive and expressed interest in Shirley. True blue, she told him she was in love with an enlisted man who had just shipped out. The captain, a meticulous, detail man, checked around until he found out the name of Shirley's lover.

Checking Carl out was no problem, and when he found out his Oklahoma rival was married, he immediately took the informa-

tion to Shirley. Naturally, he acted as though finding out Carl
was married was as painful to him as it was to Shirley. He offered
a shoulder to cry on, to be her comfort in her time of need.

Emotionally destroyed by Carl's deception, Shirley yielded to
the young captain's charms. It was done out of vindictiveness toward Carl more than anything else, but the end result was pregnancy. That was okay, though, because a captain's pay would be
much more adequate than a private's in bringing up a child. Unfortunately, however, the captain was also married. And he told Shirley that if she wanted to accuse him of being the father, he was
sure that he could prove otherwise. He would bring forth witnesses
who would testify that she had been sleeping with several other
men.

Shirley knew he was not making idle threats. Initially, she
thought about killing herself, but decided such a course of action
would not be retribution enough against the two deceivers. She
did make one positive decision, however. She decided to quit
going to church, at least temporarily.

Shirley really did love Carl, in spite of his deception. So, she
wrote him and told him they were going to have a baby. She did
not bother to tell him she had discovered his marital status.

Shirley had written Carl twice a day the first two weeks after
he left. She was sure that he had not gotten all those letters to
date, because she had received only two from him. Besides, if
he questioned the absence of letters from her over a period of
time, she could claim they were lost by the army. Why shouldn't
she lie to him. He had lied to her.

She sent the letter about her pregnancy before receiving Carl's
letter telling about his wound. After reading his letter she was
pricked by the god of sympathy and thought about writing Carl
and telling him the truth. Vindictiveness triumphed, however,
so she decided to let well enough alone.

Vivian had no suspicions about Carl's lack of fidelity. Well, almost none. She thought he might sleep with an Italian or French
girl in some village liberated by the Forty-Fifth Division, but
that could be expected of any soldier. Sort of the spoils of war.
She didn't like thinking about it, though, so she tried to keep
such images from her mind.

Carl didn't write often, but that didn't bother her either. He wasn't the writing kind. She treasured the letters she did get, reading them over and over, and keeping them safely stored in an old shoebox that she kept in a closet.

From the tone of Carl's letters, Vivian was sure that he had found himself in the army, that he would be his own man when he returned. She felt her husband had been his mother's baby too long, and that the army had broken the fetal cord, something she had been unable to do while living in the same house with his parents.

Vivian had great plans for Carl. Carl had ability and could be successful in practically anything he chose to do. Vivian was confident of it.

CHAPTER
SIXTEEN

W HEN CARL did come marching home, he marched to a different drummer than the one planned by Vivian. Carl was a hero. A real bona-fide hero. He had a silver star, a bronze star, and a couple of purple hearts. And though none of the local people knew exactly what feats of heroism Carl had performed, they were proud that one of their boys had done his part to make the world safe for democracy.

A gala celebration was planned for Carl's return, so the day he stepped off the train he was met by most of the people from Bethel. The Bethel Lumberjack band, twenty-four strong, plus five majorettes, stood at attention in their bright orange and black uniforms and played the school song. It was while they were playing that the school principal decided he had to do something about getting a new band director.

After Carl had hugged and kissed Vivian, Carl Henry, and his mother, and shook hands with his father, he was led through the back-slapping crowd to a platform where he was greeted by the mayor and lumber company owner, K. K. Keyser.

"Good to see you, Carl, good to see you," Keyser said.

Carl grasped his hand firmly and said, "Good to see you, sir."

Keyser motioned for Carl to sit down on the platform with other town notables, including the constable, all of whom were patting him on the back and shaking his hand. Keyser called for silence on the part of the crowd, then motioned to the band.

The band director began waving his arms in a frenzied sort of way, and the band played an almost discernible rendition of the *Star Spangled Banner*. Of course, the crowd stood at attention for the playing, and the men removed their hats. Some of the women even cried. Most of the tears were from parents of band members.

As soon as the band had finished playing The National Anthem, they played a special arrangement of *God Bless America*. Completion of the melody was a signal for the Reverend Rector Redfield, pastor of Holy Ghost Penecostal Church, to launch into one of his famous fifteen minute prayers.

"Most gracious, holy and marvelous heavenly Father, who in times passed hath brought salvation to thy children, purge us of our iniquities at this most solemn occasion, whereby we might fully take of thy cup of grace, which is so freely given.

"We thank you, Lord, for bringing Carl back to us, and we thank you for the part he had in destroying thine enemies. His vengeance was thine, O Lord. His hand was thy hand, his mouth thy mouth, his legs thy legs, his courage thy courage. . . ."

The prayer continued until the mayor tapped the preacher on the shoulder, so he completed the oration by saying, ". . . in Jesus' blessed holy name, amen."

Those who checked their watches found that the preacher had outdone himself. Twenty-one minutes. Some of the women murmured and whispered about how wonderful it must be to be that close to God, to carry on a twenty-one minute conversation with the Almighty.

Reverend Redfield also checked his watch and sat down on the platform with a self-satisfied smirk on his face. It was his best ministerial smirk, and was primarily for the benefit of the mayor. So touched by the Spirit was Reverend Redfield, that he believed he could have prayed for hours. He was contemptuous of Mr. Keyser, because he was a Baptist, even went to some Baptist school in Arkansas, while the Reverend Redfield's education had come straight from the Lord.

Henry was disgusted with the preacher and his prayer, and wondered why the hell Vivian had insisted Redfield be included in Carl's welcome home celebration. Well, he was the pastor of the church she attended, but Henry was anxious to get all the crap over, so he and Carl could go get a beer. Carl Henry was standing beside him, so he stuck his hand in the boy's hair and ruffled it. The boy grinned at his grandfather, and Henry grinned back.

"Friends," the mayor said, "this is one of the greatest occasions in the history of Bethel . . . welcoming back a native son. . . . Carl Hayder, known and respected by us all. . . . moreso now that he has distinguished himself on the field of battle.

"Many of Bethel's sons went off to fight the tyrant Hitler, and all served with honor. Some were required to stay here and serve (a reference to his sons), but wherever Bethelites served, they did so with unflinching courage and determination. That's the kind of tradition we have in this city. Our men and women have all served with distinction in every national emergency."

The mayor was speaking from a written text and didn't bother to elaborate on previous national emergencies.

"But among those who served, Carl Hayder has demonstrated a courage so brave that our great government has awarded him with a silver star and a bronze star. . . . two medals signifying the honor that he brought to our town. I am so proud of this young man that I closed the sawmill today in honor of the occasion. (The mayor failed to mention it was Saturday and the sawmill operated only occasionally on Saturday, then only for half a day. Also, by closing he was not obligated to pay overtime.)

"I have to feel that I contributed in a small way to this young man's bravery by giving him a job at the sawmill, so he could play baseball on the town team."

Bullshit, Henry thought.

"I watched him pitch many times, demonstrating on the mound the kind of courage that he must have demonstrated in fighting the Germans. He was always a scrapper. If you'll remember he was a hundred forty-five pound tackle on the football team, and I never saw a big man move him. I know my two sons, both of whom played in the backfield on the same team, appreciate the way Carl blocked for them. He was a good blocker and a good tackler. He's the kind of man we want working at the sawmill and living in Bethel."

The crowd applauded.

"I'm going on record right here and saying that Carl's got a job with the sawmill for as long as he wants it."

Sure, Vivian thought, for peanuts and a chance to grovel at the Keysers feet like the rest of these poor people. It wasn't good enough for Carl, and she was going to see that they made a new life.

The rest of the mayor's speech dealt with the contributions he and his sons made to the war effort, and a forecast of the new prosperity Bethel would encounter as a result of the sawmill. Vivian and Carl's eyes had met on several occasions, and both were wishing they were home in bed. It had been a long time. Of course, Carl wasn't quite as anxious as Vivian, because he was basking in newfound glory. Carl's actions in war had not been that much more heroic than those of other soldiers, but being in the right place at the right time had resulted in being decorated for bravery.

While a platoon sergeant, he had held a position until reinforcements arrived after the seventeen and eighteen year olds in his command had run while under heavy enemy fire.

He had made platoon sergeant because he was older than most of the new recruits being sent to the front. For holding the position he received a bronze star and a battlefield commission to second Lieutenant. Carl was no leader, though, because he was incapable of giving orders to others. For not being a leader he received a silver star.

Three German machine gun nests had his company pinned

down, and instead of ordering some of his men to knock them
out, Carl took on the task himself. With covering fire from his
men, he advanced against withering enemy fire until he could
lob grenades into the their positions. The grenades were not
thrown in the conventional way, but like baseballs. His control
as a baseball pitcher paid off, though it did take eight grenades
before the Germans who were not dead surrendered.

Like most warriors, Carl's exploits would grow with the passing
years, but for the time being it was best to act as though he did
not want to talk about the war. Carl wanted to be characteristic
of the front line soldier, who prefers to talk about something other
than the men he has killed. Dropping an innuendo here and there
would be sufficient. The rest was best left to the imagination.

People would say, "You know he's been through hell, because
he doesn't like to talk about it."

Finally, the mayor stopped talking, and Carl was asked to say
a few words.

"Folks, you all know me and I don't figure I did any more
than most soldiers," he said. "I just feel mighty lucky to be alive
and back in Bethel."

They applauded his modesty.

The merchants had gotten together, and each had a gift for
Carl, everything from socks to underwear. Each of the merchants
had to make a presentation, otherwise their gift to Carl would
have lost its advertising effectiveness.

The day grew late. The band stood slumped in disarray. There
would be a dance on Main Street that night, but the music would
be provided by a hillbilly band from Valiant. A few of the townspeople upstaged the merchants by presenting Carl with a new twenty-
two caliber semi-automatic rifle. The handshaking continued another half-hour after the final presentation and after the band had
marched with a lack of briskness back to the band hall to put up
their instruments.

"Dad, I'll join you for a beer later," Carl said. "Vivian wants
to show me the new house."

Henry understood, though he was anxious to talk with Carl.
"When you get back, I'll be in the saloon. I'll take young Henry
with me."

"Do you think we ought to take Rachael home?" Vivian asked. Rachael rarely stayed in town late on Saturdays.

"She wants to stay," Henry said. "Damn if she ain't going to stay for the dance tonight. She's just a proud mother, and she takes all these compliments about Carl as being hers, too."

There's no doubt about that, Vivian thought, a tinge of anger shooting through her mind.

"We'll go then . . . see you at the saloon in a little while," Carl said.

Driving with one hand, Carl pulled Vivian toward him and kissed her hard on the lips. He showed the passion of a man who had been without a woman for a long time. She kissed him back with the same longing, causing him to take his eyes off the road and making the car swerve. They laughed at his driving ability.

Later, they lay on the bed caressing each other. The sexual act had been brief, about three minutes, but that could be expected since he had been without her so long. Thirty minutes later they had intercourse again. This time Vivian had an orgasm, something she had not experienced the first time.

They drove back to town a short time later, Vivian cradled in Carl's right arm. She was very proud of her husband, and looking forward to the future. Carl pulled up in front of the saloon, came around and opened the door for her.

"Such a gentleman," she said.

He grinned.

Glancing down the sidewalk, Vivian noticed Reverand Redfield looking disapprovingly at her as they started into the saloon. For a split-second she hesitated, a feeling of guilt encompassing her. What the hell, she thought, who needs that stupid sonofabitch. And so, as dramatically as Vivian had found the church to be a comfort during Carl's absence, she dismissed it as being of no value on his return. Besides, it had been months since she'd had a beer, and she was thirsty.

They found Henry and their son sitting at a table with Murray Powell, the town constable, and Morgan Marks, owner of Bebo's Drugstore. Powell was a porker, with heavy jowls and bushy eyebrows. He was short and, in Vivian's opinion, stupid. Marks was just the opposite of Powell physically. He was tall, thin and almost hairless. He had married Veronica Bebo and, after her father died, had taken over the drugstore.

Henry was waxing eloquent on politics. "Now, this fellow Truman is my kind of man. Mind you, I'm not saying that I approve of his party, but I have to admire him. He doesn't take a lot of shit from anybody."

Henry sipped his beer before continuing. Carl and Vivian pulled up chairs, sat down, and motioned for Casey to bring two beers. Carl Henry was drinking root beer, something Henry insisted Casey keep on hand if he wanted any Hayder business.

"Course if I had my way, Ike or MacArthur would be President," he said. "I think we need a military man in The White House now."

Marks and Powell nodded agreement, but the conversation had to be discontinued. A number of other people had pulled chairs close to the table so they could talk to Carl. Most of the men had their chairs turned backward, straddling them with their arms on the backs and a mug of beer in one hand.

"It's on the house," Casey said when he delivered the beer to Carl and Vivian.

"My god, I never get one on the house," Henry said, laughing.

"When you go whip the Germans you can have one on the house," Casey said.

"Hell, Carl's done whipped them all," Murray said. "Looks like you'll have to go dry Henry."

Henry laughed and said, "The day I go dry is the day you'll find tits on a boar hog."

Some of the men looked sheepishly at Vivian, but she laughed.

"How was it over there, Carl . . . rough?" The questioner was Bruck Wieser, a sawmill worker about Carl's age who hadn't been drafted because he'd lost a hand to a power saw.

"Bruck, I'd rather not talk about it right now. It was rough enough."

Bruck nodded knowingly and said, "Well, hell, we're supposed to be having a good time today, not worrying about what was in the past anyways."

"Now you're talking, Bruck," Ward Slaughter said. Ward owned a little ranch outside Bethel. He had been drafted, but never left the states. "You'll like this new band, Carl."

"Who are they?"

"Baker McCoy and the Playboys," Ward said. "They're on the radio in Oklahoma City."

"Good, huh?"

"Better than good," Ward continued. "They got a fiddler named Lowry Brown that's the best I ever heard."

Henry snorted. "Corley Vickers is the best fiddler in this part of the country."

"Corley just was the best fiddler," Zack Beatty said.

"What in the hell you doing here, Zack? Why ain't you over barbering like you're supposed to be?" Henry said.

"I closed up. No law against it is there?"

Henry answered, "I guess not, Zack. You bringing a squaw to the dance?"

The other men laughed, but Zack's face colored. "Naw, I ain't bringin no squaw." Ever since Henry found that Zack had been sleeping with Choctaw women, he had been agitating him.

Vivian came to Zack's rescue by asking, "What time does the dance start, anyway?"

"Seven-thirty," Murray volunteered.

"I'm hungry," she said to Carl. "Why don't we go over to the cafe and eat before the dance starts."

Henry answered for Carl. "That sounds like a good idea. I'll get Rachael."

It wasn't what Vivian had in mind, but there was little she could do. Since Carl's arrival on the train she had shared him with her in-laws, sisters-in-law, nephews, nieces, and all the people in town. The townspeople were easier to take than some of the kinfolks. The Shipley boys seemed to be everywhere she looked, trying to get a word in with their Uncle Carl.

Conversation during the meal was strained. The cafe was filled with people who continually stopped by to say something to Carl and to congratulate Henry and Rachael on having such a fine boy. Vivian was glad when the meal was over, and they moved back out in the street.

Henry parked the car where Rachael would have a good view
of the bandstand and the street. Rachael, Vivian and Carl Henry
sat in the car to wait for the dance to begin, while Carl and Henry
mingled with men on the street. The Shipley boys were still following Carl around, hanging on their uncle's every word. Vivian suspected their mentality before, but now she was sure.

Finally, the dance began and the band was good. Carl and Vivian
danced most of the dances together, but Henry insisted on dancing
a few numbers with Vivian. She laughed at her father-in-law's
entertaining remarks while they danced. He was so spry for his
age, so very much alive.

When the dance broke up at one o'clock Sunday morning, the
dancing trio found Rachael and Carl Henry were asleep. Rachael
awoke when Henry opened the car door. He was feeling good,
having danced practically every number. Mostly, he'd danced with
Anise Marie.

By god, he thought, I'll have to go see her Monday afternoon.

After leaving Carl, Vivian and his grandson, Henry goosed the
Ford toward home. Rachael asked him to slow down, but he just
grinned at her.

Damn, it's good to be alive, he thought.

Just for meanness he reached over and grabbed Rachael and
pulled her close to him. She resisted, but he was too strong for
her. Putting his arm around her, he squeezed her right breast.
He knew she would be shocked, and he was not disappointed.

Vivian felt Sunday was one of the best days in her marriage to
Carl. They were alone most of the day, interrupted only intermit-
tently by Carl Henry.

She remembered Monday as possibly the worst day in their
marriage. It was that day that Carl went to see old man Keyser
about getting his old job back at the mill.

CHAPTER SEVENTEEN

CARL HENRY got his first piece when he was fifteen. The girl was Yvonne Marks, daughter of Morgan and Veronica Marks. She was fourteen and it was her first date.

Prior to the date with Yvonne that night, Carl Henry masturbated twice during the day just thinking about her. He ejaculated once in the white men's restroom at the Texaco station while having the car serviced, and again in his own bathroom.

While at the service station he debated as to whether to buy rubbers, but decided not to waste the money. It was, after all, a first date.

Carl Henry had obtained a driver's license at the age of fourteen, because of his grandfather's influence with the county judge and other law enforcement officials. They all borrowed money from Henry's bank. So, on the occasion of his date with Yvonne he was driving one of the family cars, a white Cadillac sedan.

The Hayders had begun to spread their money around more

freely than in the past. Carl and Vivian had bought a small ranch on the outskirts of town, enabling Carl to think of himself as a rancher. They did have a few cattle and horses on the five hundred acres, but that was mostly for show.

The ranch house was a white two-story frame, more than adequate for the family. Carl and Vivian often hosted dances and parties on weekends. There was really no lack of money to do anything they wanted, but Carl still continued working at the mill. All his cronies worked there, and they were the people he cared about impressing.

Vivian was still the real family breadwinner, managing the bank, newspaper and Henry's other investments. The old man had total confidence in her business judgement.

As for Henry, money had not changed his lifestyle at all. All money meant to him was power, and that is all he really wanted. He refused to move from the old house, saying he knew how it was built because he had done it himself. At Vivian's insistence, the house had been rennovated and had become somewhat of a showplace. It contained expensive new furnishings throughout.

When Carl Henry arrived at the Marks' home, Morgan and Veronica were as cordial to him as parents can be when sending their daughter out on her first date. They were, of course, proud of their beautiful daughter, and they over-emphasized to Carl Henry that he should be careful driving and have Yvonne home by midnight.

Carl Henry had anticipated the mini-lecture, so he listened half-heartedly. He was thinking, though, about how good Veronica Marks looked, about how he would like to crawl in bed with her.

Veronica was thirty-four, but she could easily have passed for a woman in her twenties. She had auburn hair that touched her shoulders, and soft brown eyes that accentuated a tanned and perfect complexion. She was a shapely five-feet six-inches tall, and to Carl Henry she looked better than any movie star he had ever seen.

It was hard to picture Veronica as Morgan's wife.

Carl Henry made all the promises he knew the Marks' expected him to make, then escorted Yvonne to the car. She was beautiful, a youthful picture of her mother.

As he helped her into the car, Carl Henry surveyed Yvonne with manly hunger. He was especially mindful of her small but well-proportioned breasts, and her tanned and shapely legs.

Carl Henry was handsome in his own right, certainly one of the best-looking young men at Bethel High School. He was six-feet two-inches tall, a muscular one hundred eighty pounds, with brown eyes and brownish hair slightly bleached by the sun. He had a strong chin and rugged facial features similar to those of his grandfather.

Carl Henry's good looks and several other things about him accounted for Yvonne's happiness. As a freshman he had become the starting quarterback on the football team and a starting pitcher on the baseball team. There was no telling what he would accomplish as a sophomore, and she had made up her mind to be a part of his accomplishments. It also didn't hurt that his family was rich. Maybe not as rich as the Keysers, but rich.

She didn't need an invitation to move over and snuggle close to him as they sped along the highway. There would be a great many girls envious of her. Subconsciously, she had already made up her mind to do whatever necessary to become his steady girl friend.

It was a mid-summer Saturday evening. A bloody-looking sun was falling in the west, and the hint of a gentle breeze flicked at the leaves on the trees along the highway. They were on their way to a drive-in movie at Valiant, a town some sixteen miles from Bethel.

"I'm really glad you decided to go out with me tonight," he said. It wasn't exactly what you might call a great opening line, but he couldn't think of anything else to say.

"So am I," she said. "Mother and Dad wouldn't let me go out with anyone else, but they really like you."

"Well, I hope that doesn't just go for your mother and father." Why in the hell would they like me? he thought. They don't even know me. His grandfather had taught him to be suspicious of any compliment, saying that most people who complimented you wanted something.

"Oh, you know it's not just them that likes you," she laughed. "You know that."

He took his eyes off the road long enough to glance at her, smiled and said, "I hope this movie is worth the trip."

"What's on?" she asked.

"I have no idea. Did you tell your folks that I was taking you to a drive-in movie?"

"They didn't ask, so I didn't tell them."

"I just wondered," he replied. "Some people think there's something evil about drive-in movies."

"Some people think there's something evil about everything," she said. "Gloria Redfield for one."

"You mean the right Reverend Redfield's daughter," he responded lightly. "How can you say such a thing?"

Gloria Redfield was not a funny subject to Yvonne. There were some people who said the preacher's daughter was the prettiest girl in Bethel, a title Yvonne wanted to reserve for herself.

"I can tell you this," she said, "Gloria would never be caught dead in a drive-in movie. She is oh, so pious and goody-goody. She lives and breathes the church."

"Now, now," he laughed, "not everyone can be a Methodist and enjoy all this liberty."

She was contemplative for a moment before saying, "There's really something wrong with that girl."

It angered her when Carl Henry softly said, "It's wrong in all the right places."

"Do you think she's beautiful, Carl Henry?"

Though by no means a master of the female psyche, Carl Henry had learned enough from his grandfather to structure his reply. "Not really. Now, I consider you beautiful, Yvonne, but I just consider Gloria pretty."

His answer pleased her, and she was willing to concede that Gloria was pretty.

Worked your way out of that one didn't you, mother fucker? he thought.

By the time they reached the drive-in, the sun had been swallowed up by the earth, and dusk brought forth its usual assortment of crickets and bugs. They tried three parking places to the right of the concession stand before finding a speaker that worked.

"Want anything?" he asked.

"Not now," she said.

She was looking up into his face and it seemed very natural to kiss her. Her firm breasts poked against his chest as their lips met, causing a fire in his loins. Her lips were sweet and moist against his, and he was surprised that she responded so willingly. His arms cradled her body as he kissed her on the mouth and neck. She gently caressed the length of his back with her fingernails. They kissed over and over again, so much that their lips became chapped and sore. There was almost two hours of continual kissing, until the movie was over and the drive-in lights signaled intermission. Carl Henry had moved his hands, in seemingly accidental fashion, all over Yvonne's body. She didn't seem to mind.

As they began the drive home, she snuggled up close to him, her head against his shoulder and chest, her right hand inside his shirt caressing his stomach. About halfway back to Bethel, he slowed the car and turned down a dirt road. When they were out of sight of the main highway, he killed the engine.

Pulling her roughly against him, he kissed her and put his hand between her legs. He ran the hand along her legs until he could feel the smoothness of her panties. She protested then, trying to move his hand, but unwilling to take her lips from his. He struggled with the tight-fitting panties until, in frustration, he tore them.

He pushed her down in the seat and lay on top of her, while fighting to unzip his pants and free his penis. Finally, it was free.

She was a combination of both surrender and struggle as he searched for the opening between her legs. Passion overcame her and she began to help him. Then he was in her, feeling the heat and wonderous delight of her body. Moments later his sperm was running inside her, and they both tasted the ecstacy of the moment.

"I love you," she said.

"I love you, too," he responded.

They cleaned sperm from the car seat with some tissue Yvonne had in her purse. He was worried that it might leave a spot.

"It's late," he said. "I'd better get you home or your parents won't think I'm all that wonderful."

"I wish we could stay out all night together," she said.

"I wish that myself, but we'll just have to wait a while," he replied.

"You are just so wonderful, darling," she cooed. "I just love you so much."

It was all Carl Henry could do to keep from laughing aloud, because her verbalizing sounded a lot like a line from a movie he had seen a week before. In fact, she had seen the movie, too. He had seen her there with some of her girlfriends.

It was like his grandfather always said, "Words don't mean a damn thing." Like telling Yvonne he loved her. How could he be sure of something like that? It did make her happy, though, and he knew most of the guys in school would give their left nut to be where he was right now. So, what the hell. He wasn't sure if he was lying, but even if he was it made her happy.

As they drove homeward, Yvonne told him she planned to be a majorette with the high school band. Just a mental picture of her decked out in a majorette's uniform, exposing her beautiful legs, caused his penis to get hard again. He wished they had more time.

"What about your panties?" he asked, remembering his earlier frustration.

"That's no problem," she assured. She tossed them out the car window. "Mother and Dad will be in bed when I get home."

"Maybe you shouldn't have thrown them away," he laughed. "I might have wanted them for a memento of the evening."

"There will be lots of evenings."

"Are you sure your parents will be in bed?"

"I'm sure."

"You just think so."

"I know so."

She was right. Her parents had left a light burning, but they had trusted Carl Henry to get their daughter home at the proper time. He made a mental note that the Marks' were nice folks. He appreciated their trust.

He kissed Yvonne in the car and on the porch before saying goodnight.

"Will you call me tomorrow?" she asked.

"What time?"

"Tomorrow afternoon," she said. "I have to go to church in the morning." He had told her he would miss church, that he would be fishing with his father and grandfather.

"Okay, goodnight."

"Carl Henry . . ."

"Yes."

"I love you."

"And I love you."

It was eleven-thirty and he wished there was some place else to go. The night had been exciting and he sure wasn't sleepy.

God, I never dreamed I'd get a piece tonight, he thought. And what a piece.

He laughed at his thought processes then, because he realized he had no basis for comparison. But, he thought, if it's all as good as Yvonne's, I'd like to spend the rest of my life just fucking.

He decided to drive to Ella's Cafe. Some of the guys would be there, and they could shoot the shit about football. It also wouldn't hurt for them to know that he had laid claim to Yvonne.

Parking in front of the cafe, Carl Henry saw through the plate glass window that four members of the football squad were sitting in a booth eating french fries and drinking cokes. They were all seniors, but that didn't matter. He had bridged the age gap on the football field.

"Pull up a chair, Carl Henry, and order yourself some fries."

The invitation came from Sherill Wesley, a squatty-built youngster whose clothes were always well-worn and ill-fitting. They were *hand-me-downs* from two older brothers.

"I'll pass on the fries, but I will have a coke," Carl Henry said.

"Hey, Ella, get your ass over here with a coke for Carl Henry," Dale Thorne shouted across the half-empty cafe.

"Get up and get it yourself you little sonofabitch," she yelled back. She was a coarse woman, heavy, with a bulldog-like face but twinkling eyes. Her bark was much worse than her bite.

Dale, a gangling youth whose body had not caught up to his

height, grinned, got up, and went behind the counter to retrieve
a coke from the cooler.

"Better watch it, Ella," Dale teased. "The kind of service you
give, we might just take our business someplace else."

"Go ahead you little bastard," she said affectionately, "if you
can find another place in this fucking town that's open."

"The saloon's open," he replied.

"They won't let you little shitheads in the saloon. The coach
would have your asses and Casey's if he found you there."

"With your attitude, I don't know how you ever get a tip,"
Dale said, winking at his friends and handing the coke to Carl
Henry.

"It's a cinch I'm not going to get a tip from you little bastards.
All you're going to do is use up all my catsup. I can't understand
how you can use a whole bottle on one order of french fries."

"As much as you water it down, we have to," Dale said.

The banter was discontinued as another customer came in and
sat down at the counter. Ella had been sitting at the counter
herself, so she had to get up to pour the man a cup of coffee.

The other seniors were Bill Dwayne and Charles Thom, both
ends on the football team. Dale was a halfback.

"Where have you guys been?" Carl Henry asked.

"Ah, we all had dates," Bill said. "We took them to the show
and decided to meet back here. I had to walk because the old
man wouldn't give me the wheels."

"Fuckin' big deal," Charlie said. "You sound like the Lone
Ranger."

"Charlie's pissed because we double dated and I did promise
I'd have the car," Bill said. "Shit, I wouldn't blame Bonnie if
she never went anywhere with me again. The old man really fucked
me up."

"He fucked me up, too," Charlie said, "because I promised
Margaret you'd have the car. It was just one fucked up evening."

"You mean you don't want to go on another walking double
date," Bill laughed.

"Why don't we go on a jogging double date next time, shithead,"
Charlie responded good-naturedly. It's hard to do a lot of hunching
while you're walking. Maybe it would be easier jogging."

"Your problem is that you need a taller girl," Dale said. "Margaret's so short that your pecker hits her in the tits when you all are facing off against each other."

"Height doesn't mean anything," Bill responded. "You have to lay'em all down anyway."

"Where were you tonight, Carl Henry?" Dale asked.

"Yvonne and I drove over to Valiant to the drive-in."

"Yvonne Marks . . . that's the goddam best-looking girl in this town," Dale said. "Did you do any good?"

Carl Henry laughed and said, "That depends on what you mean by doing good."

"You know what I mean," Dale said.

"Well, we are going steady. I guess you can read that any way you want."

"Umh, boy," Bill said. "I know some little sophomore girls, even a couple of juniors, that are going to be mighty upset that old Carl Henry is out of circulation. That's fine with me, though. There's a couple of those girls that I wouldn't mind hunching, and I can do without old Carl Henry as competition."

"You'd hunch a fuckin' pig," Charlie said.

Carl Henry stayed with his companions until about one o'clock before excusing himself. He needed some sleep before going on the fishing trip with his father and grandfather.

It wasn't until he had crawled into bed that he remembered that he had screwed Yvonne without a rubber. That recollection sent his mind spinning into frenzied anxiety.

What if she's pregnant, he thought. I'll have to marry her. Oh shit, grandad will skin me alive.

He found it difficult to picture himself as a sixteen-year-old father, even more difficult to picture Yvonne as a fourteen-or fifteen-year-old mother. He would be sixteen in September. He wasn't sure about her birthdate.

It makes a helluva lot of difference when her birthday is, he thought. That's not really the issue here.

He made a mental note to buy rubbers the next time he went to the service station. He sure as hell couldn't buy them at the drugstore.

It won't be all that bad, he thought, because she is tremendous pussy. He laughed at himself, again remembering he had no basis for comparison.

God, a sixteen-year-old father, he continued in thought. I guess I'll have to leave town and get a job. Getting out of this fucking town is no big deal, but getting a job might be tough. I could get enough money from grandad to do whatever I want, but he'll really be pissed about me getting myself in this situation.

From conversations with his grandfather about women, he had gathered that the old man's philosophy was to "find'em, fuck'em and forget'em."

Henry had once told his grandson that there was no such thing as a bad-looking woman when it came to screwing, to just work your way through the culls first.

Carl Henry had then mentioned Eva Nepps, whose face would stop the proverbial nine-day clock.

"Dammit, boy," Henry laughed, "there are always exceptions to every rule. I guess you could drape a flag around her head and do it for Old Glory."

Carl Henry had heard numerous stories about his grandfather's sexual escapades. One man told him, "If you're half the cocksman your old grandpa is, there ain't a safe pair of drawers in this county." He couldn't remember who had told him that, nor could he remember who had told him the story about Henry fucking three whores in one afternoon . . . in a period of two hours.

The Negroes in town always listened to the stories about Henry and smiled, like they knew something. They didn't contribute anything to the tales, but they did talk about pussy a lot. They called it "poontang."

Damn, what a mind I've got, Carl Henry thought. Here I am up to my ass in trouble, maybe even going be a daddy, and I start thinking about Niggers talking about poontang.

He finally dozed off into a fretful sleep, dreaming about Yvonne and the whiteness of her thighs, reliving the moment when he had pushed his cock inside her. Less than an hour later, something crawling on his face woke him. A roach. He slapped it away. Revulsion gnawed at his stomach and he felt like vomiting.

He propped himself up in bed with a couple of pillows and,

for some reason, started thinking about the period of time after his father returned from the war. It had been about a year after his return that all hell broke loose.

The woman's name was Shirley. He had been sent to another room, with orders to keep the door closed. But he had heard.

He had heard his mother crying angrily, and he had heard the woman tell his father that she loved him and that he had another son in Virginia. He couldn't hear what his father said because he was talking so softly, mumbling a lot. He didn't know how long the conversation went on because he fell asleep.

After his father went to work the next morning, his mother packed their clothes, called Henry, and then they drove to New Boston, Texas, to visit one of her sisters. He remembered that his mother cried the entire trip.

His father came to New Boston the next day. He watched through a bedroom window as Uncle Joe, a gaunt-looking man with a long nose, talked to his father in the front yard. He had watched his father pace nervously in the yard after Uncle Joe came back into the house.

He recalled hearing his mother saying that she wouldn't talk to his father, but Uncle Joe and Aunt Grace kept insisting. She finally relented and went out into the yard. He remembered that they didn't touch, just talked a while. Then his mother came back into the house and his father got back into his car and drove away. He recalled that he worried at the prospect of having to stay with his long-nosed uncle.

The next day Henry came. Uncle Joe met him in the yard, too, but his grandfather walked right past him and into the house. Henry told Aunt Grace that he was there to see Vivian and that she had damn better have her come out where he could talk to her.

His mother did come out of the bedroom to talk to Henry and, after they talked about fifteen minutes, she started packing their clothes for the return trip to Bethel. The most unpleasant thing about the ordeal was having to kiss his aunt and uncle goodby. He hated kissing kinfolks, especially Aunt Grace. She always smelled like burnt grease.

His mother hadn't really been the same since that time. It was like all joy had been ripped out of her. Even her laughter sounded phony, not like it did in the past. He suspected that she really hadn't wanted to return to Bethel and his father, that she did it only to assure that her son got what was coming to him from the Hayder estate. He knew Henry was not above using any type of threat to get what he wanted.

Carl Henry had to take a leak. He didn't bother to turn on the light in his bathroom. The window shade was up and the moon filled the room with yellow light. Standing there, shaking his cock after pissing, he felt anger toward his father. His mother deserved better.

The sonofabitch, he thought. The goddam sonofabitch.

His thoughts then turned to Yvonne's mother.

My god, she looks good. So fuckable.

He got a hard on thinking about Veronica Marks, so he masturbated. Afterward, he started to go back to bed, but remembered that he was supposed to go fishing with his father and grandfather in a few hours.

He will be up in a little while, Carl Henry thought about his father, making coffee and looking forward to getting to the creek. I've never known anyone who could get as fucking excited over a fishing or hunting trip. I guess he might as well, though. Mother probably never lets him in her pants anymore, and grandad would have his ass if he tried to run around.

What a stupid-assed fucking mind I've got. A guy ought not to think about his parents screwing.

He wondered if anyone other than his father had screwed his mother. He couldn't blame her if she had found comfort in someone else.

He thought about Yvonne then, wondered if she was asleep. She's probably sleeping like a baby. God, she has beautiful legs.

He found a pencil and wrote his father a note telling him that he wouldn't be going on the fishing trip.

I can imagine how disappointed he will be, Carl Henry thought, but dammit, I've heard all his war stories. He's such a fucking failure, all he wants to talk about is what he did in the war.

Except for the parties and dances at the house, his parents

were like strangers. His mother always seemed sad, except when
he talked to her. He could always make her laugh. Carl Henry
knew that she delighted in everything he did.

His father was sad, too, though he tried to hide it by drinking
excessively. The chain-smoking gave him away, betrayed him as
a nervous shell of a man with little or no purpose in life. He
certainly wasn't a social climber, preferring the company of labor-
ers at the lumber company to everyone else.

The stupid sonofabitch doesn't realize that they listen to his
war stories for the free beer he buys them, Carl Henry thought.
Or maybe he does know and just doesn't care.

He started thinking about himself, how many of the more prominent people in town were always commenting on his politeness
and smile. He hated their fucking guts and someday, when he
took over the bank and newspaper, they would discover that his
grandfather was a saint compared to him.

Carl Henry joined the church when he was twelve, because it
was the right thing to do. It seemed he was always doing the
right thing outwardly, feeling altogether differently inwardly.

Finally, he fell asleep.

He awoke to the smell of frying bacon, put on a T-shirt and
jeans, slipped his bare feet into houseshoes, and went into the
kitchen where his mother was fixing his breakfast. He hugged
her and sat down at the breakfast table.

She smiled and asked, "Did you have a good time last night?"

He nodded affirmatively. He had slept poorly, felt groggy as
hell.

"Where did you take Yvonne?"

"We drove over to Valiant to the drive-in movie."

"Was the movie any good, or do you even know?" she asked
with a bit of a laugh.

He liked that about his mother, that she enjoyed kidding him.
He was also pleased that she was wearing the blue robe that he
had given her for Christmas. It seemed that she was always wearing it.

"I have no idea about the movie," he said, "because Yvonne
had me down in the car seat most of the time."

Vivian laughed and said, "She looks the type. I hope you didn't let her take advantage of you."

"You know me, Mom, I'm saving myself."

"I'm sure you are," she responded with humorous sarcasm, "which is what I would expect of Henry Hayder's grandson. By the way, why didn't you go fishing with your father and grandfather?"

"I wasn't up to it. I had a headache."

"Did you take anything for it?"

He nodded and said, "Three aspirins." Taking his first sip of coffee, he grimaced. "Why does Dad have to make the coffee so strong?"

She smiled and replied, "He prides himself on making it strong, so strong that he can hardly drink it himself. Let me make you some more."

She took the cup from him as though he was a small boy, poured the remains in the sink and began brewing another pot of coffee. It was pleasant being in the kitchen with his mother. Talking to her, having breakfast with her, was always pleasurable.

After breakfast, he showered and dressed for church. From his closet he selected dark brown slacks, a cream colored shirt and a tan sports coat. His brown shoes were polished to perfection.

It was a hot but beautiful day, still early enough that the sun had not begun to sear the ground. As he drove the Cadillac toward the church, he tried to think of some way to discuss the situation with Yvonne.

How in the hell, he thought, do you tell a girl she might be pregnant?

The church building appeared all too soon, its steeple jutting upward into the blue sky. Laughing inwardly, he thought the steeple made the church look as though it was giving God the finger.

Such thoughts, he surmised. I should have my mind washed out with soap.

He was often amused by his own thoughts and wished there was someone with whom he could share them. He could, of course, share his off-the-wall thoughts with his mother and grandfather. And he often did.

He was greeted warmly at the church by his friends and by numerous adults who were not timid in declaring him one of the finest young men in town. He wondered how many of them would verbalize that if his grandfather did not own the bank and newspaper, and if his mother was not the final say on whether they received a loan.

If the fucking hypocrites only knew what I did to Yvonne last night, and what I think of them, he thought, they might not be so friendly. His grandfather had taught him to distrust everyone, saying that people showed interest in you only when it was in their best self-interest.

"The fucking hypocrites at church don't really give a shit about anyone," Henry had said. "They wouldn't give you the sweat off their balls, or cunts, as the case might be, if they didn't think they could get something out of you. People are just no damn good, but you need to be in the church to keep up with what they're doing and thinking. I want you in there, boy, so you can nail their asses when you take over the business."

Carl Henry had been around many of the churchmen enough to know they weren't all that pious.

The sanctimonious bastards like to kick a man when he's down, though, he thought, and the women are just as bad with all their gossip.

He saw Yvonne briefly before the worship service began, long enough to tell her that he had to see her after church. She was surprised that he hadn't gone fishing. He would have sat with her during the service, but he had been railroaded into singing in the choir.

Unfortunately, the minister chose this day for one of his longer sermons, pouring great ridicule on those not in attendance and belittling the entire congregation for its lack of evangelical fervor.

Carl Henry wondered why ministers preached to people who weren't there. He had begun to think the man would never stop preaching, but he finally did.

I guess nothing lasts forever, he thought, maybe not even hell. It's the heat, the fucking heat. It has addled my brain.

He met Yvonne outside the building and pulled her over under the shade of a tree where their conversation could not be heard.

He had already decided there was no smooth way to approach the subject, especially since they had so little time.

"About what happened last night, Yvonne, you may be pregnant."

She was startled, puzzled. "I may be what?"

"I said you might be pregnant. I didn't use anything."

"Didn't use anything, what does that mean?" She was naive, and Carl Henry, while he knew a little, certainly was no expert on sex.

"If you don't use a rubber, the girl can get pregnant." he said.

"Oh, my god, what are we going to do?"

"Nothing for the moment because nothing is certain, but I thought you should know."

She was close to tears. "Carl Henry, I don't know what to say."

"There's nothing to say, Yvonne. We just have to get together and work things out. I love you. Remember that. And don't cry, just leave everything to me."

Sure, he thought, leave everything to me. What the hell am I going to do?

"When can I see you?" she asked.

"Do you think your parents will let me take you to church tonight?" He didn't mind going to Methodist Youth Fellowship on Sunday night, because they always had a dance afterwards in the church basement.

"I'll ask, but they may not let me go out two nights in a row. Call me later."

"I wondered where you two made off to," Morgan Marks said, walking to where they were standing. Your mother's waiting in the car Yvonne. Can we give you a ride Carl Henry?"

"No sir, I have a car."

"Well, we'll see you later then. C'mon Yvonne."

"Mr. Marks . . ."

The man turned back to face Carl Henry and said, "Yes . . ."

"Would it be okay if I took Yvonne to M-Y-F tonight? I promise to have her home early."

Marks laughed and said, "I'll have to check with her mother. No, on second thought, she can go. I don't want you going around telling everyone that Veronica wears the pants in our family, even if it's true."

Carl Henry liked the response, and he liked Marks, though he detested the blue suit he was wearing.

Morgan also liked Carl Henry, and he expressed it when he and Yvonne joined Veronica in the car. "I really like that Hayder boy. He looks you right in the eye and states his business."

"And what was his business?" Veronica asked.

"A date with our lovely daughter tonight. I said okay. Is it okay?"

Veronica laughed. "I certainly don't want to overrule you in front of Yvonne. We want her to think that her parents agree on everything."

Yvonne smiled and thought, You had better like that Hayder boy because he might just be your son-in-law.

She felt as though her insides would never stop churning.

CHAPTER EIGHTEEN

Y VONNE WAS not pregnant. Her period was on schedule, so she and Carl Henry did not have to initiate their emergency plan. Had she missed her period, they had planned to go to Oklahoma City and get married. Carl Henry had told her that his grandfather could put pressure on the right people to take care of the age problem.

She knew he wasn't keen on letting the old man know he was in trouble. It would have been a big blow to her folks, too, but they would have gotten over it in time.

She was both excited and scared at the prospect of being pregnant. It would have been a great adventure, but it would have destroyed her dreams and aspirations, that of being a majorette in the high school band, of being elected most beautiful girl in her class, and of being homecoming queen. While being married to Carl Henry was something she ultimately wanted, she also wanted her pictures dominating the high school yearbook.

There would be full-page pictures in her majorette uniform, and full-page pictures of her as most beautiful and as homecoming queen. There would probably even be pictures of her with Carl Henry as most handsome couple, or something like that.

I'll probably be named homecoming queen my junior year, she thought, since that's Carl Henry's last year in high school. Surely, I'll be the queen that year. I just don't want to think about my final year in school without Carl Henry being there.

Maybe we'll get married after my junior year. I can finish high school wherever he goes to college. She was sure he would go to college because he had talked about it often.

He will probably even get a football scholarship, she thought.

For Yvonne, the most pressing problem in the coming year would be to be named most beautiful girl in the freshman class. Her only real competition was Gloria Redfield, and she feared some of the boys might vote for the preacher's daughter. She didn't figure many girls would vote for Gloria because of her overbearing religious attitude.

As for the boys, they might vote for Gloria instead of her because she was going steady with Carl Henry. But Carl Henry could probably straighten out the male vote. Most of the boys, especially the athletes, would do what he said.

Yvonne's parents had let her date Carl Henry once or twice a week since he has spoken to her father at church that day. He also visited her home twice a week, all of which would end with the beginning of football season.

Yvonne wanted Carl Henry at her home every night, but he said, "I don't want to wear out my welcome with your folks."

There was little chance. At least half the time he was there, Carl Henry and her father talked football. She resented her father taking time with Carl Henry she felt belonged to her, but she decided it was for the best. She also resented Carl Henry's attentiveness to her mother, thinking he was taking an abnormal interest in Veronica.

They were careful on dates now, always using a rubber. Occasionally they would sneak a few moments of pleasure without the rubber. It was exciting, but it worried her.

Just thinking about Carl Henry made her body quiver with want. Knowing he belonged to her caused a pleasant sensation throughout her entire body.

It had not taken the rest of the girls in town long to get the message. They were jealous, of course, which pleased Yvonne a great deal. She was sure Gloria Redfield, in spite of her pious ways, was the most jealous of all.

Gloria would like to be right where I am today with Carl Henry, she thought.

She worried that some of the girls might suspect that she was *putting out* to Carl Henry. There were very few girls in school who would actually sleep with a boy. She knew of only two, and they were seniors. Most of the girls would do some heavy necking, even hunching, but few would go all the way.

I might have regretted going all the way, she thought, if it hadn't been with Carl Henry.

She thought about Marlene Friel, and what had happened to her when she dated a college boy from Broken Bow. The boy was young-looking, went to the University of Oklahoma. Marlene, a high school sophomore, saw no reason to tell her parents that she was dating someone already in college.

Marlene told Yvonne that on her date with the boy, his name was Jerry, they had necked a lot and that he kept gnawing at her breasts. Then he asked if he could eat her. Marlene said at the time she didn't know what he meant, but figured he just wanted to take off her blouse and brassiere so he could suck her breasts.

"I like to have my breasts sucked, so I agreed," Marlene had said. "But before I realized what was happening, he had my panties off and his mouth was on my thing. I didn't know what he was going to do or I would have told him that I was menstruating.

"You should have seen him," Marlene laughed. "He got blood all over his face and his white shirt. He was wearing a suit that night because we had just been to church.

"You talk about a dumb-ass, he even took off my Kotex before eating me. You'd think a college man would know more about sex than that."

Marlene told the story to all the girls in her Sunday School class, and said she couldn't wait to tell it to Gloria Redfield.

"I just want to see the look on her face when I tell her about Jerry eating me," she said.

"I'd also like to hear the tale Jerry told his mother about his bloody shirt. She's probably still looking for the wound her sweet boy received. Maybe he threw the shirt away and claimed he had been beaten up by a bunch of bullies from Bethel.

"Well, enough of sweet Jerry. The next time he's hungry he'll probably want to eat somebody besides me."

While Yvonne did not find Marlene's story all that amusing, she laughed anyway. She wondered why Carl Henry had not eaten her, and decided it probably wasn't something decent people did.

And though she had no real fondness for Marlene and her crude talk, Yvonne wanted to see Gloria's expression when she heard the story.

Some of Marlene's talk really bothered Yvonne, especially when she told about how all the boys in school were screwing Choctaw and Nigger girls.

"There's not a night that passes," Marlene said, "when some of those bastard boyfriends of ours aren't out screwing some Nigger or Choctaw girl. And who's to blame them. They have to dump their sperm somewhere, and I'm sure as hell not going to let any of the little bastards in my hole."

Jeanette Vannoy asked Marlene when she was going to let someone in her hole.

"In college, that's when," she replied. "If you get knocked up there, at least you have a chance of getting a man that might make a decent living. Half these little bastards will wind up working for the sawmill or the highway department."

When Yvonne was alone with Carl Henry, she had asked him about some of the boys sleeping with Nigger and Indian girls.

"I understand that some of the guys do," he said, "but I think a lot of it is just talk. Some guys want to brag all the time about their sexual powers, but it's usually guys who have never had a girl."

"You mean you never tell your friends about sleeping with me," she teased. "I'd think you'd want them to know."

"There are some things they don't need to know, and that's one of them. They'll know someday, but it will be when we're married."

"I'll be glad when that day gets here." As an afterthought she added, "Carl Henry, have you ever slept with a Nigger or Choctaw?"

"Are you kidding? If I ever did that my Grandad would skin me alive."

CHAPTER NINETEEN

Rachael died on her grandson's birthday, while Carl Henry was screwing to Yvonne. Henry was fucking Anise Marie about the same time.

Carl Henry learned of his Grandmother's death about eleven o'clock, when he took Yvonne home. The Marks did not break the news to him, simply told him to go to Henry's house as quickly as possible. He immediately sensed, of course, that there was a death or serious illness, and he feared it might be his Grandfather.

When Vivian met him at the door and told him it was his Grandmother who had died, he was relieved.

He didn't cry when he heard the news, couldn't be sure that he felt anything. He had never felt close to his Grandmother, only to his Grandfather. He considered his Grandmother weak, like his father.

He cried a little at the funeral, of course, primarily because it was expected. He was surprised at the number of people who

attended, then remembered what his Grandfather had once told
him.

"You can't get ten people together to make this town a better
place to live, but let somebody die, then the whole damn bunch
gets together. People are like buzzards. They like the dead better
than the living."

Carl Henry watched his aunts, uncles and cousins sobbing at
the funeral and thought, what assholes. His father had cried from
the time he learned of his mother's death. Other than himself,
the only family members who weren't crying were Vivian and
Henry.

All of Rachael's cronies were crying. So were some people she
barely knew. He couldn't help but notice that Anise Marie was
teary-eyed.

It's a circus, he thought, a fucking circus. Nobody really gives
a shit that she's dead, surely not Anise Marie. This ought to elimi-
nate her guilt for fucking the old man all the time.

The preacher likened Rachael to a great patriarch of God, who
had left her children and grandchildren to carry on the Lord's
work.

Bullshit, Carl Henry thought.

That night, after he had witnessed emotional displays by his
father and aunts at the graveside, Carl Henry stood on the porch
of his home and drank in the beauty of the fall night. The stars
glittered from their perches in the sky, and the moon was like a
rounded heap of glowing embers in the fireplace on a winter evening. The evening was still, warm, and the smell of freshly mowed
grass filled his nostrils.

Smelling the grass made him remember that the first football
game of the season would be played the next Friday night.

Thinking about football beats the hell out of thinking about
death, he thought.

A few miles away Henry sat in his favorite rocker on the big
porch taking in the night sounds. An almost empty gallon jar of
muscadine wine occupied a place beside the rocker.

Henry had been crying, not because Rachael was dead but because their life together had not been as full as it should have been. He would miss her, even her condemning stare when he was profane.

She was a good woman, he thought. A damn good woman. I was lucky to have her as long as I did. Life is so short, so fragile.

He didn't want to go to bed. It would be the first night since he had built the house that Rachael would not be in the bed beside him.

CHAPTER TWENTY

I'LL TELL you, she can do more tricks on a four-inch dick than a monkey can do on a long vine."

Zack Beatty was telling Henry about a forty-seven year old widow named Rozella Moss, who had recently moved to Bethel. And, for once, he had the old man's undivided attention.

"Bring us a couple more beers," Henry told Casey. The bartender had also been listening to Zack's evaluation of the woman's screwing ability. With exception of the trio, the saloon was empty. Zack and Henry were standing at the bar, Casey behind it.

"Where did you meet her?" Henry asked.

"Damned if she didn't come to the barber shop to have her hair trimmed. One thing just led to another. We just started talking about things in general. Then, after she found out I wasn't married, she invited me over to her house for some coffee. That was on Tuesday.

"Anyways, come Thursday night I was at her house like a bore hog in heat. We talked a long time, getting cozier by the minute. After we'd had some coffee she broke out some beers that she just happened to have handy. Things really loosened up then.

"I figured she hadn't had a man in a long while, but I was a little nervous about making a play right away. After a few beers, though, I thought *what the hell* and made my move.

"By god, before I hardly even knew it she had a hand inside my pants playing with my balls. From then on it was katy-bar-the-door."

Henry wasn't sure how much of Zack's tale he could believe. He took a swallow of beer and said, "Where did you say she was from, Zack?"

"I didn't say, but she's from around Idabel, and you can flat tell it."

"How in the hell can you tell when a woman's from Idabel?" Casey wanted to know.

Zack pondered the question before answering, then said, "Women from bigger towns like that just act a lot different. They're more . . . what's the word I want, Henry?"

"Refined . . . sophisticated."

"That's it," Zack said.

"That's also a crock of shit," Henry said. "Women from Idabel don't act any different than women from Bethel. All they're looking for in either place is something hard to go between their legs."

"That ain't the case with every woman," Zack defended.

"Well, it's the case with every one of them that I ever knew," Henry opined.

"Either of you ever seen a queer woman?" Casey asked.

"Not me," Henry replied, "but I'd find it mighty queer to find one that wouldn't fuck."

The old man was sometimes almost too crass for Casey and Zack.

"Hell," Casey said, "I was just wondering if there were any queer women in Bethel."

"None that I know of," Henry said. "I've only known of one queer man in this town, and I ran into him when I was sheriff. That has been some years ago. I pistol whipped the shit out of him and ran him out of town. I can't remember his name, but I think he was a barber."

Zack took exception to Henry's jibe. "You're making that barber part up, Henry. There ain't never been no queer barber in Bethel."

Henry laughed. "I was just kidding you. Let's leave the queering to the boys in Tulsa, Oklahoma City and Dallas. We fuck here. Now finish telling me about this Rozella."

"Like I was saying, I ain't never had nothing to compare with this woman."

"That doesn't surprise me," Henry interrupted. "Is Rozella the first white woman you've ever laid? Or is she white?"

Zack was livid. "Dammit, Henry, don't get started on that shit about me sleeping with Choctaws again. I ain't slept with one of them in a long time. And Rozella sure ain't no Indian."

"You sure she hasn't got a little Indian blood in her?" Henry teased. "I just can't figure you sleeping with a pure white woman."

"Okay, Henry," Zack said, waving his hands in resignation, "I'm through talking because I'm tired of you pestering me about sleeping with Choctaws. You've been ribbing me about it for years, and enough is enough."

"Whoa, don't get so heated up," Henry said. "I'll back off and you can tell us some more about Rozella Moss."

Zack was upset with Henry's condemnation and refused to drop the subject. "You just don't know when to quit badgering a man, Henry. I can't ever recall coming in this saloon when you were here that you didn't start that shit about me sleeping with Indians. I admit that I done it in the past, but for god's sake, let dead dogs lie. I don't like Choctaws anymore than you do."

"Henry wouldn't kid you if he didn't like you," Casey said.

"You don't have to intervene, Casey," Henry said. "If this silly mother fucker doesn't like what I say, he can kiss my ass. And if he gets too mad, I'll take him outside and beat the dog shit out of him."

Zack grunted, knowing full well that Henry meant what he said. "Dammit, Henry, I just think the joke has gone far enough."

"Fine," Henry said, "but I told you I was backing off. Just

don't get smart-ass with me, because I'm still not too old to beat the living shit out of you."

Zack cleared his throat and said, "I'm not looking for trouble, Henry, just a little respect."

"You got it, asshole. Now finish telling us about Rozella."

Henry wondered what Rozella looked like. Couldn't look like much or she wouldn't sleep with Zack. Still, you never can tell. Some women are drawn to ugliness. I'll have to see what she looks like, and soon.

The old man listened as Zack told about his night with Rozella, but his thoughts drifted to a young girl in a barn in Arkansas. That was so long ago, and yet the memory was as fresh and clear as yesterday. He had for years searched for that girl in every woman he had known, but he had never found her.

He had lived with one woman for years, had watched her die without really feeling much for her. They had been husband and wife, but they had also been strangers. He could never talk to Rachael about his dreams and aspirations, because she would not understand. She had never understood him, up until the day she died.

Still, she was a good woman, he thought, and she deserved better than me. But she is responsible for what happened to Carl. She made him weak. He is capable of being more than he is, or is he? I don't guess it matters anymore. Carl Henry, he's got my strength.

It's hard to imagine Carl being a war hero, shuffling around like he does with a cigarette hanging from his mouth. He could have parlayed being a war hero into a political office. That's what I would have done.

Zack interrupted his thoughts with, "You boys can kid me all you want to, but I'm sticking to that little woman from now on."

"You thinking about marrying her?" Casey asked.

"Well, that's a little drastic, but the thought has crossed my mind," Zack said.

"Zack's too tight to marry anybody," Henry said. "He'd be scared silly that Rozella would spend all his money."

"That's not true, Henry. Just because I don't throw money away doesn't mean I'm chincy. If I was to marry the woman, she'd have equal rights to my money."

"If that's the case, you're a bigger damn fool than I thought," Henry said.

Casey didn't want the conversation to evolve into a money argument, so he said, "I hate to break up all this stimulating talk, but what do you think about the football team this year?" While asking the question he set three new beers on the bar.

"Casey, you're a gentleman and a scholar," Zack said, always grateful for a free beer. "I think we're going to have a helluva team this year, and a lot of it's on account of this old bastard's grandson."

"I just as soon we not have a football team at all," Henry said. "The boy's a fine baseball player, could be a big leaguer if he doesn't get himself hurt playing football."

"Football's not as dangerous as it used to be," Casey said. "They wear a whole lot more padding now."

Zack nodded agreement and opined, "And I tell you something else, Henry. Football is the coming game. It's going to pass up baseball."

"Dammit, Zack, just because you don't know nothing about baseball, you've suddenly become an expert on football," Henry angrily chided. "There's no way football's ever going to pass up baseball, even if the WPA builds six more football stadiums in Bethel."

Henry still blamed the Roosevelt administration for most of the country's ills, including every problem in Bethel. During the depression, the WPA had built a football stadium in Bethel that seated twenty thousand people. Bethel's population was only eight thousand, had only been about six thousand when the stadium was built.

"Look at it this way," Zack continued, "colleges are offering boys full scholarships to play football, but they're not offering anything for baseball. A boy that plays football can get himself a good education free."

"By god, if he signs with the Yankees or Cardinals he doesn't need an education," Henry said. "Baseball is where the money is. Besides, Carl Henry sure doesn't have to worry about money to go to school on."

Henry thought that if his dream for his own son was not fulfilled, it might be through his grandson. He had seen Carl Henry play football and he worried about him getting hurt, because he played with a kind of reckless abandon.

He's like I was, Henry thought. When he does something, he goes at it like it is the last thing he will ever do. He liked that about the boy.

Henry recalled all the days he and Carl Henry had spent together, days of hunting and fishing and daily swims when the boy was not in school. The boy had been a willing pupil, so it had been easy to teach him to track game. But lately he seemed preoccupied with other things.

Probably girls, he thought, smiling inwardly. If that Yvonne Marks is any indication of the kind of girls he's interested in . . . well, he's doing all right.

Yvonne reminded Henry of the girl in the barn in Arkansas.

I should have married that girl, he thought. Regardless of the consequences, I should have married her.

It was getting late, but he didn't want to go home.

Anise Marie will be there, he thought. She's always there. Ever since Rachael died she's been there. I'm sick of Anise Marie. Anise Marie is the most boring woman in the world. I hate screwing Anise Marie. It's all I can do to get up a hard for Anise Marie.

He wondered what Rozella Moss would be like.

If I was a few years younger, I'd go by and see, he thought. Shit, she's probably not much better than most, if at all. Fucking any of them gets boring after a while.

The important thing is waking up in the morning, feeling the coolness of the creek water when you go for a swim, smelling frying bacon, tasting cold beer, and seeing the moon bob up from behind the mountains.

And the memories. They're important. I like to remember what things were like once.

Zack interrupted his thought process by calling his name.

"What is it?" he asked.

"I'm going back to the barber shop. Drop by tomorrow and I'll buy you a beer."

"Yeah, I'll do that," Henry replied.

Henry didn't seem to want to talk after Zack left, so Casey busied himself washing and drying glasses. Henry stood at the bar with a fresh beer, sipping it and thinking.

The town has changed and the people have changed, he thought. It's grown some, but maybe not for the better. Seems to be more Niggers than when I first moved here. The sawmill can be blamed for that. The Keysers like to hire Niggers because they don't have to pay them much.

Hell, I guess I've changed some, too. Having the Niggers and Indians around don't bother me that much anymore, as long as they stay in their place.

To hell with them. Old Lady Roosevelt's going to see they get all that's coming to them and more.

Maybe I'll wander over to Carl's and Vivian's for supper. See how the boy's doing. Don't get to see him much anymore because of that damn football and his girlfriends. But I have to give him credit for the work he's doing at the newspaper. He's really learning the business. Might even be as good a writer as I am already.

In a way he wished the boy hadn't spent the summer working at the paper. He would have preferred that they spend the time together fishing the creeks and talking.

This might have been my last summer, he thought with sadness.

He didn't believe it, though.

God, how Viv's changed, he thought. Still pretty as a picture, but so hard. Most of that's Carl's fault, though I can't really blame him for sleeping with that woman from Virginia, being away from home for so long and all.

He still could have salvaged things, though, if he had been smart. But the boy never did use his head. If he had, he probably could have been a congressman or senator.

Anise Marie will probably have supper fixed for me, but dammit, I didn't ask her to fix supper. I wish the hell she would quit hanging around the house all the time. I could hire me a Nigger to clean up the place and fix my meals. By god, that's what I'll do. I'll send the bitch packing.

Things sure have changed. There was a time when I'd like to have had her around so I could get in her drawers.

"Henry . . ." It was Arlo Shipley, calling to him across the semi-darkness of the saloon. "Rosie thought you might be in here. She wanted to know if you wanted to have supper with us tonight."

"I'll let you know if I ever want to eat with you, Arlo," he said. "I'm going over to Carl's and Viv's."

"You want us to give you a lift over there?"

"You know damn well my car's parked out front," he replied.

"We were just trying to be helpful," Arlo said.

"I'm sure you were, Arlo. I'm sure you were."

Well, some things haven't changed, he thought. Arlo is still the stupidest sonofabitch in ten counties.

CHAPTER TWENTY-ONE

CARL HENRY had been visiting the Marks' home on a regular basis for almost a year. During that time, both Morgan and Veronica had shown more than a passing interest in the relationship he had with their daughter. Morgan, perhaps, because he depended on Hayder financing for his business. And neither Vivian nor Henry were persons to be crossed if you wanted to do business in Bethel. Of course, he also saw Carl Henry as a prospective son-in-law, one who could provide Yvonne with everything she ever wanted.

But Veronica, she felt an unexplainable physical attraction for Carl Henry, and she suspected he felt the same way about her. It was obvious from the way he looked at her, and from the way he seemed to accidentally touch her on occasion. It caused a sensation within her she had never felt before.

Veronica did sometimes feel guilt about the strange feelings she had for Carl Henry. She couldn't comprehend what the feelings meant, but she was sure a married woman should not have such intense emotions toward a boy, especially a boy her daughter cared for so much.

In the context of her feelings for Carl Henry, Veronica felt no guilt where Morgan was concerned. She often found herself comparing the two, and subconsciously finding more strength in Carl Henry than in her husband. He was, of course, larger than Morgan, certainly more physical looking. She often imagined how Yvonne must feel when Carl Henry was holding her in his arms. She even felt jealously toward her daughter.

So pronounced was her feeling for Carl Henry that when Morgan was making love to her, Veronica's thoughts would be of the younger man. In fact, thinking about Carl Henry during lovemaking with Morgan had become a necessity if she was to achieve an orgasm.

Veronica had married Morgan when she was only seventeen, just graduated from high school. He was thirty at the time, working as a pharmacist in her father's drugstore.

It seemed a perfect marriage. Morgan was kind, caring, receptive to his wife's every need. For Veronica, who had been raised in a protected environment by smothering parents, he was the perfect mate. He was never too demanding, and she felt very safe and protected when with him.

There was absolutely no doubt in Veronica's mind that she loved Morgan. As to the magnetism that existed between Carl Henry and herself, she was sure that it was not love, and she was just as sure that it would eventually go away.

There had been the normal flirtations in high school, even a steady boyfriend when she was a junior, but Veronica had never known any man sexually other than Morgan. And, because she was perfectly content with her situation, she doubted that she ever would. There certainly was no overt desire on her part.

But this thing with Carl Henry bothered her, stirred emotions she did not know existed. She had become helpless in dealing with her feelings where he was concerned.

Such was her mental condition that night Bethel experienced the worst storm in its history.

The fury of the storm took the town's residents by surprise. It came roaring into the area . . . without warning . . . spawning minor tornados, knocking down power lines, and pouring forth a drenching rain that caused flash flooding. The loss of electricity, plus the high winds and hail that shattered windows, paralyzed the attempts of residents to move from one location to another. They were pretty well stuck wherever they happened to be at the time.

Both Morgan and Yvonne were trapped at the drugstore. Veronica and Carl Henry were trapped in the Marks' home.

Yvonne often helped her father at the drugstore when she was not in school, and on this particular day he had been forced to stay at the business later than usual. Yvonne was anxious to get home because she had a date with Carl Henry, but they had to wait for a perscription pick-up.

Yvonne pouted about the delay, but her father was adamant about waiting because, "This medicine is for Mrs. Bates and she's very sick." The storm hit before Mrs. Bates daughter arrived to pick up the medicine.

Carl Henry arrived at the Marks' home just before the storm moved in. Veronica greeted him at the door, told him Yvonne would be home soon, and suggested he be seated on the couch in the living room.

"Would you like a coke?" she asked.

"That would be fine."

He liked watching her as she walked away from him, the firm buttocks, the beautiful legs. He was much more interested in watching Veronica than in the thunder, lightning and wind that had suddenly moved into the area.

Then the lights went out.

"Mrs. Marks," he called out, "are you okay?"

"I'm fine," she called back. "I can't see very well, but I have some candles here someplace."

The phone started ringing.

"Carl Henry, will you get that? The phone's on the table at the end of the couch."

"I've got it . . . hello."

"Carl Henry, I'm glad you're there," Morgan said from the other end of the line. "Is Veronica okay?"

"She's fine," he replied. "She's in the kitchen looking for some candles."

"I'm glad you're there," Morgan repeated, "because Veronica is afraid of storms and this is a bad one."

"We're fine here, but what about you and Yvonne?"

"It's bad here, but we're in no danger. I think it's headed your way. We're getting heavy hail and high winds so we're just going to have to sit it out until . . ."

The phone started crackling, then went dead.

Veronica was back in the living room, light from a candle accentuating the beauty of her face. "Was that Morgan?"

"Yes. The phone went dead, but Mr. Marks said they were safe. He said it might be quite a while before they got home. The storm must have hit the downtown area pretty hard."

"It's bad here, too," she said. "Would you look at all the lightning."

He was more interested in looking at her, but said, "It looks like a war outside. I don't think we have anything to worry about though."

Veronica put the candle on the coffee table, sat in a chair facing the couch and said, "I've always been afraid of lightning."

"I'm not too fond of it myself."

They sat quietly for a while, listening to the sounds of the storm. The candlelight created a mood quite different than the sporadic eerie glow outside that was caused by the lightning. Neither Carl Henry nor Veronica were afraid. They were savoring the moments, grateful for this act of nature that caused them to be alone together, though not fully comprehending why.

"How is your mother?" Veronica asked, breaking their self-imposed silence.

"She's fine. Working too hard, as usual."

"I don't know anyone who doesn't admire your mother, all that she has accomplished."

Carl Henry knew it was a lie, but it didn't matter. He realized she was just making conversation.

As to everyone admiring his mother, he knew most of the women in town resented her. She was all that they were not, because she had boldly entered a man's world and had succeeded.

And to the men in town, Vivian represented a threat to all they held sacred. She was a bitch from hell, destroying their egos, making decisions about their fates they thought only another man should make.

"I don't think Mom considers herself as having accomplished all that much," he said. "It's just a job to her."

That was true. Vivian did not consider bridging the gap from a woman's to a man's world as some noble cause. Nor did she consider herself a child of destiny. Carl Henry knew she had stepped into her role to ensure his future. His mother didn't even solicit praise, though she appreciated it when it came from his grandfather.

"I forgot to get your coke," Veronica said.

"That's okay."

"It won't take but a second. I wouldn't mind having one myself."

"I'll come along and hold the candle," he said.

"That's not necessary."

He had, however, already picked up the candle and started toward the kitchen. She followed closely behind.

As they entered the kitchen, a draft snuffed out the flickering flame. The room was in total darkness, wind and rain hammering at the tightly-closed windows. The air was heavy, so much humidity.

Before their eyes became accustomed to the darkness, they brushed against each other. It was like some prearranged signal. Suddenly, she was in his arms and he was kissing her passionately. Initially, there was a tenseness on her part, but then she responded willingly.

He lifted her into his arms and carried her toward the living room couch, but enroute she directed him to the bedroom. There, with animal-like fierceness, he made love to her with a roughness she had never known. She whimpered her pleasure while the storm raged outside.

At the drugstore, Morgan and Yvonne worried about Carl Henry and Veronica. They anxiously awaited a break in the storm, so they could go home and make sure the people they cared most about were alright.

Now that they had found each other, neither Carl Henry nor Veronica wanted continuation of their relationship to be dependent on acts of nature, such as the storm, or on accidental opportunities of being alone together. They wanted each other regularly. And since they obviously could not carry on their affair in the Marks' home, they needed a place of their own.

Carl Henry had the perfect place. It was the family lake house, located just a few miles from town. The lake property was one of the numerous acquisitions Henry had made over the years. It was very private, fenced, and had a locked gate. Carl Henry had a key to the gate, and had one made for Veronica.

The house was located about a mile from the gate, so there was no danger of Veronica's car being seen. The only possibility of discovery was if Henry visited the property, which was unlikely. Though the house overlooked twin lakes that were teeming with fish, the old man preferred fishing in streams. To Carl Henry's knowledge, the only time his grandfather visited the lake house was when the two of them inspected the property together.

"Carl Henry, have you ever brought Yvonne out here?" Veronica asked. They were on a bed in the lake house, having just finished their lovemaking.

"No, you're the only one I've ever brought here," he replied.

"Good," she sighed. "Promise me that you won't bring anyone else here. I want this to be our special place."

"That's a promise that will be easy to keep."

She surprised him with, "How do you feel about Yvonne?"

"What do you mean?"

"Do you love her?"

He hesitated, then replied, "I don't know."

"Do you love me?"

It was a question he didn't want to answer, but he said, "I don't know that, either."

It was not what she wanted him to say. She wanted him to

love her, and only her. It was not a matter of wanting him forever, because she knew that was impossible. But at this particular period in her life, she wanted his complete love and devotion.

For Veronica, these stolen moments represented her first and only real romance. Her courtship with Morgan had been so contrived, so well-planned. But this thing with Carl Henry was a romantic adventure, one that she wanted to be as important to him as it was to her.

"Am I too old for you to love?" she asked.

Realizing her sensitivity he said, "No, it's not that at all. It's . . . well, you are married and I don't feel like I have the right to love you."

"What has that got to do with anything?" she replied, annoyed.

He shrugged. "Nothing . . . I don't guess."

"The fact that I'm married doesn't make me love you less," she said. "It might even make me love you more."

"You know how much I care for you, Veronica. I care for you very much."

"I don't know that at all." She could be testy at times.

"It's all that I can do to keep my hands off you, even when Mr. Marks is around."

She was now becoming more pleased with the conversation. "I feel the same way around you, and I have to admit that it's not very pleasant seeing you and Yvonne being so cozy."

It was the first time she had verbally communicated her jealousy, and he found it amusing. He knew not to show that emotion, though, but said, "If I hadn't been seeing Yvonne, we wouldn't be here now."

"That's true, but it's not necessary now."

"Are you telling me that you don't want me to see Yvonne anymore?" he asked.

Unwilling to be cornered, she replied, "I'm saying you don't have to see Yvonne in order to see me."

"That would seem kind of funny, wouldn't it, just all of a sudden stopping seeing Yvonne?"

"I don't think so," she answered, then as an afterthought added, "You're not fucking my daughter, too, are you?" She couldn't believe she had said it, especially the word *fucking*. She couldn't recall ever having said it aloud before, not even in her most intimate moments with Morgan and Carl Henry.

Carl Henry couldn't believe she had said it either, not Veronica. But his mind responded quickly and he said, "No, of course not." There was a time for truth and a time for lying.

Her own statement had flustered her. "I bet the two of you do some heavy necking, though."

"Veronica, what's the purpose of all this? Why bring up all this stuff about Yvonne and me?"

"I don't know," she confessed. "It's just that I hate that she gets to spend so much more time with you than I do. No, that's not true. The truth is that I hate that she gets to spend any time with you."

Her acknowledgement pleased him. "You're jealous of Yvonne?"

She didn't like it articulated, but replied, "Yes, I suppose that I am."

He countered, "Well, I guess I could get all upset about you and Mr. Marks. Maybe you shouldn't be seeing him and me at the same time."

"That's different."

"What's so different about it? And you sleep with him. I don't sleep with Yvonne."

"I don't have any choice about that," she reasoned.

"We all have choices, Veronica." With such logic he began to think he was taking control of the mini-argument.

"I don't feel the same about Morgan as I feel about you."

"That doesn't alter the fact that you have sex with him. I don't like that any better than you disliking my being with Yvonne once in a while."

She realized the conversation was going nowhere, so she began kissing him and caressing his genitals. He was quite willing to respond to her, so the conversation ended in lovemaking, the way all their conversations ended.

CHAPTER TWENTY-TWO

WHEN CARL Henry was a senior, he played in the most meaningful football game in the history of Bethel High School. It was the game for the state championship.

The Bethel Lumberjacks had never before played in the championship game, though in the previous two years the school had fielded teams that came close. When Carl Henry was a sophomore, the team that beat Bethel 28–27 in bi-district won the state title. And the following year Bethel was beaten 35–28 in the regional playoff by the eventual state champion.

In those two previous years, it had been a lack of defense that caused Bethel's downfall. The offense, under Carl Henry's leadership at quarterback, had been more than adequate.

When a sophomore, Carl Henry was named to the all-district team. And when a junior, he was honorable mention all-state. Everyone expected that he would be named first team all-state as a senior.

In that fall of his senior year, the coaches put a great deal of emphasis on defense. They were confident the offense would jell as it had the previous two years, but that confidence was almost shattered in the first game of the season.

In the opener, powerful rival Broken Bow struck for an early touchdown but missed the extra point attempt. Initially, the early Broken Bow lead did not bother the partisan Bethel crowd. After all, it was a rare game when their team did not score four or five touchdowns.

However, on this particular night the Lumberjacks offense was a comedy of errors. They fumbled. And then they fumbled some more. Each time they got within striking distance of the Broken Bow goal line, they erred.

The coaches fumed and paced the sideline in frustration. And the mood of the crowd turned sour. This was not what they had come to see. They had wanted a slaughter, and now their team was in danger of losing.

On the visitors side of the field the Broken Bow fans whooped it up. Bethel had beaten them three consecutive years, so there was cause for jubilation.

With less than two minutes left in the game, Broken Bow was forced to punt from its own twenty-five yard line. It was a low wobbly kick that Carl Henry fielded on the dead run at his own forty. He broke three tackles before finally being brought down at the Broken Bow twenty.

The partisan crowd was in a frenzy as the team broke from the huddle. Carl Henry took the snap from center, rolled to his right, and rifled a pass to Ward Montague. The slender end took the impact of the ball on his chest at the goal line, smothered it in his arms, and stepped across for the touchdown. Carl Henry calmly kicked the ball through the uprights for the extra point and a 7–6 Bethel lead.

They kicked off to Broken Bow, but for all practical purposes the game was over. There was no way Broken Bow's desperation passing attack could succeed against Bethel's defense.

In the next eight games the Bethel defense held their opponents scoreless, while the offense was averaging close to fifty points a

game. It was not until the final game of their regular season schedule that Bethel was scored on again, and then only in the fourth
quarter when they had a 56–0 lead.

The football mystique in Bethel was not unlike it is in numerous
small cities in the United States. The school had brought in a
new coach in Carl Henry's sophomore year at the highest salary
allowable. The school board wanted a winner, and board president
Kurt Keyser said they would have to pay to get a winner. There
was some under-the-table money, some of which came from
Henry. He was pissed about it, of course, but Keyser appealed
to him on the basis of Carl Henry getting the best possible coaching
in order to realize his full potential.

The former coach had been allowed one assistant. The new
coach, who came in with a reputation as a bad-ass, had six.

Of course, all the coaches had teaching assignments. They were
forced into teaching subjects like history, biology, government,
algebra, geometry, and so on. The fact that they had all been
physical education majors in college and didn't know shit about
the subject matter was of little consequence. They all had their
teaching certificates from the state, so from that standpoint they
were qualified.

No athlete had to worry about passing a course at Bethel High
School. It wasn't just a matter of the coaches passing anyone who
wore a jock strap, either. All the teachers had been thoroughly
intimidated by the townspeople, the administration and the school
board.

Though there was no need, Carl Henry studied diligently. He
enjoyed the fact that he knew and understood more about the
subject matter than the coaches. But more important, he knew
how important it was to his mother and grandfather that he be
well prepared for the future.

For a time he felt sorry for some of his teammates, the fact
that they were getting nothing resembling an education. Henry
straightened out his thinking though by saying, "The dumb little
fuckers are just going to work for the sawmill or highway department anyway."

By god, Carl Henry thought, Grandad's right. If a person wants an education, he can get it. If he doesn't, then it's no skin off my nose.

The new coach instituted new rules, the most inane one being that a football player could not speak to a girl at school during the week. If a player was seen talking to a girl, he was used as a tackling dummy during an afternoon practice session. Players were required to swear an oath that they would tell on any teammate seen talking to a girl. The coaches wanted players minds on football, not girls.

These new rules allowed a player to date a girl after a Friday night game, and on Saturday and Sunday nights. But Sunday through Thursday nights during football season, coaches called the homes of players to make sure they were in bed by ten o'clock. Parents were as caught up in the rules as were the coaches and players.

Carl Henry thought the rule about talking to girls was as stupid as the coaches, but he obeyed it. The only time he broke it was the day after his Grandmother died. He spent the noon hour that day with Yvonne, then reported his treasonable action to the head coach.

He was told to forget about it under the circumstances, but he insisted on taking his punishment. The coach winced every time he was tackled. He was well aware that an injury to his starting quarterback could mean a mediocre season.

Carl Henry did not particularly enjoy playing football. The games were okay, but he hated practices. And the coach believed in practice and more practice.

Practice started at three-thirty in the afternoon and usually went on into the night. It was not unusual for the stadium lights to be on at eight o'clock.

The coaches had seen to it that afternoons were free for their varsity players. After lunch the players were all assigned to study hall, followed by a physical education class. Those two periods were actually skull sessions in the locker room, studying the game plan for the following Friday night and going over scouting reports on the opponent.

Practices were gruelling, the coaches making the players work on fundamentals like blocking and tackling constantly. Scrimmages were long and there was always the demand to run . . . run . . . run.

Carl Henry was pretty sure that most of his teammates hated the coaches and football as much as he did, but peer group pressure kept them all plugging away, knocking heads with the zeal of lunatics. He had already decided that football was a game of lunacy, that the coaches were keepers of lunatics who had reverted to being animals.

He couldn't explain why he played, except that he did like the games, the glory. It was not that he was afraid people would call him a coward if he didn't play.

"Hayders don't have to explain why they do things," Henry told him. "The people in this town don't have enough balls to call a Hayder a coward. Not where we can hear it anyway."

There were some boys whose athletic skills were so negligible that they played in the band. Their fathers stayed away from the stadium. They had nothing in common with the fathers of football players.

The coaches were aware of the pressure to play, so they were ruthless in their treatment of the players. In later years, when girls decided boys didn't have to be jocks to be manly, the coaches would have to revise their thinking. But for the time being, it was their ball game.

Carl Henry's senior year held more happy memories for Yvonne than it did for him. Not only was she the steady of a football captain destined to be named to the all-state team, but she was also homecoming queen and head majorette. She had been a majorette since her freshman year, and twice she had been named most beautiful girl in her class.

Carl Henry continued to make love to both Veronica and Yvonne as often as time and circumstance permitted. Veronica's ardor continued to increase, and she became more resentful of Carl Henry's relationship with Yvonne. He refused, however, to be intimidated by her. He did have strong feelings for Veronica, but they were equally as strong for Yvonne.

After winning the district championship Carl Henry's senior year, the Lumberjacks annihilated their bi-district, regional and semi-finals foes by scores of 40–6, 35–7, 56–13 and 21–0. Only the big one was left, the state championship.

The competition was the Ringling Wranglers, a team that sported an identical 14–0 record. The game was to be played in Oklahoma City.

Because of pride in the team, Bethel was in a festive mood. Stores throughout the small city displayed banners with slogans like: *Wreck the Wranglers, Bethel is Best, Rip Ringling*, and so on.

Henry observed the signs, listened to people talk about the big game, and came to the conclusion that it was idiocy's finest hour. He was not impressed with the town's togetherness.

At a pregame skull session with players the coach said, "Their noseguard, Slaughter, is the key to their defense. He's a big sonofabitch, about two hundred seventy, and he's fast.

"They use a five-four-two most of the time, and I think we can get around the corners on their outside linebackers, especially the one on the left.

"Problem, though, is this big mother fucker at noseguard. You've got to hold him out anyway you can. Coach Porter's been scouting Ringling and he says he's seen Slaughter rattled just once. That was when he was mad, so make the sonofabitch mad if you can. I hope that ain't bad advice.

"I'm telling you fucking offensive linemen something, though. I don't care if Slaughter is the meanest bastard in the world, you keep him off our backs. If you don't . . . well, you better give your hearts to Jesus because your asses belong to me."

It was one of the coach's favorite expressions, perhaps because he was a Sunday School teacher. He was a Sunday School teacher because Mr. Keyser wanted him to be, because it was good for the image of the athletic program.

"Now another thing, goddamit," the coach continued. "We're going to be in Oklahoma City a couple of days before the game. We're going there to get adjusted to the field, and to get away from all these people who think you're all so goddam great. If you listen, they'll have you believing that you can walk on water, that you're the best thing to come along since pussy.

"I want you to know that right now you're just shit, and you'll be nothing but shit until you win that game next Saturday.

"Anyway, while we're in Oklahoma City . . . Rhodes, quit whispering to Stewart back there or I'll give you a good ass-kicking. We can't watch you all the time in the motel, so don't go around acting like a bunch of wild Indians and hicks."

There were six Indians on the team, but the coach never seemed to notice them.

"We're not going to Oklahoma City to play around. We're going up there to win a football game. Any questions?"

There were none.

"Okay, that's it. Rhodes, I want to see you and Stewart. The rest of you can go."

"Doug and Frank are really going to get their asses chewed," Boyd Arnold said to Carl Henry as they were leaving the locker room. He was referring to Doug Rhodes and Frank Stewart.

"I hope that's the worst they get," Carl Henry replied. The coach was known to administer punishment at times with a heavy oak paddle. It had holes in it.

"I'm gonna be different if I ever coach," Boyd said.

"I didn't know you were thinking about being a coach," Carl Henry answered.

"Hell, everybody's got to be something."

"That's true, but I didn't know you were into being a saddist."

"I don't know what the fuck that even means," Boyd said.

"It's just someone who enjoys inflicting physical and mental pain on someone else," Carl Henry explained.

Nodding his head Boyd said, "That sure as hell describes our coaches."

"Say Boyd, you want to come over to the house, play a little catch and have supper with us?"

Since they were out of school for the Christmas holidays, the coaches had conducted practice in the morning and the skull session right after lunch.

"I don't know," Boyd said, "but it sounds good."

"C'mon and go. I'm going over to Yvonne's tonight, and I'll drop you by your house."

Boyd was one of the meanest guys Carl Henry had ever come in contact with on the football field, but he had a fear that very few people knew about. He was afraid of the dark. A couple of the other players lived in the same block as Boyd, and when they practiced after dark he would walk home with them.

Carl Henry's willingness to drive him home settled the issue, so he got in the car and said, "Sounds great. Mom won't expect me until after dark anyway. But say, aren't you afraid the coach will find out about you going over to Yvonne's?"

"Let's call it a technicality," Carl Henry replied. "We're not supposed to see girls on a school night, or talk to them at school. Hell, school's out. It's not my fault the stupid sonofabitch forgot to change the rules for the holidays.

"Besides, Yvonne and I are just going to sit in the swing on her front porch and talk, if it's not too cold. If it is, we'll sit in the living room. I can't see the harm in that, especially since I'll be home by ten."

"I didn't say there was any harm in it, but you know how the bastard is. He's always looking for something to hang on a guy's ass."

Carl Henry pushed down on the accelerator to speed up the Cadillac and said, "Well, let him look. After this game he can stick all his rules up his ass."

"What about baseball?" Boyd wanted to know. "You are going to play baseball, aren't you?" One of the assistant football coaches was baseball coach, and he also had strict rules.

"I plan to play, but I'm not taking a bunch of shit off the coach."

"Goddamit Carl Henry, you've got to play. We can win the championship this year."

Carl Henry had pitched the team to the district championship as a junior, but two errors had cost Bethel the bi-district crown. It was Carl Henry's only loss of the season. His grandfather had told him that with the kind of support he got, he wouldn't blame him for not playing.

Boyd played centerfield for the team, and was well-known for his bench jockeying. He never stopped talking to the opposition. Carl Henry recalled a game where Boyd had singled, bringing Doug Rhodes to the plate. Just before Doug laid a bunt down the first base line, he noticed the first baseman laughing. Whatever was funny had obviously taken his mind off the game because he didn't field the bunt.

Later, he had questioned Boyd about the incident and discovered the centerfielder had challenged the first baseman to a jackoff contest.

There was no way anyone could beat Boyd in a jackoff contest. He had beaten everyone on the football team who had dared challenge him. Carl Henry hadn't, because he now had a better place for his sperm.

"Lots of people figure you can sign a pro baseball contract right out of high school," Boyd said. "Of course, you're going to get plenty of football scholarship offers, too. Any idea where you might go?"

"O.U., I guess. I really don't know what I'll do at this point."

"By god, if O.U. offers you a scholarship, you'd better take it," Boyd advised. "They tell me the people up there will really lay some bread on you. They'll get you a summer job making a bundle, maybe five hundred or a thousand a month."

"I'll have to see it to believe it. You hear a lot of shit about what the colleges will do for you, but I don't know how much of it's true. Besides, money's not a problem for me."

"That's true," Boyd said, enviously. "What are you going to major in if you go to college?"

"Journalism, English. I don't really know."

"Hell, if I get to go I'm going to major in P.E.," Boyd said. "No point knocking your brains out studying those tough subjects. About the only chance I have to make something of myself is to be a teacher and coach. Shit, I already know more than most of the coaches."

"Saying you know more than those stupid bastards isn't saying a lot," Carl Henry said.

"Amen, brother."

Carl Henry knew there would be a great temptation to skip college in favor of professional baseball. At one time that was what his grandfather would have counseled, but now the old man had sort of changed his tune. He had been talking more of late about the importance of education.

"Baseball's not what it was once," he had said. "Getting so there's too many Niggers in the game. A good education is important because you have to be smarter than the next man."

One thing that bothered Carl Henry about pro baseball was that there was the possibility of spending several years in the minor leagues, then not making the majors. He was confused as to what he should do, but figured he had plenty of time to decide.

Yvonne's father had encouraged him to go to college. So had his English teacher, Mrs. Webster. He had to admit that he liked the possibility of studying literature, maybe journalism. Mrs. Webster said he had the makings of a good writer. He liked that.

They played the championship game on a Saturday afternoon, two days before Christmas. It was the largest crowd the Lumberjacks had ever played before, and there were rumors in the dressing room that more than a hundred college scouts were in the stands.

Carl Henry tried to approach the game with his usual calm self-assurance, but as game time approached he tingled with nervous excitement. One of the halfbacks, Bill Powell, vomited and teammates applauded. Bill had a nervous stomach, and he had vomited prior to every Bethel victory, all fourteen of them. It was a good sign.

The weather was cool and crisp. Snow clouds lent a grayness to the afternoon, and an icy north wind cut across the stadium with the sharpness of a carving knife. The weather could not dampen the enthusiasm of Bethel fans, though, and when the Lumberjacks ran onto the field, more than two thousand supporters stood and cheered. The support was enough to make a chill run up the backbone of every player, if the weather wasn't.

Carl Henry and Murray Conradt, co-captains for the Lumberjacks, met the Ringling co-captains at mid-field for the coin toss.

One of the Wrangler co-captains was the big noseguard, Slaughter. The other was the quarterback, Tim Barrilleaux.

Carl Henry did not catch Slaughter's first name during introductions, but thought it was Cortney. He sized the opposition up without apprehension, noting that they both had on their game faces . . . grim, determined. He often wanted to laugh at the ridiculous importance people put on football games.

Hell, I'm here, he thought. I wonder if Murray and I have our game faces on?

He laughed inwardly, filled with elation at the thought of the big game. Finally.

Carl Henry's call was correct, so Bethel won the toss and possession of the football. The wind was a negligible factor in the decision to take the ball. It was blowing across the field. Ringling chose to defend the west goal.

It all seemed like a dream to Carl Henry as he stood on the goal line listening to the National Anthem, then the Bethel and Ringling school songs. It was hard to stand still, not because of the cold but because of the nervous excitement. He wanted to jump up and down, to feel the wind in his face, to feel the crunch of body against body. He wanted to be the first to get the ball, so he could be tackled first, so the butterflies would disappear from his stomach.

Suddenly the ball was coming toward him, spinning crazily end-over-end. He could no longer hear the noise of the crowd, nor could he feel the bite of the north wind. All feeling was seemingly drained from his body. He could only see, know and feel what he had to do.

The ball settled in his arms like a feather, and he was conscious of tucking it under his right arm as he began to run toward the right sideline.

Protect the ball.

Protect the ball.

Protect the ball. It was a continuous refrain that ran through his mind.

He could see a wave of blue coming toward him, a wave of orange and black going away from him. He could see blue and orange smashing together, leaving open gaps for him along the brownish-colored grass. He felt light, as though his feet were not touching the ground. He was flying, skimming along the earth.

Then he was hit by a patch of blue . . . then another . . . and another. As his body was slammed to the frozen turf, he was shaken from his hypnotic state, back to reality.

He was calm in the huddle, deliberate. "Thirty-two on two. Thirty-two on two. Break."

They took their positions with the precision of a team that had won fourteen straight games. They were together. As Carl Henry took his position behind the center, he looked across the line of scrimmage at Slaughter and remembered what the coach had said. Then he started laughing, so softly the officials could not hear him.

"What's up?" his center said, raising up slightly and cocking his head to the right.

"Haven't you noticed?" Carl Henry said. "Slaughter is the stupidest-looking sonofabitch I've ever seen."

The Bethel center and guards grinned, Slaughter's face turned crimson and he whispered, "I'll get you, you mother fucker."

It was a completely rehearsed act on the part of Carl Henry and his teammates, one designed to make Slaughter mad. There was no doubt that they had accomplished their purpose.

"Hut, hut." Carl Henry handed the ball to fullback Tob Westmoreland over right guard. He was following through on his fake to the left halfback when he was smashed from behind. It was Slaughter.

The tackle was perfectly legal, but an official caught Slaughter pounding at Carl Henry's ribs with a fist. The play had gained three yards, so there was no real decision as to whether Bethel would take the penalty. It was fifteen.

Carl Henry had taken the opening kickoff on the ten and had returned it to the Bethel forty. The penalty set the Lumberjacks up with a first down at the Ringling forty-five.

"Let's do that again," he said in the huddle. "Thirty-two on one. Thirty-two on one. Break."

Because Slaughter played Carl Henry instead of his position,

Tob was able to break through for twelve yards and another first down. Bethel was on the Wrangler thirty-three.

Back in the huddle Carl Henry said, "Okay gang, forty-two trap on one. Forty-two trap on one. Break."

The hard-charging Slaughter was trapped with ease, allowing speedy Bill Powell to break for nine yards. Only a shoestring tackle by a defensive back prevented a touchdown.

"Okay," Carl Henry said in the huddle, "they're going to be drawn in expecting us to try to punch out a first down up the middle. Let's go with a fake forty-one, twenty-seven power sweep on two. Make sure you get that outside linebacker, Tob. Fake forty-one, twenty-seven power sweep on two. Break."

Carl Henry had properly anticipated the Ringling defense. They converged on the middle, allowing little Bruck Wieser to skitter down the left sideline for a touchdown.

Slaughter had continued to smash into Carl Henry on every play, but it didn't matter. Bethel had scored quickly on a team that was supposed to be their toughest competition of the year. They had scored quickly because Ringling's great lineman had lost his cool.

But Ringling quarterback Tim Barrilleaux would not be denied. Mixing his plays beautifully, he led the Wranglers on an eighty-yard march in the second quarter, covering the last six yards himself.

Somehow, Boyd got through the big Ringling line and blocked the extra point attempt, so Bethel took a 7–6 lead to the dressing room at halftime. The Bethel offense had moved the ball well, but had been unable to put together a sustained drive following their initial possession.

Slaughter had gotten control of his anger and was giving Carl Henry and his teammates all kinds of trouble. He had smashed tackle Joe Redfield's nose, causing the preacher's kid to say, "I'll get that goddam sonofabitch if it's the last thing I do."

Bethel had given up two costly fumbles and a sure touchdown pass had been dropped, so the coach raged, "Goddamit, I've seen some piss poor football in my time, but nothing compared to what

I've seen this first half. You had them on the ropes. You had them on the goddam ropes and you let them get away. We could have had two more touchdowns, but hell no. Here we are hanging on to a one point lead, and we wouldn't have had that if it hadn't been for Boyd.

"As for you, Wieser, what the fuck's wrong with you . . . fumbling on the ten yard line. You'd better hold on to that fuckin' football or I'll get someone in there who can. You've been carrying the thing like it's a damn watermelon.

"In fact, all you backs act as though you've never been hit before. All of you cough up the ball like you don't want it. Tob . . . Bill . . . shit, let's hang on to the ball.

"And you, Slaughter . . . are you kin to that big sonofabitch with the same name? I can't figure out any other reason for you to drop a sure touchdown pass. Right in your hands and you drop it . . . damn. Is Carl Henry going to have to throw it and catch it, too? You bitch all season 'cause we don't throw it to you enough, and when we do you drop it.

"You defensive backs had better be glad Barrilleaux ain't thrown no more than he has, because I believe he owns you. He's completed six out of nine and he's had a couple dropped. All that means is that you haven't done a damn thing to stop him.

"And you linemen aren't putting any pressure on the fucking quarterback. Now get your asses in gear for this second half and let's win ourselves a football game."

The coach then outlined the game plan for the second half, which was to continue running straight ahead . . . at Slaughter. Carl Henry and most of his teammates thought it was a stupid plan, but theirs was not to reason why. They were conditioned to take orders.

In the third quarter the Wranglers seemed content to punch at the Bethel line, and to skirt the ends on occasion. They ate up a lot of the clock and a great deal of yardage, but it was in two, three and four-yard chunks. First downs were hard to come by for both teams, so it became a game of position. Each team was waiting for the other to make a fatal mistake.

The Wranglers sensed that Carl Henry had been ordered not to throw the football, so they threw up eight and nine man lines. Bethel's backs kept punching away, but without success.

In the fading moments of the third quarter, Barrilleaux punted from mid-field. The high spiral was pushed southward by the icy wind.

Carl Henry stood motionless at his own fifteen, waiting for the ball to descend. Blue-jerseyed defenders converged on him, anxious to smash him to the frozen earth, to perhaps cause the fumble for which both teams seemed to be playing.

Using his peripheral vision, Carl Henry watched the ball falling from the gray sky about ten yards from where he was standing and at about a forty-five degree angle. The defenders were watching him, not the ball, so he bolted past them and took the ball on the dead run.

He tucked the ball under his left arm and hurried up the left sideline, watching orange jerseys topple what was left of the blue in his path. Seconds later he stood in the end zone, relishing the hugging, cheers and backslapping of his teammates. It had been a great run and, moments later after he kicked the extra point, Bethel had a 14-6 lead.

That's when Barrilleaux took control of the game. After the kickoff he threw seven straight complete passes to move the Wranglers in for a touchdown. His uncanny accuracy had the Bethel coaches talking to themselves.

Though his team was ahead 14-13, Bethel's head coach had a premonition that the lead would be shortlived if Barrilleaux got his hands on the ball again. Bethel's defensive backs hadn't faced anyone in his class the entire year.

On the sideline the coach told Carl Henry, "Son, we have to hang on to that football. Tell those fucking backs that they'd better hit the line like they've never hit it before. Tell them that they'd better hang on to that ball or I'll have their asses. We've got to score."

Tob returned the kickoff and was stopped hard at his own twenty. Then the Bethel backs smashed into, sometimes through, the big blue line time and time again, the clock ticking off precious seconds and yardage coming in small chunks. Still, they were able to control the football, moving sixty yards to the Wranglers' twenty.

With a first and ten, Carl Henry called the option, which had been the most productive play of the drive. He was stopped after a one yard gain. Then he called a twenty-four, a dive play between guard and tackle with the right halfback carrying the ball. Another one yard gain. Facing a third down and eight, he called a time out and trotted to the sideline for a conference with the coach.

"Want me to keep it on the ground, coach?"

"We need a touchdown. We can't let that Barrilleaux kid get his hands on the ball without one."

"What do you think we ought to run?" Carl Henry asked.

The coach countered with, "What do you think will work?"

"Well, they're using a nine man line, so we ought to be able to use a quick down and out."

"Use what you think will work," the coach said, "but get us a touchdown."

Back in the huddle Carl Henry said, "Okay, we're going with a P-seventeen on two. A P-seventeen on two. Break."

The play called for Ward Montague to fake inside from his end position, then to run a flat route toward the left sideline. In the meantime, Carl Henry would roll to his left and hit Ward with a pass almost immediately on his cut. It had been a bread and butter play during their fourteen game win streak.

The Wranglers didn't disappoint Carl Henry. They threw up a nine man line.

Carl Henry took the snap, rolled left and cocked his arm. Ward made his cut and the ball was delivered, traveling straight and true toward the target. The defensive back had not reacted quickly enough, but Carl Henry saw the beginnings of a nightmare unfolding as he went down under Slaughter's driving charge.

The ball ricocheted off Ward's shoulder pads and into the arms of the defensive back who had been so badly beaten on the play. Pinned down by Slaughter, Carl Henry watched the blue-jerseyed defensive back racing up the sideline. There was no chance of an orange jersey catching him.

"How do you like that, mother fucker?" Slaughter said.

Carl Henry trotted to the sideline, head down. There was nothing left in him.

"Of all the goddam stupid shit I've ever seen," the coach said. "Didn't you know that if they intercepted in the flat they'd have clear sailing for a touchdown?"

He didn't bother to remind the coach that he had agreed to the play. It wouldn't have done any good.

It was a good play, the right play, he thought. We had them dead to rights.

Carl Henry was angry when he returned to the field, and his anger showed itself as he fielded the kickoff and headed upfield. He broke four tackles before being dragged down by Slaughter and two other opponents. There was less than four minutes left, so he initiated his game plan, not the coach's.

He called one rollout after another, sometimes passing and sometimes running. The team moved down the field with the precision of a finely tuned engine.

I could have been doing this all day, he thought, angry because the coach's game plan had been so unimaginative.

With fifteen seconds left they were on Ringling's one foot line. That's when Charles Houston came running onto the field with a play from the coach.

Carl Henry had already called an option in the huddle, but the coach wanted a twenty-four. That meant Houston, a sophomore who had replaced Bruck Wieser at halfback, would be running the ball. Houston just happened to be the grandson of Kurt Keyser.

Carl Henry considered disobeying the order, but decided against it. Charlie fumbled and the game was over.

As they left the field Charlie kept saying over and over, loudly so everyone could hear, "It wasn't a clean handoff. It wasn't a clean handoff."

Charlie's parents were on the field with him and they were giving Carl Henry condemning looks. He wanted to shoot them the finger, but he didn't. He didn't even know whether it had been a clean handoff or not. He didn't really care. He only knew it felt as though his guts had been ripped out.

Barrilleaux and Slaughter made their way through the crowd

to shake hands with him. It was a kind of grudging respect given to those defeated, but not beaten.

Yvonne found him, kissed and hugged him.

He felt as though he was going to be sick.

CHAPTER TWENTY-THREE

CARL HENRY was not named first team all-state. He was named to the second team. The first team honor went to Tim Barrilleaux.

Some said Carl Henry ruined his chances for first team when he unleashed a profane assault on the coach following the championship game, all duly recorded by the press. Henry told his grandson that his chances for the honor went down the drain when Bethel lost the game, that to the victor belonged the spoils. Henry also told him that in terms of importance, the game and the all-state honor ranked right along with the debate as to whether horseshit or cowshit made the best fertilizer.

Following the championship game, while the two teams, their fans and coaches were walking off the field, Bethel's head coach began berating Carl Henry for mistakes he had made in the game. He was, of course, angry and frustrated because the game represented his whole world. Still, most of the disappointed Bethel fans felt the coach's cruel and sarcastic comments were out of line.

Henry heard some of the coach's statements to his grandson, and had to be physically restrained by Carl, Vivian and others or he would have attacked the man. As it was, he was able to get in some choice words not meant for delicate ears.

"Does that stupid sonofabitch have a note at our bank?" he asked Vivian in an above normal voice.

"Yes," she replied.

"Call it in," he ordered. "I want the stupid bastard to know that you don't fuck with the Hayder family."

The coach already knew that, and when he heard Henry's outburst he realized that in the heat of the moment he had made a mistake. But before he had a chance to rectify it, Carl Henry's emotional bubble burst and he spewed forth his entire vocabulary of profanity. And had he not been restrained by teammates, he would have punched the coach.

All of this was witnessed by sportswriters who, though they have no aversion to using profanity themselves, wrote that such behavior was a disgrace to high school athletics. In their articles they depicted Bethel's coach as representing all that is good, pure and holy. Such reporting of the incident could have well been a deciding factor in whether Carl Henry was named first team all-state.

Carl was upset by his son's outburst against authority. Both Henry and Vivian applauded it. Carl was, of course, worried about what people might say. Neither Henry nor Vivian gave a damn.

The Saturday afternoon following Christmas, just a week after the game had been played, some men in Casey's saloon were discussing its outcome, more specifically they were discussing Carl Henry's verbal assault on the coach.

When one man said the boy's language could not have been topped by the world's most profane man, Zack Beatty said, "Ain't no way the boy can top his grandpa when it comes to cussin'. Henry can come up with cuss words people have never heard before. You can tell they're cuss words just by the sound of them. I'll tell you something else, too. The old man is proud of the boy for laying into the coach like that."

"Well, I ain't blaming the coach for jumping on the kid's ass," James Roe said. "The boy flat threw away the game."

"Hold on there a minute," Bruck Wieser commanded. "If it hadn't of been for that kid, we wouldn't have been in no championship game. And we couldn't have even stayed in the game against those big-assed Ringling boys if it hadn't of been for Carl Henry."

"But . . ."

Bruck interrupted Roe with, "That kid's carried this team on his shoulders all year, and it sure wasn't him that lost the game. What lost the game was trying to make a hero out of Kurt Keyser's grandson."

"Ain't you just pissed because the coach took your boy out of the game and put the Houston kid in?" Roe asked.

"No, I ain't pissed because he took my boy out, but I am pissed that he put an inexperienced kid like Houston in the game when he had a fine senior halfback sitting on the bench. I'm talking about Boyd Arnold. But then, his grandaddy don't own no sawmill and ain't president of the school board."

Roe's face was a bit flushed. "Well, why in the hell did the Hayder kid give the ball to Houston then?"

"Because the coach called the play dumb-ass, not Carl Henry."

"The Houston kid said it was a bad handoff," Roe countered.

"Bullshit."

"The Hayder boy ain't denied it," Roe contended.

"No, and he won't," Bruck said. "He doesn't make excuses, and he sure doesn't blame a teammate when something goes wrong."

"He's like his old grandpa in that respect," Zack said. "Henry don't make excuses for anything he does. He figures there's nothing he can't handle on his own, and he doesn't give a shit what people say or think about him."

"That's a fact," Casey chimed in.

"Well, it still looks to be like the Hayder boy fucked up the town's chance for a state championship," Roe said. "But you fellers have a right to your opinion."

Bruck surveyed some of the nodding heads agreeing with Roe and said, "You're a real fine bunch of assholes. You want to blame Carl Henry for losing the game because none of you have balls enough to put the blame where it belongs, on the coach and

Kurt Keyser's grandson. He's the little fucker that fumbled. But
I don't blame him because he shouldn't have been in the game
anyway.

"You fuckers want to blame Carl Henry because most of us
work for Keyser in one way or another. I'll tell you about me,
though. I may work at the sawmill, but I'm my own man. I'll
not bow down to anybody. You fellers may have to kiss ass to
keep beans on the table, but I don't."

Bruck was not an articulate man, and he was a bit drunk. But
he got his point across.

"This is a scared town," he continued. "Most of us felt we could
act a little braver, maybe talk a little tougher, if our kids won
the state championship. But we'd still be as phony as a three
dollar bill, though. The Keysers would still own us . . . lock,
stock and barrel. Old Keyser has a lot of us by the balls and we
ain't got guts to make him turn loose.

"I tell you, boys, you'd better be glad the Hayders live here
because they're the only ones who will stand up to the Keysers.
I'm talking about Henry and Vivian. Carl Henry, too, from what
I've seen."

His omission of Carl's name was obvious to everyone present.
Men who worked at the sawmill moved uneasily in their chairs.
They wished he would quit talking about the Keysers. Some of
them would have left, but they were afraid he might single them
out for a sarcastic comment. Bruck was mean enough to fight a
circle saw, so none of them were interested in a confrontation.

"How do you know the coach called the play?" Roe wanted to
know.

"Because my boy said so," Bruck replied. "Carl Henry had
already called an option play before the Houston boy came into
the huddle to replace my kid. The Houston boy told Carl Henry
the coach wanted him to call a twenty-four."

Roe was considering arguing, but he certainly wasn't going to
suggest that Bruck's son was a liar, not with the mood the man
was in. So he opted for, "I'd guess I'd better go. Man can get
himself in real trouble here. Figure it must be Hayder territory."
He drained the last of his beer before exiting.

"Who the hell is that feller?" someone asked.

"He's fairly new in town," Casey replied. "Been here about three months. Works as a foreman at the sawmill."

"Couldn't you tell?" Bruck laughed. "He has a shit-eatin' grin and a brown nose."

"Getting back to Carl Henry," Zack said. "What do you think they're going to do to the boy for cussin' out the coach?"

"Ain't you heard?" Casey asked. "Henry made the coach write a letter of apology to Carl Henry. It's going to appear in the next issue of the newspaper."

"My god, ain't that old fucker something?" Zack marveled, laughing. "Who would have thought that he would turn the tables on the coach?"

"The coach didn't have a helluva lot of choice," Casey replied. "Henry's bank owns the sonofabitch."

"You know old Keyser thinks the coach hung the moon," Bruck said. "How's he going to take Henry making his boy kiss ass?"

"He's got no choice, either," Casey related. "Seems that Henry has liens on a lot of the sawmill property. He has Keyser kissin' ass, too."

"That damn Henry is as crazy as a fox," Zack said, laughing.

CHAPTER TWENTY-FOUR

ARL HENRY had not planned to screw his high school English teacher. It just happened.

Dianne Webster was thirty-three, divorced, and though not a natural beauty her talent for makeup and dress made her one of the most desirable unmarried women in Bethel.

She was slightly built, dainty, only five feet three inches tall. Her legs were shapely, her breasts firm. Short brownish hair accentuated the smoothness of her face. She had hazel eyes and a few faint freckles across the bridge of her nose.

Dianne was one of the few teachers who had mentally stimulated Carl Henry. She was always encouraging him with his writing, always encouraging him to expand his literary knowledge.

Initially, she invited Carl Henry to her home to discuss a one act play he had written. It was his first attempt at writing a play, and Dianne was unable in class to give him the personal attention she thought his effort demanded.

On that first visit they sat together on the couch and discussed his play. The discussion was so enjoyable, so very pleasurable, that they began to look for opportunities to be together in the evenings. At first he was visiting her home once a week, then twice a week.

He enjoyed her company because she stimulated his mind, encouraged his ideas and aspirations. She enjoyed him because he was so eager to learn, had so much potential. And there was also a definite physical attraction.

Dianne was considered a bit stuck-up by many of the townspeople, primarily because she had spurned so many local suitors. A couple of eligible bachelors who worked at the sawmill would each have given a nut to get in her pants, but she rejected their every attempt at courtship. Most of her dates were with professional men from out-of-town . . . teachers, lawyers, doctors. There were very few professional men in the area, especially unmarried ones, so she often had relatively long periods without male companionship.

"I wish you would call me Dianne instead of Mrs. Webster," she said. "I'm talking about when we are alone together, not at school."

"That's pretty hard to do."

"No it's not. Try it."

"Okay, Dianne."

"See, that wasn't so hard was it?"

"I guess not. But it seems strange, you being my teacher and all."

"Is it because I'm older?"

"Probably. I don't know. Grandad always told me to be respectful to my elders, at least on a face-to-face basis."

"Do you consider me that much older than you?" she asked. "Do I look old and decrepit?"

"No, of course not," he responded. "I think you're very pretty."

"As pretty as Yvonne?"

"Sure, prettier." A time for lying, a time for truth.

"Would you do something for me?" she asked.

"Sure, if I can."

"Would you hold my hand?"

I'll be damn, he thought. His heartbeat increased and, though he tried to fight the feeling, his penis fought against the front of his shorts. He took her hand and moved closer to her on the couch.

"I've been wanting to touch you for a long time," she said. "I hope you don't mind."

"I don't mind at all," he said.

"I think you're one of the best-looking, smartest young men I've ever known."

He was a bit flushed by the compliment, not knowing what to say, so the words he blurted out were awkward. "I think you're the prettiest, smartest woman I've ever known."

She was looking directly into his eyes, and he was sure that she was reading his innermost thoughts, which were that he would like to shove her down on the couch, tear her panties off, and plunge his cock into her. No matter if she did know what he was thinking, he couldn't control his thoughts.

Her face seemed to be moving closer to his. He wanted to pull her closer to him, but he was still unsure as to how she might react. He decided to hell with it, he had to have her.

Suddenly, her hands were on his shoulders, then his back. Her tits pressed against his chest, and her lips searched for his mouth. He responded with all the pentup emotion inside him. He could taste the cigarettes she had been smoking but he didn't mind. He didn't mind anything.

She took his left hand and put it up her dress, on the lace of her panties. He put his hand inside the panties and began fingering her. The warmth he felt inside her seemed to run up his arm, into his brain, and down to his penis.

As they continued kissing, he began pulling her panties off. She raised her smooth, firm buttocks from the couch to help him. When the panties were off, he unbuckled his belt and unzipped his pants. She reached inside his shorts and freed his penis.

He would have pushed her back on the couch and taken her, but instead she pushed him back and took his penis in her mouth. Neither Veronica nor Yvonne had ever done that.

He didn't know what to do, whether to go in her mouth or
not. However, as she massaged his balls with her fingers and
moved her mouth up and down on his penis, he had no choice.

"Did you like it?" she asked a few moments later. They were
partially upright on the couch, her head resting on his chest.

"Yes, I liked it very much." She raised her lips for a kiss. He
paused momentarily, remembering where her mouth had been
moments earlier, then kissed her. Under the circumstances, it
would have been discourteous not to do so.

"I want to fuck you. Do you want to fuck me, Carl Henry?"

"Yes, very much." Her word usage shocked him. It was not
what he expected from a woman with such broad literary knowledge.

They had to wait a while before he could perform. When he
did, Dianne seemed very pleased with his effort.

Carl Henry felt no guilt about making love to Dianne, though
it was assumed he and Yvonne were engaged. To this point he
had made love only to Yvonne and Veronica. Unless, of course,
you counted the Choctaw girl and Nigger girl he fucked. He certainly didn't count them.

He had told Yvonne that he would never stick his dick in an
Indian or Nigger pussy, but to do so had become somewhat of a
test of manhood around Bethel. Besides, fucking a Nigger was
supposed to change your luck, according to some oldtimers around
Bethel, and Carl Henry had felt the need for a change of luck.

He reasoned that the Indian girl and Nigger girl had merely
been receptacles for his sperm. Dianne was something else again.

"My ex-husband was such an asshole."

"Really."

"He used to tell me that I was no good in bed. Do you know
what I did after my divorce?"

He shook his head. How in the hell would he know?

"I had to prove to myself that I was a real woman, so after I
had been divorced for about six months I started looking around
for a man. I selected one I was attracted to with the intent of
going to bed with him. That's how I've selected men over the
past few years. All this time I've been working on my technique
in bed. Do you think I'm good?"

He wanted to tell her she wasn't too bad, but said instead, "You're fantastic." The oral sex had been good, and he wondered what other surprises she might have in store for him.

Carl Henry screwed Dianne regularly during the spring of his senior year, the summer following graduation, and periodically while he was in college. Finally, when he was a senior in college, she married a bookkeeper who worked for the lumber company.

Carl Henry was glad, because sleeping with her had become more of a chore than a pleasure, a mercy fuck simply because he liked her. He agreed with her ex-husband. She just wasn't all that good in bed.

CHAPTER TWENTY-FIVE

Following Rachael's death, Anise Marie visited Carl and Vivian often. Carl Henry figured it was because she was, more or less, living with his grandfather. He also figured she was thinking in terms of becoming his father's stepmother.

Fat chance of that, he thought. Why should the old man marry pussy he's already getting?

Carl Henry didn't particularly dislike Anise Marie. Of course, he didn't particularly like her either. His feelings toward her were . . . well, sort of noncommital.

The thing about her that annoyed him most was the constant twittering about her son Edward. She was always talking about Edward's exploits, as though he was the Lone Ranger. Edward's exploits were, of course, job-related. He was an accountant, a certified public accountant.

What in the hell exciting is there about being an accountant? Carl Henry thought.

Edward worked for an oil company in Oklahoma City and, according to Anise Marie, the damn thing would have gone under if it hadn't been for her son. He was the savior of the company.

Bullshit, Carl Henry thought.

He could understand the pride she had in her son, but he hated listening to her constant bullshit.

Things were different when his grandfather was at the house the same time Anise Marie was there. On those occasions Anise Marie was relatively quiet, knowing the old man would tire of her bullshit and tell her to shut-up.

However, when the two of them were there, they usually stayed for supper. And at the table Anise Marie would always inquire about Carl Henry's activities, tease him about Yvonne. He didn't like her questions, but he went along with the inquisition to keep from being impolite.

Carl Henry was sure that his mother considered Anise Marie a real air-head, but she was polite, too. He was sure it was in deference to Henry, though the old man was generally pretty sarcastic to Anise Marie.

Being around Anise Marie, listening to all her talk about Edward, generally depressed Carl Henry into thinking that he had little, if any, control over his own life.

Surely, he thought, if Edward had any control of his destiny, he wouldn't be an accountant. Maybe I don't have any choices either.

"It just doesn't seem possible," Anise Marie said, "but Edward's baby will be in the second grade this year."

"I know," Vivian replied. "It seems like only yesterday that Carl Henry was a baby."

"And look at him now," Anise Marie said.

"What's there to look at?" Henry asked.

"How big he is," Anise Marie answered.

"Somehow I knew you were going to say that," the old man said. "You always have had a knack for stating the obvious."

It always amazed Carl Henry that Anise Marie never seemed to know when his grandfather was being sarcastic. And he had noticed the old man was becoming increasingly intolerant of her, which indicated to him that Henry allowed Anise Marie in his life only for the sake of convenience.

Not a noble reason for keeping the woman around, he thought, but it's hard to knock availability. That's what I've got with Yvonne, Veronica and Dianne.

Anise Marie continued to wax eloquent about Edward and her grandchildren, but Carl Henry noticed that she never mentioned Edward's wife. He surmised that it was because the couple didn't get along well, or that Edward's wife didn't put up with any of her mother-in-law's bullshit.

Anise Marie particularly enjoyed talking about Edward being the organist for his church, teaching a Sunday School class, and sometimes substituting for the preacher.

Fuckin' triple threat man, Carl Henry thought. Bet the sonofabitch even cleans up the church restrooms.

Henry tired of Anise Marie's banter, so he said to his grandson, "Are you going to be playing baseball this spring?"

"I guess that's up to the coach."

"The hell it is," Henry responded. "If you want to play, you play. And if the sonofabitch says one cross word to you, I want to know about it. It's time some of these little asshole coaches know who's running things in Bethel. And if they think old man Keyser can save them, they've got a rude awakening coming."

"Henry, I wish you wouldn't be so profane," Anise Marie reprimanded.

"Goddamit woman, you stick to talking about Edward and his organ playing," Henry commanded. "You're a guest here and that's all. Remember that."

Anise Marie's face turned red, and it was hard for Carl Henry to keep from laughing. She went into a deep sulk, which she was often prone to do when he shouted at her.

From the way she acts, Carl Henry thought, you'd think her relationship with the old man is platonic, that she visits him, fixes his meals and cleans the house as an act of Christian compassion. Fucking whore. All you want is his dick in you. That's all most women want.

"I want to play," Carl Henry said, "but I hate to play under forced conditions."

"Forced conditions is what the world is all about," Henry said. "Boy, you've got to realize how the world is, that it's made up of the strong and the weak, the leaders and the followers. The Hayders are leaders and we've got the means of leadership because we've got the power. You've got to learn to use the power because we can't let the sheep get in control."

Vivian laughed and said, "That's pretty heavy stuff, Henry."

"I know it is, Viv, but you understand what I'm talking about. If the boy doesn't play, some asshole will think he's intimidated us. We're the ones who intimidate, not them. Do you understand what I'm saying, Carl Henry?"

"Yessir, I do."

"Make them kiss your ass, boy," Henry commanded. "It will be good for their souls. If any of them ever make it to the Pearly Gates, they're going to need a little humility. God put us Hayders on earth to teach humility to the people of Bethel, especially to goddam dumb-ass coaches."

Carl Henry looked at his father, who seemed oblivious to the conversation. He rarely said anything, during or after meals. After meals he just drank bourbon and smoked cigarettes.

"Yessir," Henry continued, "you're going to someday be in charge of everything I own, so you've got to learn to use the power of money. Money is the most powerful thing there is."

Anise Marie interrupted with, "God is more powerful than money."

Henry looked at her incredulously, then snarled, "What in the fuck do you know about money or God? You're one of the sheep, Anise Marie. One of the goddam sheep.

"That's because every Sunday you listen to some asshole preacher tell you that you're supposed to be a sheep, that you're supposed to turn your cheek when somebody slaps you in the face, that you're supposed to let people walk all over you in the name of Christianity. Hell, that's not Christianity, that's stupidity.

"If Jesus ever did come to Bethel, which is highly unlikely, He would do some real ass-kicking here."

She began, "The *Bible* says . . ."

"Woman, you don't know what the *Bible* says," Henry interrupted. "And you sure as hell don't know what it means. I know more *Bible* than any person in this town, maybe in this state. The *Bible* tells you to be decent to people, but if they don't respond to decency it tells you to kick ass."

"I like your interpretation of the Scriptures," Vivian said, laughing.

"Mother knew a lot about the *Bible*," Carl injected.

"Your mother didn't know shit," Henry said. "That's not saying she wasn't a good woman, because she was. I'm sure she made it right on into Heaven, no questions asked. But she didn't really know or understand the Scriptures. I don't think it was meant for everyone to know and understand them, just a few of us."

Anise Marie had reverted to her sulking attitude. Carl Henry figured she wasn't likely to attempt another contribution to the conversation.

"Grandad, you don't have to worry about me," Carl Henry said. "I'm not going to take any shit from anyone."

"I know that, boy, but it's not just a matter of not taking any shit from these assholes. It's a matter of making them afraid to give you any. We don't want them to even think about it."

"Isn't it a little hard to keep people from thinking?" Carl Henry questioned.

"Not in this town," Henry said. "An ant could carry all the thought in this town in its peewee brain and have plenty of room to spare. That's fine. We'll do the thinking for the good people of Bethel."

Carl Henry had never before realized just how much contempt Henry had for his fellow man.

"I can attest to the fact that people around here don't think," Vivian contributed. "If they did, they wouldn't sign some of the notes I draw up at the bank."

"That's a good point, Viv," Henry said. "We sure do have a lot of people by the balls, including Mr. Keyser. So, you don't really have to worry about the coaches, boy. They can't even run to their principal benefactor for help."

"Oh, I wasn't worried a bit," Carl Henry said. "I knew they didn't have a chance against you and mother."

If Carl Henry's statement bothered Carl, he didn't show it.

He just kept drinking and smoking. He pretty much stayed in a drunken stupor.

"Anise Marie, don't you think it's time you went home and I went home?" Henry asked.

She nodded affirmatively.

"Young Henry, you let me know if anybody gives you any bullshit," the old man said.

CHAPTER
TWENTY-SIX

CARL HENRY was apprehensive when he saw the black Cadillac parked in front of the house. It was Mr. Keyser's car.

It was Saturday afternoon and Carl Henry was returning from his usual rendezvous with Veronica. When he walked into the living room, Keyser got up from the couch to shake his hand.

"Good to see you, son. Your folks and me have just been talking about you."

"Well, I hope it wasn't all bad," Carl Henry responded. He hated the man's folksy demeanor.

"No, no . . . not bad at all. In fact, I'd have to say that it's been all good."

Then you must want something, he thought, you stupid sonofabitch.

Carl and Vivian were sitting in chairs facing the couch. Carl Henry noted that his father looked pleased, but that his mother looked disgruntled.

"Mr. Keyser's been telling us about Bosque University," Carl said. "He . . ."

Vivian interrupted, "He wants you to go there, but I told him you have a scholarship to Oklahoma."

"I know you've had an offer to Oklahoma, Carl Henry," Keyser said, "and to a lot of other schools. But the coach at Bosque asked me to talk to you. Of course, he wants the opportunity to talk to you, too.

"In fact, the school president called and asked if I would go to bat for them in recruiting you. Bosque is my old school, you know, and they thought I might swing a little weight around here. I told him it was mighty little, but that I'd try, which is why I'm here."

Carl Henry wanted to say, I knew it wasn't a social call, mother fucker, but opted for, "Well, I appreciate your interest, but I have sort of committed to Oklahoma."

"But you haven't signed anything yet," Keyser said.

"No, not yet."

"Well then, Oklahoma doesn't have a legal claim on you."

"No legal claim," Vivian injected, "except his promise to the Oklahoma coach."

"That's right, I did promise the O.U. coach that I'd sign with them."

"And when someone makes a promise, they ought to keep it," Vivian quickly added.

In his most patronizing tone Keyser said, "I'm certainly not advocating breaking a promise, but you know how these things are, Vivian. A boy's got to look for the best deal, and coaches don't expect a kid to keep a promise if something better comes along."

"Carl Henry doesn't have to look for the best deal," Vivian spouted back. "Perhaps you haven't noticed, but we're not destitute. Carl Henry doesn't even have to have a scholarship. We can afford to send him to any school he wants to attend."

Keyser, a bit flustered said, "My gosh, I know that Vivian. It's just an honor for a young man to receive a scholarship."

"If it's such an honor, then a young man should be honorable in obtaining it," she said.

"Viv, why don't you make us some coffee?" Carl suggested. He wanted to get her out of the room.

"I don't want any coffee," she responded.

"Well, Mr. Keyser may want some," he countered.

"Then you make it for him," she said.

Carl Henry almost laughed. He liked his mother's temper.

"I don't want any coffee," Keyser said. "I'm not trying to cause a rift here, but would you at least listen to what the school is willing to offer Carl Henry?"

"There's sure no harm in that, is there Viv?" Carl asked.

She sighed, "I guess not."

"Obviously," Keyser said, "he'll get full tuition plus room, board and books. There will also be fifty dollars a month in laundry money."

Carl Henry smiled at the mention of laundry money. It was a method schools used to give athletes spending money without incurring the wrath of the National Collegiate Athletic Association.

"What about a summer job?" Carl Henry asked. He really didn't need one, but what the hell.

"That's all taken care of, too," Keyser said. "The school will get you a summer job that will pay at least one thousand a month."

"And what if I get married while I'm in school?" Carl Henry asked.

"Thinking about marrying that little Marks girl, huh? Well, I'd advise against it while you're in school, but if you do the athletic department will furnish you an apartment with all bills paid, plus two hundred a month for food. Your wife can have a full scholarship, too, if she wants it.

"Another thing. There's a new car dealer that will furnish you a new car every year. Of course, the car is just a loan and you'll have to sign papers as though you're paying for it, but you'll never have to make a payment. You get to keep the car after you finish your senior year of eligibility."

It was pretty much the same deal other schools had offered.

"It sounds fair," Carl Henry said, "but I do have this obligation to Oklahoma."

"Did Oklahoma offer you more than we are?" Keyser asked. "I mean . . . we can negotiate this thing. The coach at Bosque really wants you. I wouldn't be surprised if you're weren't the starting quarterback by the time you're a sophomore."

"I'd be surprised if he wasn't the starting quarterback at Oklahoma by the time he's a sophomore," Vivian said.

"It's not a matter of what you're offering," Carl Henry said. "It's the promise I made to the Oklahoma coach."

"Couldn't you at least think about Mr. Keyser's offer?" Carl asked.

The problem with my father, Carl Henry thought, is that he still kisses ass. He's never really comprehended that we are in control now, not the Keysers.

"I don't guess it will hurt to think about it," he said, "but I've pretty much made up my mind. Besides, isn't Bosque a Baptist school?" He knew it was, but wanted to get Keyser's reaction.

"It's a Baptist school, boy, but they don't jam religion down your throat. There are a lot of non-Baptists on the team. The coach doesn't worry about a player's religion unless he's just a borderline athlete. Good players don't have to worry about going to chapel or taking religion classes. The school chaplain is a former player and he excuses all the athletes from chapel services. He also teaches the religion courses for athletes.

"Now, the normal students have to take two *Bible* courses and go to chapel three times a week for the first two years."

What the hell is normal about that? Carl Henry thought.

"Another thing about Bosque," Keyser continued, "is that it's a small school . . . I mean in comparison to Oklahoma. You will get a lot of personal attention there that you wouldn't get at Oklahoma.

"And the coach at Bosque believes in the passing game. I know you like to pass the football, and you won't get much chance to do that at Oklahoma."

"I'll tell you what we'll do," Vivian said. "We'll talk to Henry about it. I'd like to know what he has to say."

She knew that Keyser feared Henry, that he didn't want the old man involved.

After Keyser left the house Vivian said, "That pompous asshole has promised the Bosque coach that he will get you to sign. I can just see him now talking to the school president, bragging about how powerful an influence he is in the community. He's made a commitment to Bosque University and he'll go to any lengths to fulfill it."

"I think you're being unfair in your judgement of the man," Carl said.

"For god's sake, dad," Carl Henry said. "He doesn't give a shit about me. It's a matter of pride with him."

"All we have to do is turn the deal over to Henry," Vivian said. "He'll take care of everything from now on."

Carl Henry did sign with Bosque, after Henry negotiated with Keyser. The deal was struck after Keyser bought several thousand acres of worthless land from Henry, at a premium price.

Henry put the money in the bank in Carl Henry's name.

CHAPTER TWENTY-SEVEN

CARL HENRY probably never would have really known Gloria Redfield if Yvonne had stayed in Bethel the summer following his graduation. That was the summer Veronica took her to Europe.

He was opposed to the trip but Yvonne explained, "Mother wants to take me to Europe because she thinks we might get married next summer. She thinks this might be the last time we'll get to go on a trip like this together."

The real reason for the trip was that Veronica was pissed at Carl Henry. She wanted to punish him because he had missed a couple of Saturdays at the lake house, and she figured spending part of the summer away from him might revitalize his interest in her. She imagined that his interest in her was slipping. It wasn't, but the situation demanded constant reassurance and he wasn't good at giving it.

So, mother and daughter went on their trip, leaving Carl Henry

with no one to screw except Dianne. And she was becoming somewhat of a bore.

A summer with limited screwing required imaginative planning,
so he spent considerably more time working at the newspaper
office and playing touch football. It was at one of the touch football
games that he began to have serious thoughts about Gloria.

Since there was very little to do in Bethel, a number of girls
came to watch the boys play touch football. Most of the girls
who came were dating players, except for Gloria. She came to
watch her brother, Joe, play.

Most of the guys who knew Gloria considered her aloof, a real
cold fish. In fact, not one of them could even lay claim to ever
having kissed her.

She was beautiful, with long blonde hair colored by the summer
sun. She was always tastefully dressed, always with just the right
amount of makeup. Her preacher-father did not approve of cosmet-
ics at all, but her mother did, in moderation. She never wore
shorts or slacks.

While Carl Henry considered Gloria beautiful and wondered
about the mystery between her legs, he considered her a waste
of time. For most of his friends a girl who wouldn't neck was a
waste of time. For him, a girl who wouldn't screw was a waste of
time.

Joe Redfield, much to his father's chagrin, did not fall into the
prudish or super-religious category. In fact, with his profanity
and other vices, Joe seemed to always be trying to compensate
for being a preacher's kid.

On that particular summer afternoon, ten of the guys had gotten
together for a game of touch football. It was no coincidence that
nine girls showed up after they had been playing about thirty
minutes. The nine girls were steadies or semi-steadies of the players. It may, or may not, have been a coincidence that a tenth
girl showed up a short time later. That girl was Gloria and she
came, presumably, to visit with Evelyn Hogan, a short, redheaded,
freckle-faced girl who dated her brother.

When the game was over, the couples decided to go to the
Dairy Mart for cokes. Carl Henry was invited to go along. He
suggested that Gloria ride with him and she accepted.

Two tables had to be pulled together inside the Dairy Mart to accommodate the five couples. The place was new and fairly crowded.

Since Gloria was a year behind him in school and also one of Yvonne's rivals, Carl Henry had never talked to her much before. He discovered she was pleasant company, very intelligent and interested in many of the same things that interested him. He spent a little more than an hour with the group, and the time with Gloria passed all too quickly. He had to excuse himself, however, because he needed to shower before visiting Dianne Webster.

While in bed with Dianne that night, he couldn't get the memory of Gloria out of his mind. As their bodies moved rhythmically together, he imagined it was Gloria beneath him. He wished it was her. The thought of her excited him to faster, more urgent movements, causing Dianne to groan with pleasure.

On Sunday afternoon he called Gloria, suggesting that they meet at the Dairy Mart for a coke. She declined his invitation because it was too close to church time, but she did invite him to call again.

It was the following Friday night when they finally got together. Because of her father's opposition to the Hayders, he didn't pick her up at the parsonage. Joe delivered her to the Dairy Mart where Carl Henry was waiting. They arranged to meet Joe back at the Dairy Mart at a specified time.

That night Carl Henry discovered Gloria was not all that prudish, at least not with him. They drove around a while and listened to music, then parked.

Nothing ventured, nothing gained, he thought, then reached over and pulled Gloria toward him.

She resisted momentarily, then came into his arms. They kissed. It was obvious that she wasn't well-versed in the art, but that made her even more desirable. He wanted to force her down in the car seat, but restrained himself.

Don't press your luck, he thought.

Gloria knew her parents did not approve of Carl Henry, or of any of the Hayder family. That's why they had to arrange meetings in various places.

She also knew that Carl Henry and Yvonne were serious about each other, though she suspected Yvonne was more serious about him than he was about her. At least, that's what she wanted to believe. She had been interested in Carl Henry for a long time, but this had been her first chance to get close to him. She wasn't about to blow it.

Though Gloria's dislike for Yvonne had never surfaced openly, primarily because she was cast in the role of the super-Christian, she detested her rival. Gloria thought Yvonne had received numerous high school honors she could have had were it not for the fact that her father was a preacher.

She didn't really like the role she was forced to play, but she did not deviate from it. To do so would displease her parents, and pleasing them was important to her. Joe was enough of a rebel.

So, she didn't wear shorts, tight sweaters, slacks and jeans. She wanted to, but she didn't. She could have gotten a great deal of pleasure out of showing off her beautiful legs and large, firm breasts. She was aware that her figure was exceptional. Even the old men looked at her lustfully.

Her secret dates with Carl Henry were the closest she had ever come to rebellion against her parents. To see him, she was having to lie. She had never lied before, except maybe to herself. Joe was very adept at the art of lying, but not her.

Strangely, she felt no guilt.

Before the lies she had always felt that she had done nothing to feel guilty about, even though her father was constantly preaching that all have sinned and come short of the glory of God, whatever that meant.

Gloria did feel she should experience some guilt about the strange way she felt when Carl Henry was kissing her, but she didn't. He made her entire body tingle, and it felt too good to be wrong. She even wished that he would touch her breasts and put his hand between her legs while he was holding her close and kissing her. He had been very gentle with her.

Gloria's dating had been limited, and she had never let any of those boys kiss her, though some had tried. It was different with

Carl Henry, though. She wanted him to do everything to her that she had been missing. She was sure she loved him.

But her father's comments about Carl Henry made him seem like the forbidden fruit Eve gave to Adam in the Garden of Eden. Her father considered all the Hayders evil people, possessed of the devil.

Carl Henry's not like that at all, she thought.

She determined to do her best to win him away from Yvonne, no matter what it took.

If Carl Henry was capable of respecting any woman other than his mother, it was Gloria. He even convinced himself that his delay in screwing her was done out of respect. The real reason was that initially she wouldn't let him, not until she extracted a promise from him of his undying love toward her.

He made the promise, of course, and began screwing her regularly. But then Yvonne and her mother came home, making continuation of their summer romance difficult. It had been a quiet, secretive affair from the start. Gloria wanted to keep it from her parents, and Carl Henry certainly didn't want Yvonne or Veronica to know. The problem was that he felt he might be in love with Gloria.

Carl Henry talked the situation over with his grandfather and the old man told him that love was a word made up of "two vowels, two consonants and two fools." He said love was like a chigger bite, that it would itch for a while and then go away.

Joe and Evelyn, of course, knew about the summer romance of Carl Henry and Gloria, but they were pledged to secrecy. Neither were worried about Carl Henry's relationship with Yvonne being shattered, but they did want to protect Gloria. Joe had hoped things would work out between his sister and Carl Henry, because he liked his former teammate a great deal. He realized, however, that any serious relationship between them probably would have ended in tragedy because of his father's attitude toward the Hayders.

The Reverend Redfield's distaste for the Hayders stemmed from two factors. First, he felt Vivian had used him during the war.

She had been faithful to the church then, and he had prayed diligently for her husband's safe return. When he did return safely, she rejected the church.

Such rejection was like a slap in the face to Reverend Redfield and, in his mind, that was like slapping the face of God. He had visited her repeatedly, but long prayers were ineffective in moving her back into the House of God. He could only surmise that her continual rejection of God had caused the Almighty to turn His back on her, and he was convinced that the Lord did not want him associating with sinners.

Carl Henry was another matter. He was much like his mother in rejecting God, except that he did go to the Methodist Church. Reverend Redfield might have been able to accept his going to the Methodist Church if it hadn't been for the fact he had taken time personally to discuss a true religious experience with the boy. He had labored in telling him about the true way, and Carl Henry had rejected the truth for the social activities of the Methodist Church.

The boy was once upright, hardworking and respectful of his elders, thought Reverend Redfield. Now he is cynical, sarcastic and profane.

While the preacher's attitude toward Carl Henry lacked a certain Christian nobility, he was right about one thing. The boy had changed.

What Reverend Redfield would not admit colored his thinking about the Hayders was that he had been turned down for a loan at their bank. And Vivian was the one who turned him down. He thought she did it almost gleefully because she had become a disciple of Satan.

Carl Henry didn't give a damn about the preacher's attitude toward him, but he was concerned that Yvonne might hear about him seeing Gloria. A few people had seen him with Gloria, but it was usually in a group setting. He would have to casually mention the chance meetings with Gloria during the summer, which would really piss Yvonne. She would be angry, mostly jealous, and that could actually work in his favor. She would be anxious to please him.

That summer Carl Henry told Gloria he loved her, and she told him that she loved him. He learned from dealing with Yvonne, Veronica and Dianne that telling a woman you loved her was an effective way of getting what you wanted. His grandfather had told him that women were suckers for declarations of love, and he found the old man's logic to be sound with the four women.

He was hard-pressed as the summer began to wind to a close. It became tough satisfying four women, covering his tracks so none of them would know about each other. He was, however, pretty sure Veronica was becoming suspicious of his relationship with Yvonne.

That became obvious just before he left for Bosque University. Yvonne told him her mother wanted them to stop going steady, because if they continued she would miss a great many important senior activities. He was livid with anger but acted casual about it, as if he didn't care. She could see the ice in his eyes, his chilling indifference.

"It's just something mother suggested. It's not like I'm going to be intimate with anyone else. She just doesn't want me left out of any of the senior stuff."

"Fine."

"You don't act like it's fine."

"How in the hell do you want me to act? You want me to jump up and down, turn cartwheels . . . what?"

"Please don't act that way, Carl Henry."

"Goddam, Yvonne, what in the hell do you want from me? You want me to be thrilled about you going out with some dumb-ass? You want me to cheer because he may top you in the front seat of his car? All that going on while I'm working my ass off on a fucking football scholarship. Well, two can play the game."

"I don't care about anyone else. I'd never even let anyone else touch me." She was on the verge of tears.

"I don't really give a damn, Yvonne. There's probably a lot of stray pussy around Bosque University. Baptist girls put out, too."

"Are you saying you don't care about me?" she cried. Tears were streaking her makeup. "I can't stand it when you talk about being with another girl."

"Tough when the shoe's on the other foot, huh?" Her tears always bothered him. "When are you going to get it through that damn thick head of yours that I love you?"

"I love you, too," she said, a faint smile tugging at the corners of her mouth.

"Maybe you just love your mother better."

"You know that's not true. She just doesn't understand about us."

"I'm beginning to wonder if I do. It seems to me that when two people love each other, they're just not interested in going with other people, for any reason."

He was capable of sounding as pious and authoritative as the Reverend Redfield.

"I'm sorry, I don't know what I was thinking," she said. "I really don't want to be with anyone else."

"Let's cut the bullshit, Yvonne. You have a mind of your own, so use it. Your mother doesn't know best about everything."

"I know," she said. "I won't let anything come between us. Mother just thought some things were important to me that aren't. The most important thing for me is belonging to you, waiting for you."

He knew social functions were as important to Yvonne as they were to her mother, but he didn't say anything. He just sat there with false hurt in his eyes. She kissed him on the neck and mouth, giving assurances of her faithfulness.

He laughed to himself and thought about breaking out into song, the church hymn *Great is Thy Faithfulness*. Then he wondered why his mind rambled so.

Yvonne's faithfulness was important to him. So was the faithfulness of Veronica, Gloria and Dianne. He wanted all of them to be faithful.

He knew he didn't have to worry about Yvonne, nor her mother. He did, however, plan to chew Veronica's ass the next time they met at the lake house. The nerve of her, trying to screw up his relationship with Yvonne.

CHAPTER
TWENTY-EIGHT

CARL HENRY's freshman year was a good one. He laid his share of coeds and played exceptionally well for an undefeated Bosque freshman team. In the meantime, the varsity was being smeared from Syracuse to California. So, Baptist alums looked forward to the highly-prized freshman crop joining the varsity with the same eagerness they claimed to have for the second coming of Christ. And as quarterback, Carl Henry was cast in the role of messiah. Football was serious business at Bosque.

He married Yvonne the summer after his freshman year. It was a big wedding. Veronica saw to it.

Practically the entire town turned out for the wedding. At least, anyone of importance. The Methodist Church was filled to overflowing. Even Henry came, though he had previously stated he would never darken the doors of a church in Bethel.

Veronica had decided she was happy about the union, though she now felt a continued relationship with Carl Henry was out of the question. It just wouldn't be right, making love to her daughter's husband.

They spent their wedding night in Durant, Oklahoma, enroute to Oklahoma City. Henry had suggested they might want to spend part of their honeymoon in St. Louis, maybe catch a few Cardinals games. Yvonne had laughed, thinking he was joking. Carl Henry knew the old man wasn't.

"Hell," he told his grandson, "you can only spend so much time in bed. You'd better have something else to do because screwing is easier for a woman than it is for a man."

"I don't guess this compares much with Paris or London," Carl Henry said. They had just made love in their motel room and he was lying on his back watching a bug make its way across the ceiling. He wondered how anything could walk upsidedown.

"It doesn't matter where we are," she said. "The important thing is that we're together. Having you is better than all those exotic places rolled into one."

The bug had made it to the other side of the room and now seemed to be trying to decide whether to come down the wall or traverse the ceiling again.

"You've had me since I was fifteen, Yvonne."

"I know, but not like this. Now we really belong to each other. It's different somehow. I just feel more a part of you. Do you know what I mean?"

The bug had decided to come down the wall.

"Sure, I know what you mean."

"Are you happy with me, Carl Henry?"

"What kind of stupid-assed question is that? I married you, didn't I?" The old man had told him that you could never really anticipate the dumb-ass questions a woman might ask.

"People marry all the time and aren't happy with each other," she said.

"This is one helluva conversation to be having on our wedding night. What am I supposed to do if I'm not happy with you, take you home?"

"I just want some reassurance."

"Okay, I'm happy. I love you. Now, are you satisfied?"

"Well, it's better if I don't have to ask for reassurance."

He couldn't help it. He started laughing. She was so damn serious. Then, realizing the ridiculousness of the situation, she also started laughing.

"Dammit, we've been married only a few hours and you're already nagging me," he said. "What are you going to be like in five years?"

She made what she considered a tiger-like sound and crawled on top of him. "I'm going to love you all up in the next five years. I'm going to love you so much that you'll become a weak, feeble and toddering old man with gray hair."

"Whoa," he laughed. "Are you telling me that I'm going to be pussy-whipped within five years?"

"That's exactly what I'm telling you, and I'm ready to start right now." She began kissing him and he faked fighting her off.

"Wait a minute, baby," he laughed. "I've got to have some time to regroup. I've already spent my manhood and you've got somewhat of an advantage on me."

"I can feel you regrouping rather quickly."

"It's true that you don't have much of a problem in getting me up for the occasion, but just give me a minute to go to the john. I'll soon return and you can begin your five-year program."

"Deal," she said.

On the way to the bathroom he noticed that the bug had reached the floor. He killed it with his shoe.

CHAPTER
TWENTY-NINE

T HINGS MIGHT have been different if Carl Henry hadn't been injured during his junior year, and if Yvonne had not been pregnant during his senior year.

He passed and ran Bosque to a convincing victory over Oklahoma State in the season opener of his junior year. And he was having another big Saturday the following week when a Florida State tackle crunched his knee. The injury occurred in the third quarter with Bosque holding a two touchdown lead.

His replacement was Tim Barrilleaux, the same guy who had quarterbacked Ringling to the Oklahoma state championship when Carl Henry was a senior in high school. Barrilleaux had been breathing down his neck since the season began, and there was a great deal of pressure on the coach to play the sophomore because of his tremendous freshman year.

Many of the alumni felt Carl Henry had failed the school the previous year when Bosque managed only a break even season.

Barrilleaux had been sensational in the annual green and white spring game. In that game he had led the underdog white team to a two touchdown victory over the green team, which was quarterbacked by Carl Henry.

Seeing Barrilleaux go in the game hurt Carl Henry worse than the knee.

Sophomore jitters or whatever, Barrilleaux did not do well. Carl Henry sat on the sideline with his knee packed in ice and watched with satisfaction as his rival fumbled twice. The fumbles gave Florida State the impetus for a touchdown and field goal. Bosque had to stave off a frantic Florida State passing attack to preserve a four-point victory.

By Wednesday the swelling in the knee had gone down, and by Thursday Carl Henry was operating at almost top speed. He would start against Auburn that Saturday.

Auburn got on the scoreboard early in the first quarter with a thirty-seven yard field goal, but on the ensuing kickoff Bosque came roaring back. Utilizing his running backs with short play action passes, Carl Henry took the team on a sustained march into Auburn territory.

Facing second down and five at the Auburn twenty-three yard line, he faked to his fullback crashing over left guard and rolled right looking for a receiver. The Auburn linebacker seemed to come from nowhere, smashing into him and dislodging the ball. There was a wild scramble and Auburn recovered. Carl Henry lay still on the field.

Through hazy eyes he could see the team doctor and trainer kneeling beside him, and he could feel an intense pain in his shoulder. It was like a dream because everyone seemed to be moving in slow motion.

"Looks like a shoulder separation," the doctor said.

The coach mumbled, "Goddamit, I wish the sonofabitch had held on to the ball."

It was all crazy. He wanted to get up, to tell them that he could still play. But they were putting him on a stretcher and the trainer was talking to him. He couldn't understand what the trainer was saying, couldn't even remember the trainer's name.

Auburn won the game 24–21.

With his damaged right shoulder, there was no way Carl Henry could play. Barrilleaux became the starting quarterback. He was still the starting quarterback when Carl Henry began his senior year, even though the shoulder had healed.

The one thing Carl Henry couldn't take was being second to anyone. He became moody and a complainer. He made his dislike for Barrilleaux known to anyone who would listen. He didn't worry, as the coaches did, about dissension on the team. He didn't give a fuck about the team.

There were those who said Barrilleaux was given the nod at quarterback because he was a Baptist. Carl Henry liked to believe that, though he had difficulty with such logic since the head coach was one of the most profane men he had ever encountered. The coach was, however, a big cheese in the Fellowship of Christian Athletes. Initially, Carl Henry had been involved with the organization, but decided it was nothing more than organized bullshit.

"Just a bunch of superstitious jocks trying to get God on their side," he told Yvonne, "so they can make an extra yard or level some poor sonofabitch on another team. There is no fucking way to make Christianity and football compatible."

One of Carl Henry's favorite teachers at Bosque taught speech and considered football over-emphasized and a complete waste of time. One day in class she had asked a ministerial student, who played on the team, to explain the difference between Christian and non-Christian football. The teacher was just being sarcastic, but hearing the clown try to explain the compatibility really opened Carl Henry's mind to the ridiculousness of trying to justify a game of violence.

The more he thought about the game, the more he felt it was one of sheer lunacy and idiocy, men crashing against men, and spectators screaming for them to crash into each other even harder.

Still, he could not stand the thought of not being the number one quarterback, nor the thought of not having the crowd's adoration. He realized that he was a contradiction, but he was caught up in the madness.

Carl Henry blamed Barrilleaux for his imagined destruction,

the destruction of his perfect grade point average, his stature as a football player, and his relationship with Yvonne.

The destruction of his relationship with Yvonne was really imagined. She was just pregnant, somewhat cranky, and she wasn't up to going to bed with him every night. But Carl Henry was like his grandfather in that he could not tolerate even the mildest forms of rejection.

He also knew there had to be a way to get even with Barrilleaux. There was, and he found it, though it was entirely unintentional.

Carl Henry was in a history class with Barrilleaux's wife, Tommie Jean. He was always very charming to her, so she began to believe her husband was wrong in some of the things he said about his rival. Carl Henry never had a problem striking up a conversation with Tommie. She was pretty, he liked her, and he didn't blame her for his troubles. After all, anyone could make a mistake and, in Carl Henry's mind, Tommie's had been in marrying Barrilleaux.

Everything just seemed to fall into place.

First, on Wednesday Carl Henry hurt his knee in practice. The doctor advised that he not suit up for the game the following Saturday, which would be against Georgia Tech at Atlanta. Another player took his place on the traveling squad.

The team left for Atlanta on Friday and Yvonne left the same day to visit her parents. She wanted him to go with her, but he just wasn't in the mood to visit Bethel. The wife of a teammate made the trip with Yvonne.

On Saturday morning he saw Tommie at the campus drugstore. He had gone there to read the newspaper and have a cup of coffee, maybe shoot the shit with some other students. Tommie was there to buy hairspray. There was nothing sinister in him suggesting that she join him for a cup of coffee. By this time he had started calling her T. J.

They talked a lot of trivia, the conversation finally getting around to the game that would be played that night. When she discovered Yvonne had gone home, she invited Carl Henry to have dinner with her and to listen to the game. He agreed, of course, provided she would allow him to bring the steaks.

T. J. was a small town girl, naive and very religious. A part of her fascination with Barrilleaux was that he aspired to some type of religious vocation. She had become increasingly fascinated with Carl Henry, but considered her strange feelings toward him nothing more than a special friendship. She had never told her husband that she even knew Carl Henry, because Tim fostered a special dislike for him.

Carl Henry arrived at the Barrilleaux apartment about six. After the initial formalities, he tended the steaks on a charcoal grill on the patio while she busied herself with other kitchen duties.

She finished her tasks before the steaks were done and joined him on the patio. It was chilly so she had one of Tim's sweaters draped around her shoulders. She stood with her arms crossed, as though she was cold, and that accentuated the size and firmness of her breasts. Carl Henry could not help but notice.

Dinner was good, the conversation easy and relaxed. T. J. was aware that Yvonne was expecting and wanted to know if Carl Henry was excited about the baby. He told her he was, though he really hadn't given much thought to it.

There was time to do the dishes and listen to music before the kickoff. He could have cared less about the game, would have preferred to have watched television.

She tuned in the radio and they sat on the couch, comfortably apart. There was the usual pregame bullshit, interviews with the coach and players about their chances against Tech. The coach and head bullshitter said the team might miss the services of veteran backup quarterback Carl Henry Hayder. To be publicly acclaimed as a backup quarterback didn't set well with Carl Henry.

The announcer did his best to make the contest sound exciting, but he was pissing into the wind. Both teams were seemingly content to let their backs bang into the line for two or three yards. After three unsuccessful rushes, there would be a punt. Each team was waiting for the other to make a mistake.

Carl Henry knew Barrilleaux was following the coach's conservative game plan to the letter.

That's why he's quarterback and I'm not, Carl Henry thought. He follows orders to the letter. I would have made something happen by now.

Interrupting his thoughts T. J. said, "The game's pretty boring."

"Your husband's doing what the coach wants him to do. He could pick that Tech secondary apart by passing. Their game films showed us they are very weak against the pass."

"Why doesn't the coach want Tim to pass?"

"He's scared of the pass. Thinks it's a sign of offensive weakness."

Changing the subject abruptly she said, "Do you want some coffee?"

"I could drink some, but I don't want you to go to any trouble."

"It's no trouble. I'd like some myself."

"Can I help?"

"No, you just sit there and listen to the game. Tell me if anything exciting happens."

She walked toward the kitchen and, though she was wearing a loose-fitting dress, there was enough movement to stir his interest. He remembered having seen her in shorts that summer and thinking what great legs she had.

"Your husband just fumbled on our nineteen," he said loud enough for her to hear. "Tech's got the ball." He tried not to show elation at Barrilleaux's mistake.

I hope Tech beats the living shit out of them, he thought.

She came to the door and said, "God, he's going to be in a foul mood when he gets home. He fumbled three times last week."

The announcer for the hometown radio station practically cried as he described Tech's nineteen-yard drive for a touchdown.

"What do you want in your coffee?"

"Just one sugar," he replied.

By halftime Tech had a two touchdown lead and Bosque was still trying to establish a running game. Carl Henry got up from the couch and stretched.

"Do you want to walk around a little bit before the second half starts?" he asked.

"Sure, let me get a coat."

Carl Henry was only wearing a sweater, but cold didn't bother him that much.

"Would you like to wear one of Tim's coats?" she asked.

"No, I'm hot natured. Besides, it's about fifty degrees."

"I just freeze to death," she said. "I can't stand cold weather."

"I used to swim in a creek when it was colder than this."

"You're kidding."

"No, I'm not. My grandfather and I used to swim when there was snow on the ground."

The apartment was adjacent to the campus, so they were walking on a sidewalk past classroom buildings.

"Is your grandfather some kind of a nut?" she asked, laughing.

"Probably, but a damn tough one."

"I was just kidding when I asked if he was a nut."

"I know that. Really, though, I don't know anyone who has lived more than my grandfather. He could teach all the professors here a lot. And I guess some people might think he's different, even a bit crazy, but I've yet to meet a man who's smarter than he is."

"You must be very fond of him."

"He's the only man I've ever really respected."

"What about your father?"

"What about him?"

"You respect him, don't you?"

"Not like my grandfather."

"It's wonderful to feel that way about somebody," she concluded.

"I'm sure you feel that way about somebody."

"Well, maybe my husband. I don't know."

The dorms were pretty well deserted. It was still too early for most students to be in from their Saturday night dates.

"I was telling you about swimming in the cold, though," he continued. "My grandfather goes swimming every day, in the nude. He taught me to swim, hunt and fish. We spent a helluva lot of time together."

"Just the thought of swimming in this kind of weather sends chills up my spine," she said. "You make your grandfather sound like Superman."

"He is one of the strongest men I've ever known. When I was thirteen and he was seventy-four, he raced me for a mile. Beat me, too."

He wanted to tell her some of the things he had heard about his grandfather's exploits with women, especially about sleeping with the three sisters. But he decided it wouldn't be appropriate.

"Say, we'd better get back if we're going to listen to the second half," he said.

"I guess so, but it's so pleasant out tonight that I'd just as soon walk as listen to the ball game. It looks like we're going to lose anyway."

"Well, I sure don't care anything about the game," he said. "We can walk until you get tired."

"Are you sure?"

"Absolutely."

They walked and talked, about trivial things. The game was already in the fourth quarter when they returned to the apartment. She reheated the coffee and they sat together on the couch to listen to the outcome. Bosque trailed by twenty-one points.

First, it was their fingers that touched accidentally. Then their eyes met and a sort of warmness enveloped them. His hand reached for hers and, though she wanted to stop the madness, her emotions were too strong. Their lips met, then their bodies. Their passion for each other became a raging and uncontrollable fire.

His sure, steady hands removed her panties and, while the announcer droned on, they made love on the couch. She had an orgasm about the same time Tim fumbled again.

Appropriate, Carl Henry thought.

He left the Barrilleaux apartment about noon the following day, two hours before Tim was scheduled to arrive. Yvonne would not be home until six.

It was a couple of months later when T. J. told him she was pregnant. They had been seeing each other two or three times a week since the Tech game. It had been difficult finding times and places to make love, but they had managed. He thought he might be in love with her. She claimed there was no doubt about her love for him.

"It's yours," she said in telling him about the child. "I've never slept with Tim without my diaphragm, and I've always used it when we made love except for that first night."

"What do you want to do?" he asked.

"Nothing," she said matter-of-factly. "Dammit . . . goddamn. It's just not fair. We love each other and there's nothing we can do."

It was the first time he had ever heard her use profanity.

He shrugged his shoulders and said, "I wouldn't say there's nothing we can do." He felt that he had to say something.

"What would you suggest we do?" she catily replied. "Yvonne is having a baby in a month. You certainly are prolific." She smiled faintly in spite of the sarcasm.

"I don't know, but there has to be something we can do."

"Okay, you go get your clothes and I'll go get mine and we'll run off to Mexico," she said.

"Be serious."

"I am."

They sat silently in the front seat of the car, watching the moonlight sparkle on the ripples in the river. They had met at a shopping center, where she had gotten into his car. It was Thursday night and the stores were open until ten. She had told Tim that she was going shopping.

"Have you told Tim about the baby?"

"Yes."

"What did he say?"

"He was upset at first because he has another year in school, but he seems pretty excited about it now."

"How did you explain it."

"I just told him I forgot to use my diaphragm one night."

"He can't tell when you're using it."

"No, why should he be able to."

"I can always tell."

"I didn't know that."

They stared at the river a while before she broke the silence. "I don't think we should see each other again under the circumstances."

"Why not?"

"It's just not a good idea. We ought to give the baby a better break than we gave ourselves."

"That's up to you. You know that I care very much about you."

"I know that."

They ended it there on the bank of the river, making love one last time before he took her back to the shopping center. She was tearful. He figured the entire affair was just one of the breaks of the game.

CHAPTER THIRTY

FOLLOWING GRADUATION from Bosque University, Carl Henry returned to Bethel as publisher of the newspaper and as president of Henry's bank. There was considerable negative murmuring by the townspeople and by the rest of the Hayder clan about his appointment to both positions. He was, after all, only twenty-two years old.

The question most often asked was, "What can a twenty-two year old boy know about running a bank and a newspaper?"

Response from some of the bolder townspeople was, "Nothing, but you'll have to live with the situation because he's Henry Hayder's grandson."

Of course, no one posed any questions to Henry about his grandson's competence.

Actually, Carl Henry had no intention of making any significant changes in the bank or newspaper. Henry had good people running both operations, and Vivian was still keeping a tight rein on the financial aspects of all Hayder enterprises. She was in control. Carl Henry was merely a highly paid figurehead, the heir apparent to practically everything Henry owned.

When Carl Henry returned to his hometown, it was to a large, newly-built two-story house, the finest in Bethel. It was a graduation gift from Henry, who said his grandson should live in a home befitting the president of a bank. Henry, of course, continued to live in the old house.

Along with the new house and new positions came a warning from Henry. "Carl Henry, I'm passing the mantle on to you, so you're going to have to be very careful about the way you conduct yourself. I have lots of enemies in this town, some in our own family, and they'll try to get to me through you.

"Just don't take any shit off of anybody, and that includes all your relatives. Your uncles, aunts and cousins will test you, try to discover your weaknesses. They're jealous of you. Some of them even think they ought to be where you are, though most of them don't have enough sense to come in out of the rain. Be firm with them, and remember that you don't have any weaknesses because you're like me.

"Also, be careful who you fuck. Not every woman is discreet, so you'll have to use some judgment. That wasn't as important years ago, but things were different then. I didn't always use good judgment, but I wasn't as much in the spotlight as you're going to be.

"The important thing is to never let your guard down, even for a minute. Don't tell these bastards here in Bethel anything, and don't become friends with any of them. They're just acquaintances, boy, and that's all they should be. The biggest lie ever perpetrated was that a man needs friends. That's a crock of shit. You need yourself and that's all."

Carl Henry had no difficulty heeding his grandfather's advice. There had always been somewhat of a schism between Carl Henry and his relatives, primarily because of the old man's favoritism toward him. As far as he was concerned, it negated any obligation to them. Henry had already provided adequate jobs for them, so Carl Henry had no plans to give them even the sweat off his balls.

In terms of women, he planned to limit his sexual activities to Yvonne, Veronica and Gloria. Veronica had changed her mind about not sleeping with her daughter's husband, and they had continued making love whenever possible while he was in college. Now that Carl Henry was back in Bethel, they could intensify their relationship.

Gloria had married an oil field worker who was gone quite a bit, so there was no problem there, except maybe from her preacher father who seemed forever present.

Though Carl Henry could have spent his days basking in newfound importance, he instead chose to antagonize county and state officials. He began to use his journalism training to develop editorials calling attention to the senility of some longtime politicians. He was particularly adept in discussing the wrongdoing of certain Democratic office holders, all of which infuriated party officials.

Since the Democrats controlled the county, party officials made the mistake of asking Henry to muzzle his grandson. Until that time the old man could have cared less about Carl Henry's feud with various politicians, but when party officials came to him with the problem he interpreted it as an attempt at intimidation. He told them to fuck themselves, then suggested to Carl Henry that he develop an even harder line attitude toward the politicians he was bedeviling.

One oldtime politician who was subjected to more than his fair share of Carl Henry's editorial ire was Bernard Snook, the state representative for the district in which Bethel was located. Snook, sixty-four years old, had been in office for more than thirty years.

In one editorial after another, Carl Henry implied that Snook was senile. He also accused the man of being responsible for gambling and other criminal activity in the county. It was an election year and every editorial called for voters to oust Snook.

The Hayders even provided an opponent for Snook, a young Republican lawyer named Drew McIntyre, who represented some of their legal interests. The opponents were contrasts in every way: Snook, a shabbily-dressed bumbling orator with limited formal education; and McIntyre, a nattily-dressed silver-tongued speaker whose educational background was more than obvious.

Still, the people might have chosen Snook were it not for fear of Hayder retribution. As it was, McIntyre walked away with the election and Carl Henry owned his first politician. McIntyre was the first of many he would own.

As for Snook, he died shortly after the election. Some said Carl Henry Hayder put the final nail in his coffin. But if there was any remorse on the part of Henry's grandson, none were aware of it.

Prior to his planned editorial attack on Snook, Carl Henry had vowed to Yvonne, "I'll get that bucolic bastard if it's the last thing I do."

"That's fine," she laughed, "but what does bucolic mean? Is it something like syphillis?"

She had a way of making light of his seriousness. He liked that and joined in her laughter.

"It means he's a country bumpkin."

"Well, I can see how a big city boy from Bethel, Oklahoma might be incensed by a bumpkin."

"I've got big city ways."

"They must be hidden somewhere."

"Nobody likes a smart-ass, Yvonne."

"I've always been a smart-ass."

"Well, it's more pronounced now that you're getting educated." She was commuting to a nearby college to complete her degree.

"You think so," she said.

"No doubt about it."

"Maybe we need more than one brilliant mind in the Hayder family."

"I wasn't implying that you're becoming brilliant," he teased. "I might if you were majoring in something other than education."

"Oh, so you're embarrassed that your wife might someday be qualified to be a teacher."

"Not at all," he countered. "I'm just embarrassed that you're having to take education courses. What are you taking this semester, sandpile and sandbox?"

"If my mind isn't playing tricks on me, I believe you have a couple of education courses on your transcript."

"Merely in the line of duty, my dear. Those were crip courses to keep me eligible for football."

"Aha, brilliant one, are you saying that you had to take crip courses to stay eligible for football?"

"Not at all," he replied. "The coach registered for me, and he decided that I needed an easy semester to help me concentrate on the main purpose of a university, that being to have a winning football team."

"God, you're cynical," she said.

"Skepticism is the hallmark of good journalism," he stated in his preacher-mimic voice. "No news organization can exist for very long if it continually registers contentment with things as they are, if it does not probe beneath the surface of events, if it fails to sound the alarm over the shortcomings of society. For change is the first law of journalism."

"My, what learning comes forth from the mouth of the Bethelite."

"Mere memorization, my dear, straight from a journalism textbook. At our newspaper a treatise like the one I just spouted would leave their mouths gaped open, but they would never understand it. Here in Bethel a major story is the piano recital of an advertiser's daughter, or ten thousand words on last Friday's football game. Journalistic values here are nothing more than a crock of shit."

He was serious now, and she sensed the change in his mood. While he was extremely self-centered, he had a definite sense of right and wrong, something that haunted him on occasion.

Yvonne put her arms around him, kissed him and said, "It's all going to work out."

"Things work out only if you make them work out," he opined. "God, how I hate politicians."

"Don't worry," she assured, "you'll win. No politician can stand up to Hayder vindictiveness."

He laughed, then asked, "How's C. H.?" The reference was to their son, Carl Henry Jr.

"He's asleep."

"Does he still have a fever?"

"No, I gave him a baby aspirin this morning and he's okay now. I took his temperature just before you came in."

"Wonder what was wrong with him this morning?"

"I don't know, but it was nothing serious. Would you like some dinner? I didn't know what time you would get in, so I didn't fix anything."

"You haven't eaten?"

"No, I thought I'd wait for you."

"You'd better start eating at the proper times," he said. "With my work load, there's no telling what time I'll get in." Gloria's husband was out of town, so he had stopped by to see her.

"In case you haven't noticed, it's not going to hurt me to miss a meal," she said.

"You're not chubby."

"I don't want to get that way."

"They tell me that a fat girl is hard to beat in bed."

"Who is this *they* that have been telling you that?"

"I can't recall right off, but it's logical that there's a lot more to love on a fat girl. I heard of a guy who married a fat girl and made love to her every night for twenty years, only to find out after all that time he had been missing the spot. She was still a virgin."

"Oh, brother," she laughed.

"Yep, it seems that he had been getting his jollies on a different wrinkle every night. He had never found the right one."

"Do you want any dinner?"

"Just a sandwich and, as long as you're up, build me a scotch and water."

"You're drinking too much lately," she cautioned.

"I've been trying to clear up a case of the worms, and worms can't live in alcohol."

After the election, when Snook died, the newspaper editor asked Carl Henry if they should use his obituary as a major story.

"Hell no," he replied. "I don't want to give the stupid fucker's relatives any more consolation than I gave him."

For the next three years Carl Henry worked diligently to assure that other Hayder-backed politicians were elected to county and state offices. With the Hayder fortune growing daily, he was very much aware the family needed political friends in high places. Some even said Carl Henry was laying the groundwork to become governor of the state, a rumor that pleased Henry.

Why not, the old man thought. The boy would make a great governor. I would have made a great governor myself.

If the governor's mansion was what Carl Henry had in mind, he never said. He assumed complete control of the newspaper, increased his authority at the bank, and began to play a more important role in Henry's land and oil dealings. Henry and Vivian turned more and more of the Hayder business over to him.

Bethel's population continued to increase, which meant more prosperity for both the bank and the newspaper. With an increase in new businesses, the newspaper became a daily. Some well-meaning people even tried to open a new bank in Bethel, but with the help of political friends Carl Henry was able to thwart their efforts.

No matter how many new businesses, no matter how many new people, the Hayders were still the most powerful family in Bethel. No businessman could alienate the Hayders and survive.

During this period Carl Henry and Yvonne had another child, a girl they named Vivian.

Carl Henry did work in a couple of affairs during the three years, one with a high school majorette, but he had come to believe he was deeply in love with Yvonne. He did find it difficult to express that love, and his mind was constantly changing about the depth of their relationship.

CHAPTER THIRTY-ONE

Henry was tired, exhausted from a week-long trek into the mountains where he had camped out and did some fishing. He had gone into the wilderness because he had felt a need to get away from civilization, from the house and especially from Anise Marie. She was always underfoot.

The mountain air, the swimming in a cold stream, the cooking of freshly caught fish over an open campfire . . . all these things refreshed him. But now he was home and he was tired.

I guess an eighty-seven year old man has a right to be tired, he thought.

He was sitting in a bathtub of hot, soapy water, Anise Marie scrubbing his back. He thought she seemed overly-delighted in washing every part of his body.

"Being out in the woods a week, I bet this hot bath really feels good," she chattered.

"If you think it feels so damn good, why don't you get in the tub with me?" he invited.

She laughed and said, "Quit your kidding, Henry."

"Who in the hell's kidding?"

"You are," she said, scrubbing his neck.

He grabbed her by the arms and pulled her into the tub. She was too surprised to scream, but merely gasped, "You've ruined my clothes."

"Big deal. You should have got naked before trying to give me a bath." He thought she looked very comical sitting in the tub with her clothes all soapy. She tried to get out, but he wouldn't let her.

"You're crazy, Henry," she whined. "You're just flat crazy."

"Hell, you've been fucking around with me for years, Anise Marie. Are you just now discovering that?"

"Let me up, Henry."

"No, by god, just sit where you are. And as long as you're in the tub, why don't you give my privates a good washing?"

"I'm not going to do it."

"Then you'll sit in this damn tub until hell freezes over."

She went into her sulking routine then, which he always found amusing.

"What's so funny?" she wanted to know.

"You are," he laughed. "The way you sulk, you remind me of an old possum."

"I don't like being compared to a possum."

By god, he thought, the woman doesn't have a humorous bone in her body.

"I was only joking," he said.

"Sometimes your jokes aren't funny, Henry."

"If you don't like the way I am," he threatened, "don't let the door hit you in the ass on the way out."

She relaxed then, knowing he was angry. He had released his grip on her, but she was now seemingly content to stay in the tub. With soap and a washcloth, she began concentrating on his penis and balls.

Stupidest fucking woman I've ever known, he thought. She loves verbal abuse.

The warm water, Anise Marie washing his penis, aroused Henry. It made him think about the girl of long ago, the one he made love to in a barn in Arkansas.

"My god, Henry," Anise Marie exclaimed, obviously delighted that she had stirred him up.

"Come here," he ordered. It was a bit awkward, but he was able to remove her wet panties. She was a willing participant in helping him position himself, so they were soon screwing.

When they were finished she got out of the tub. She knew that when he was finished, he was finished.

"That was good," she said.

"Hasn't it always been good?"

"Yes, but it's been a while."

"Did you think I didn't have any more lead in my pencil?"

"No, I didn't think that at all."

It has been a while since I screwed her, he thought, but dammit, she doesn't hold much interest for me anymore. I need a younger woman. Bet I could get one, too, if I put my mind to it.

"Are you going to get out of the tub now?" she asked.

"No, I think I'll sit here and soak a while. You could bring me a big glass of muscadine wine, though."

She brought him the wine and he sat in the hot water drinking it. The wine took effect almost immediately, bringing a feeling o melancholy. After Anise Marie had refilled his glass a couple mo times, he began to have pleasant thoughts toward her.

Maybe I should have married her after Rachael died, he thou She's not that bad of a woman. I've always been able to cou her to cook for me and to take care of the house. And even she's not that good in bed, she's always available. I ca get it up by thinking about someone else, Vivian or t the barn.

Hell, he reasoned, if I had me a young woman I another family. I could put four or five more Hayo before the good Lord takes me.

Seconds later his thoughts were contradictory, reasoning he couldn't marry Anise Marie because he was too old, that his days on earth were numbered.

He laughed to himself then, thinking about the fact that he had outlived Arlo Shipley.

That worthless sonofabitch figured he would outlive me, he thought, but I'm the one who got to spit on his grave. You can't tell me the bastard was ever a Christian, either. He was a damn Catholic until the day he died.

His mind wandered to Carl Henry and he thought, I've got to go over and see the boy this week. I wish to hell he had gone up in the mountains with me. Seems he's always too busy nowadays to go fishing. I'll have to start taking little C. H. with me. I'll damn sure make a fisherman out of him.

I can't complain about Carl Henry, though. He's damn sure got this town, maybe even the whole state, by the balls. If he doesn't, he will. If he had been a war hero like his daddy, there's no telling what he might have been able to do. He might even have been the fucking President of the United States.

CHAPTER THIRTY-TWO

CARL WAS drunk, which was not uncommon. He often drank excessively, and he never stopped smoking. He had years before accelerated to four packs of cigarettes a day. Only the few hours sleep he got each night kept him from smoking around the clock.

The drinking started in the morning, after coffee and cigarettes. It picked up as the day went on, usually reaching a peak after the sun went down.

Sometimes Carl did his drinking in Casey's old saloon, and sometimes in one of the new lounges on the outskirts of town. And because he was quite generous in providing liquor to anyone who would listen to his war stories, he was quite popular with certain elements. Those folks listened only as long as he was buying. And Carl never stopped buying. That was the advantage of having an unending supply of money.

But Carl didn't relegate his drinking to bars. He had an excellent stock of liquor at home, which he depleted and restocked on a daily basis. His entire life revolved around drinking and smoking.

Carl was an alcoholic, though he wouldn't admit it to himself. He considered himself just a good old boy who liked a drink now and then.

Vivian became completely intolerant of him. There had been a time when she would have an occasional drink with him, but no more. She was sickened by his weakness, detested him. His constant cigarette smoking nauseated her. She was ready for Carl to die. She wanted to be free of the bondage of caring for him, of loving him.

Henry was equally sick of Carl's dependence on the bottle. The old man never liked weakness in any person, but it was almost more than he could endure to see it in a Hayder. He, too, would not have been sorry to see Carl die.

Unfortunately for Henry and Vivian, Carl was not willing to succumb to their wishes. He was very much alive and, even with excessive drinking and cigarette smoking, he was in relatively good health. Therefore, with his drunken antics he continued to be a source of embarrassment to the rest of the Hayder family.

So, Carl Henry came up with a solution. They sent Carl away to a hospital that specialized in curing alcoholics.

"I don't care if they cure him or kill him," Henry said, "just as long as they do one or the other."

CHAPTER THIRTY-THREE

CARL HENRY was pissed at himself, primarily because he was depressed and didn't know why. He lay in bed staring at the ceiling, disgusted with the tenseness he felt. He couldn't really pinpoint what was bothering him.

Yvonne lay beside him, sound asleep. He envied her ability to go to sleep so quickly and to sleep so soundly. He had never been able to do that.

Maybe it's because you're always scheming, you sonofabitch, he thought. Maybe it's because you're never satisfied with things the way they are. You're a real dumb-ass. You've got it made and can't accept it.

For some reason his mind wandered to Dianne. He hadn't thought about her for some time. He tried to remember what she had been like sexually, but couldn't. He wondered if she still liked to screw as much as she did when he was in high school.

Even though he couldn't really remember what Dianne had

been like, only that she wasn't all that good, thinking about her aroused him. He thought about waking Yvonne, but knew she would be pissed if he did. In his frame of mind, he wasn't up to any hassles.

The moonlight in the bedroom was so bright that he could make out all of Yvonne's features.

She's still a beautiful woman, he thought. Even after kids and putting up with all my bullshit for twelve years. Most men would give their left nut to be with a woman like Yvonne, and here I am panting like a dog after Barbara Neeley.

He had only recently hired Barbara at the newspaper. She was fresh out of college and built like the proverbial brick shithouse. Thinking about her kept him in a constant state of arousement. The fact she was married, that her husband worked at the bank, didn't bother him at all. She certainly would not be the first married woman he had laid. And he would fuck her. He was sure of that.

His thoughts then skipped to his old high school friend, Boyd Arnold. It was probably because of the advice Boyd had given him a few days earlier.

"You stupid sonofabitch," Boyd had said. "If you don't keep your pants zipped up, you're going to get your ass in a lot of trouble. And dammit, people don't want a governor who fucks everything with two legs."

He smiled when thinking of Boyd's warning.

"I'm not kidding you, you dumb shit," Boyd continued. "Some of your sexual escapades are being talked about all over town. One of these days Yvonne's going to find out and the shit's going to hit the fan."

Boyd was one of the few high school classmates with whom Carl Henry maintained any type relationship other than business. Boyd was a salesman for a building supply company, was married to a girl named Lois, and had a baby daughter. He had become fairly successful and was a good family man, a far cry from the old Boyd who was the county jackoff champion.

"What makes you think Yvonne doesn't know?" he had asked.

"Because I know she would kick you out on your ass if she knew," Boyd replied.

"I doubt it, Boyd, but I sure as hell don't need you preaching at me. I've had enough of that shit in my lifetime."

"Well, none of it ever took," Boyd opined.

"Another thing," Carl Henry said, "let's not discuss this governor shit. I have no intention of running for governor."

"Oh, I'm sure you don't have any intention of running for office now, but that will come. There's no doubt in my mind that somewhere down the road you're going to make the race, if some husband or father doesn't shoot your ass first."

"Not much chance of that," he countered. "I'm real shifty-assed."

Their conversation had taken place in Casey's saloon, now under new ownership. Casey had died.

His thoughts raced to Lois, and he wondered what she would be like in bed. He was suddenly wishing he had met Lois before Boyd had married her.

Goddamit, what's wrong with me? he thought. I can't even keep from having the hots for my only friend's wife.

His feelings for Yvonne changed on a daily basis. He loved her one day, doubted that he loved her the next. He didn't feel all that guilty the days when he doubted his love, merely reasoned that a man either feels for a woman or doesn't.

I probably shouldn't have come back to this fucking hole, he thought. I could have gotten a job on a big city newspaper, maybe even a foreign assignment. Maybe I could have been a sports editor.

He laughed inwardly at the thought of himself as a sports editor. He had a great deal of disdain for most jocks and players, so he began to imagine interviews with coaches and players who always say the same things.

"What do you think it's going to take to win, coach?"

"We're going to have to control the ball."

Good point, he thought. If the other team doesn't have the ball, they certainly can't score, unless they're counting on a safety to win the game.

"Do you think the team's ready?"

"Ready as we'll ever be. But they've got a fine ballclub, excellent coaching."

The dialogue that passed through his mind was not really trivial enough for most coaches, he thought. He decided on an interview with a player.

"What's it going to take to beat Tech today, No-Neck?"

"We're gonna have to concentrate. We can't be thinkin' of nothin' else, just beatin'em. All them fans in the stands can't help a bit. We gotta do it."

"How do you feel about Tech?"

"I hate'em. That's what it's all about. I'm goin' into this game wild, mad and hatin' everybody."

Other than football, what sort of activities are you involved in in school? he mentally asked the imagined player.

"I'm a physical education major, so I don't have much time for anything but studyin', but I am in the Fellowship of Christian Athletes."

He switched back to the coach and asked, "How big is this game, coach?"

"They're all big, but we just have to play'em one at a time. I hope we're ready, 'cause they'll be doin' some things we ain't seen yet."

"This is your first year as a college coach, isn't it?"

"Yeah, it is. Last year I was coachin' in high school and teachin' English."

He chuckled to himself at the stupidity of his imagined interviews and thought, I'd better watch myself or people will think I have Communist leanings, making fun of something as important to American life as football.

The funny thing, the thing that annoyed him about himself, was that on Sunday he would be sitting in front of the television set, vicariously living every play with the pros. He didn't watch college football, considered it just minor league pro ball.

He got up and fixed himself a scotch and water, took the drink in the den, made himself comfortable in the recliner and started reading the newspaper. He laughed to himself while reading the sports pages, because some of the interviews sounded very similar to those he had imagined.

CHAPTER
THIRTY-FOUR

THAT PARTICULAR Monday proved to be a memorable one, though it didn't start out too well. When he came out of the house, he discovered that the left rear tire on his car was flat. In putting on the spare, he got grease on his slacks and had to change to another pair. He was pissed off about it, but Yvonne just laughed at him. She generally teased him when he got mad about unimportant things, which usually straightened out his mood.

He was in a good mood when he arrived at the newspaper office, in an even better mood a couple of hours later. Barbara Neeley had agreed to have a drink with him after work.

But then, about eleven o'clock, there was news about T. J. Barrilleaux, a woman he never expected to see again. The news came via a press release, delivered by a guy in a flashy suit. He introduced himself as the educational director of the First Baptist Church, then asked Carl Henry if he would mind running an article about the church's new pastor.

Ordinarily, Carl Henry would not have been anywhere near the city desk, but he had gone there to discuss a political candidate with the editor. The editor had gone for coffee, so Carl Henry took the press release and picture and said the paper would try to find space for the announcement.

The picture of Tim Barrilleaux surprised him.

He had over the years lost track of Barrilleaux and T. J. He knew Barrilleaux had been drafted by the Chicago Bears following his senior year, and had spent a year on the team's taxi squad before being cut. It had been his last knowledge of Barrilleaux's whereabouts.

Because he considered Bosque an unpleasant experience, Carl Henry had severed all ties with his former classmates. When the Bosque alumni magazine arrived in the mail each month, he just threw it in the trash without reading it.

But it was all there in the news release . . . Tim Barrilleaux, graduate of Bosque University, theological degree from a Baptist seminary in Fort Worth, Texas. Much of the press release stressed Barrilleaux's football exploits which, in Carl Henry's opinion, was a good indicator of the mentality of church-goers, how much they were impressed by so-called Christian jocks.

Sort of like some of the early Roman gladiators spearing and cutting up unarmed people in the arena, he thought. All of that would have been okay if the gladiator had done it in the name of Christianity.

The press release mentioned that Barrilleaux was a big wheel in the Fellowship of Christian Athletes, but the part of the story that interested Carl Henry most was in the last paragraph. The sentence said Barrilleaux was married and had one child, a son.

Carl Henry was pissed about the tone of the news release, the fact it stressed Barrilleaux's athletic accomplishments as though they were vital to his religious convictions. He had seen his share of ads in newspapers touting professional athletes as speakers in churches, as though they had some special pipeline to God.

It seemed to him that many churches demanded their religious heroes be athletes, former dope addicts, drunkards or whoremongers. There were also the weirdos who derived great satisfaction from preaching Jesus to strippers on Bourbon Street in New Orleans, who after doing so took their tales of depravity to the churches.

Another biggy in evangelical churches was the former Catholic priest who had seen the light, and who was now willing to recite all the ills of Rome to willing Protestant audiences. And there was always the Jew who had found Jesus.

It's all a bunch of shit, all a game, he thought.

He remembered a Dago girl he had slept with a couple of years before at a newspaper convention, some of the things she had told him about her experiences in a parochial school. She told him that in a marriage and family class the girls had been taught to hold their legs in a certain way after intercourse, so as not to allow any sperm to escape. He was not sure Catholic schools in the southwest taught that. He had met the girl in a bar in Oklahoma City. He couldn't remember her name, but she was from New Jersey.

He realized he was playing a game, trying to clutter his mind with all sorts of thoughts to escape thinking about the sentence referring to T.J. and the child. He couldn't get thoughts about T. J. out of his subconscious.

He told the editor to cut all references to Barrilleaux's football prowess from the story, to mention only that he played football at Bosque and that he was a member of the Fellowship of Christian Athletes.

Just like the sonofabitch to become a preacher, he thought. He was always the original Mr. Clean.

It was hard to get T. J. out of his mind. It was, in fact, impossible. Having her reappear in his life made him realize just how much he once cared for her. He wondered if he still did.

He also wondered how she would react to seeing him. It had been a long time. He tried to remember how she looked, but couldn't.

The years have probably changed her, he thought. They've changed me. For the better, though. Men seem to get better looking with age, but not women.

He wondered about the child. A boy the story said. He would be six, no, seven now. Was it possible that the child looked like him? He wanted to see the boy, and he wanted to see T.J.

Those were his thoughts throughout the day, until five-thirty when he met Barbara at the Honeymate Lounge.

With Barbara he could forget. He could forget T.J. and the child, Yvonne and his children, Veronica and her bullshit. He could forget anything and everything, because Barbara was truly a beautiful woman, all he could ever want in a woman.

She started to work for the newspaper in August, following graduation from the University of Texas. She had been married for about three months to Conrad Neeley, a youngish looking twenty-four year old who was already developing a pot belly. From the time he saw them together, Carl Henry thought Conrad and Barbara were an unlikely looking couple.

He heard Conrad's parents had money, which he figured might be the reason Barbara married him. He could think of no other reason.

It might also explain why she was driving a new Porsche and Conrad was driving a new BMW. They were not the type cars normally seen around Bethel, and the couple certainly couldn't afford them on their salaries.

As far as Carl Henry was concerned, anything and everything about Barbara's reasons for marrying Conrad were superfluous. The important thing was that they had met, he liked what he saw, and she obviously liked what she saw.

Regardless of any magic that existed between them, he knew she would not be an easy lay. It was his persistence that finally made her consent to having a drink with him. And it was no coincidence he had sent Conrad out of town on banking business.

"Here I am, Barb." He was standing to the right of the door as she entered the lounge.

She had difficulty adjusting her eyes from the bright sunlight to the dimly-lit room, but then said, "Aha, now I have you in focus. I'm glad to see you."

"And I'm glad to see you."

"God, this conversation is original," she laughed. "But let's not overdo this business of who is most glad to see whom, or whatever. Let's get a drink."

They made their way to a booth at the back of the lounge and sat across from each other. A cocktail waitress came over to take their order.

"What are you having?" he asked.

"J.B. and water."

"I'll have the same," he said. He couldn't help but notice the cocktail waitress was new, and that she had great looking legs.

"Do you have to undress every woman you see?" Barbara asked, laughing.

"That obvious, huh?"

"It sure is," she replied, "and it doesn't do a lot for my ego. Of course, you undressed me the first day you saw me, and there's no telling how many times since."

"I didn't know I was so transparent," he laughed. "What makes you think I undress every woman I see?"

"Not every woman," she teased, "only the pretty ones. Your eyes really give you away. I hope you're not going to try to deny this accusation, because I'm sure I can get numerous women witnesses to support the allegation. And you should be ashamed, being a married man, father, bulwark and pillar of virtue in the community."

"Whoa," he laughed, glad she was in a playful mood. It was a good sign. "If I wanted someone to bitch at me, I could go home."

"That's probably what you should do," she advised in semi-serious fashion. "What did you tell your wife, that you were going to work late at the office?"

"That's what I told her."

"That's awful, but I was pretty sure you didn't tell her you were meeting a sexpot like me."

"Hey, it's not just a matter of not going home," he confided. "I'm also missing football practice."

"Football practice?"

"That's right. I coach a peewee football team."

"My god, I hope the building doesn't fall in on us. I certainly don't want to be responsible for interferring with the holiest of holies, King Football."

"Hey, it's no big deal."

"Shhh. Remember where you are and watch what you say. If anyone hears you talking like that, you'll be accused of being a Communist."

"I am."

"What?"

"Just kidding."

"You'd better be. For all you know, I'm a card carrying member of the Daughters of the American Revolution."

"The possibility did cross my mind, you being a U.T. graduate and all."

"If I were fortunate enough to be a member of the D.A.R. or the National Rifle Association, I'd have you up against the wall."

"You're a bloodthirsty child."

"Not a child," she corrected. "Never a child."

"I do have to admit you don't look like a child."

"And what do I look like?"

"A very desirable woman."

"Thank god this assinine conversation is coming to an end," she said. "Our drinks are here." As the waitress placed the drinks before them, Barbara asked her, "What's your name?"

"Dora."

"You see this man sitting across from me, Dora?"

"Yes."

"This man is not to be trusted."

"I know," she replied matter-of-factly.

"You know?" Barbara questioned. "How do you know?"

"Some of the other cocktail waitresses warned me about him." Dora was young, not very sophisticated, and she had responded to Barbara's question in all innocence. Carl Henry and Barbara laughed. Dora joined in.

It was a nice evening, relaxing, no hassles. The lounge served food, so they had steaks and salads. And drinks, lots more drinks.

"Barb, I'm really glad you agreed to meet me here this afternoon."

"Well, you are the boss. I really didn't have much choice in the matter."

"Get off that bullshit."

"Oh, you know I'm glad I came," she said more seriously.

"I hope so."

"You don't have to hope."

"What time do you have to go home?" he asked.

"No special time. As you know, Conrad's out of town. You sent him, if you'll remember. But I guess you have to go pretty soon, don't you?"

"Naw. Yvonne just expects me when she sees me coming, and she probably couldn't see me now anyway. I imagine she's already in bed."

"It's just nine o'clock."

"It's not unusual for her to go to bed that early."

"For god's sake, I can think of only one reason for going to bed that early."

"Well, that's sure not the reason," he said. "We've never been very compatible in that sense, because I'm one of those people whose motor runs until about two o'clock in the morning."

"I guess her going to bed early makes for a great sex life, doesn't it?"

"There hasn't been much for the last few years."

"I bet you tell that to all the girls."

"Sure," he laughed, "and it's amazing how effective it is. Most of them feel so sorry for me that they can't wait to get their clothes off."

"It's probably not all sorrow that they feel."

"What else could it be?"

"You are an extremely handsome man, a very sexy one."

"And you're a very beautiful woman, a very desirable one."

"Well, now that it has been established just how fantastic we are, let's have another drink," she said.

"I'm for that." He signaled the waitress for two more of the same, then asked, "Where are you from, Barb?"

"Boerne, Texas."

"Boerne, Texas? Where in the hell is that?"

"It's pretty close to San Antonio."

"What in the hell does a person do for fun in Boerne, Texas?"

"About the same thing you do in Bethel."

"Nothing, huh? Do your folks still live in Boerne?"

"Yes, but didn't you read my resume before you hired me?"

"Hell, I never got past your legs."

"Male chauvenist pig."

"Those words are music to my ears."

"Which reminds me," she said, "I want to talk to you about the so-called society section of the paper."

"What about it?"

"I didn't get a degree in journalism to be a damn society editor. Any moron could handle all that assorted bullshit about parties, dances and weddings."

"What do you want to do?"

"Anything except that bullshit."

"Okay. Tomorrow I'll have our erstwhile editor assign you to something more befitting a U.T. grad. We'll see just how good you are."

"I'm goddam good."

"At everything?" he teased.

"At everything."

They sipped their drinks in silence for a few moments before he asked, "Where did you meet Conrad?"

"At the university."

"I do remember from his resume that he's from Corpus Christi. That's because I didn't bother checking his legs. Are his folks in business there?"

"Damn, you're full of questions," she said. "Didn't you interview Conrad before hiring him?"

"No, my mother hired him, not me."

"Well, his folks own a couple of dry cleaning stores in Corpus. They're pretty well off, which is why I have the Porsche. They gave it to me for a wedding present. Of course, they're certainly not in the same financial league with the Hayders."

"What makes you think I'm interested in that?"

"You're transparent as hell."

"Don't be so touchy," he said. "What does your dad do?"

"He works for the railroad, my mother's just a housewife, and I'm an only child," she said in hurried-up fashion.

"Don't get agitated," he said. "I'm just interested in knowing you better."

"Bullshit, Carl Henry. I've sat at the same table with you in the coffee room at the newspaper office, and I've listened to you question people. You just pry and pry until there's not a drop of information left in them. You know everything about everyone at the newspaper, but no one really knows a damn thing about you."

"I'm not very interesting."

"Bullshit again. Order me another drink."

He motioned for the waitress to bring two more.

"You keep everyone on the defensive," she continued. "No one has the nerve to ask you any questions because you're so intimidating. And that's just the way you want it."

"I'll tell you anything you want to know."

"Okay," she said, "how come a man like you, wealthy and with a beautiful wife at home, is spending the evening putting the make on me?"

He gave her credit for bluntness. "What makes you think I'm trying to put the make on you?"

"Oh hell, don't play games with me? Why don't you just come out and say what you want?"

"Okay, I want to fuck you," he angrily replied. "Is that simple enough?"

He was sorry he said it, saw she was sorry, too. They didn't talk for a while, just nursed their drinks. He broke the silence by asking, "Do you want to go for a ride, get a little fresh air?"

She nodded affirmatively, so he paid the tab and they stepped out of the lounge into the fall night. For the time of the year, it was cooler than normal, but not too cold to put the top down on the Cadillac convertible. He opened the door on the passenger side for her, then went around to the driver side. He felt a bit tipsy.

"This sonofabitch will really go," he said as they drove down the street. The car was powerful, a pleasure to drive, and he couldn't help but accelerate.

"Don't drive so fast," she commanded. "It wouldn't look too good if we were picked up together drunk and speeding."

"Don't worry," he said. "We own the fucking cops in this town. We own the fucking state police, too."

She played with the radio dial until she found some good music. Moments later they were heading down a winding country road that led to the river. They sat quietly, listening to the hum of the car's engine and to the music.

After several miles she interrupted their silence. "Stop the car when you come to a side road."

Moments later he found one and did as she asked. The moon was so bright it was almost like daylight.

"I told you not to play games with me," she said, "and all the time I've been playing games with you."

He didn't respond, just leaned back in the seat and looked straight ahead.

"From the first time I saw you, I've been interested in you," she confessed. "I fought my feelings because you're married and I'm married. I've been afraid I would eventually give in to my feelings and today I did, by agreeing to have a drink with you after work.

"I convinced myself it wouldn't do any harm, that we'd have a drink and thirty minutes later we'd both go home. The problem is that I didn't want to leave you in thirty minutes, and I don't want to leave you now."

"You don't have to leave me."

"But I do. You're another woman's husband and I'm another man's wife."

It sounded like a recording to Carl Henry. He had heard similar statements from numerous married women over the years. When he heard them, he knew one thing for sure. He was going to score.

"The problem is that I care for you very much," she continued, "and I really can't explain why. It's crazy. I have everything a girl could want, a loving husband, a . . ."

He turned off her guilt. "Look, baby, I don't hassle anybody, and I'm sure not going to hassle you into doing something you don't want to do. Probably the best thing would be for me to take you back to your car right now, and I'll do that if it's what you want."

He knew it was the last thing she wanted.

"I don't know," she whimpered. "I don't know what to do."

That's when he played his trump card, one he thought would have made his grandfather proud.

"Look, Barbara, it's crazy and I probably shouldn't say it, but I think I'm in love with you."

"But we've known each other such a short time."

"Who says time has anything to do with love?" he asked. "What's the set amount of time you have to know someone to love them. I get a little pissed off about this business of time. Knowing someone a long time doesn't assure that you'll love them. I've known my wife for years and I don't love her."

"You don't."

"No, I don't," he said emphatically. "I thought I did when I married her, but it was really just a case of feeling an obligation to her. I got in her pants when we were in high school, so I figured I was indebted for life."

"I don't love Conrad."

"I know that."

"How did you know?"

"The two of you don't match up," he said. "You're a beautiful, intelligent woman and he's a clown." He knew women liked to be told they were intelligent, even moreso than being told they were beautiful. Using the two compliments in combination normally worked miracles. In truth, he never gave women much credit for being intelligent.

"He's good to me."

"Is that what love is, being good to someone?"

"No," she responded, "love is what I feel for you."

"I hope that's true."

"It is."

He pulled her over and kissed her tenderly, though passion

boiled within him. The passion could be released later, but he didn't want to frighten her now.

She responded to his kiss and whispered, "Just hold me."

They all want to be hugged, he thought. They clutch at something that's not there.

They were soon driving to the house where she and Conrad lived, touching but not talking the entire way. He helped her out of the car and they walked up on the porch. As they entered the door she would have turned on the light, but his hand stopped hers at the switch. He pulled her body against his and kissed her, this time releasing all the passion within him. He scooped her into his arms and she directed him to the bedroom.

He undressed her first, then himself. Then they made love.

"Oh, darling," she whispered, "I didn't know it could be so different."

After their lovemaking, he was ready to go home. Then Barbara reminded him she had left her car at the lounge. By the time he drove her back to the lounge, he was ready for her again. He fucked her in the front seat of the Cadillac, with the top up.

CHAPTER
THIRTY-FIVE

CARL HENRY went to church the Sunday after the affair with Barbara began. He didn't go out of a sense of guilt. He was past that. He didn't even go to his own church. He went to the First Baptist Church, the church where Tim Barrilleaux was pastor. He wasn't anxious to see Barrilleaux, but he was curious about T. J. and the child.

At breakfast that morning, Yvonne tried to persuade him to go to church with her. But he begged off, pretending to be too tired. Yvonne accepted one excuse from him as well as another. She knew he just didn't want to go, and lately there had been enough conflict in their marriage without starting an argument about religion.

He was still at the breakfast table, working on his fourth cup of coffee and reading the paper, when Yvonne and the children left. They left early because they were going to Sunday School. He admired Yvonne's persistence in seeing that their children attended church regularly, because they didn't want to go either.

After they left he shaved and showered, applied stick deodorant to his underarms, rubbed his body with a generous portion of Johnson Baby Powder, splashed on some cologne, and admired the nakedness of his body in the mirror when combing his hair.

He selected a dark gray suit and light gray dress shirt from his closet. Choosing a tie was more difficult. He always had difficulty selecting a tie. He finally settled on a blue and gray striped one.

After dressing, he checked himself in the mirror and liked what he saw.

He arrived at the First Baptist Church at eleven. The congregation was already standing and singing.

Amazing, the fervor of these Baptists, he thought. They drink, fornicate and steal like everyone else, but they sure do like their religion hot and heavy. Maybe that's an unfair assessment of Baptists, because I don't guess you can judge all of them by the sonofabitches that I know. I should be more objective, being a journalist and all.

His thinking amused him, because he didn't know any objective journalists.

Glancing about at the singing Baptists, Carl Henry thought, Grandad's right. Most of these bastards don't know what Christianity is all about. They're just a bunch of fucking sheep. They'd screw their neighbor in a minute if they could benefit from it.

He tried to spot T. J., but the church was too crowded. He certainly had no trouble spotting Barrilleaux. He was sitting in a high-backed chair on the platform, piousity all over his face.

Piousity, is that a word? he wondered. Who the hell cares? I might not be able to recognize T. J. It has been a while.

As the service continued he stood, sang, sat and bowed his head on command, thinking all the while, we're all just like robots. We do what we're told and never question why.

He kept scanning the congregation for T. J., but with no luck. He did spot several beautiful women he figured would be worth knowing.

Some fine looking snatch here, he thought. I always spot a lot of stuff I'd like to screw when I go to church. I must really be fucked up in the mind. Religion does that to you, though. It really fucks up your mind. Joe Bob Stewart's a good example of that.

Joe Bob was a former seminary student who had given up his life's commitment to God to work for Carl Henry's newspaper. Carl Henry and Joe Bob had gotten drunk one night and the former seminarian had told his boss about his first attempt at getting a piece of ass. Carl Henry could remember the tale vividly.

"I was fifteen," he had said, "and this friend of mine told me if I'd take this girl out she would fuck on the third date. I was the last guy in school to even know she was putting out.

"Anyway, I asked her out and she said yes. Hell, I was so anxious for the third date that I bought a pack of rubbers before I went out with her the first time. I kept them in my wallet, which wasn't all that unusual. I guess everybody who was anybody kept a pack of rubbers in his wallet back then, though most guys eventually gave up on getting a piece and just jacked-off in them.

"On those first two dates we did a lot of necking and hunching, and I even tried to get some, but she was strictly a three-date girl. Shit, I thought I might even be in love with her. She would get me so stirred up that I'd come in my shorts, and back then I equated sperm and love equally.

"But shit, there was also the church to think about. My mother was always sending me on a guilt trip, bouncing all this religious stuff around in my head. My mother, the preacher and my Sunday School teacher laid so much Scripture on me that I was convinced that the only Christian thing to do with a girl you were fucking was to marry her.

"And I'll say this without apology. When that girl put her hand on my dong the second time we were out, I was ready to propose. I didn't, of course. Even back then some infinite wisdom was looking out for me.

"Finally that third date came around. Now, keep in mind that I was wrestling with my religious convictions at the time and maybe, just maybe, you can understand what happened.

"There was no doubt she was ready. We started out in the front seat of the car and ended up in the back. I don't mind admitting that my hands were trembling, but I finally got her

panties off. All this time we were doing some hot and heavy necking, and she had hold of my old dong. I swear I felt like I was
going down for the third time, because it was all I could do to
keep from shooting off all over the car.

"Of course, that worried me. I was afraid I might stain the
seats or not be able to get the smell out. And my mother has
one of the best noses and best sets of eyes in the world.

"It took some doing, but I got the rubbers out of my wallet
and opened them. I'd never used a rubber before, even to jackoff,
so it took me some time to comprehend how you unroll one onto
your dick.

"After discovering how to get the first one on, I began to wonder
why they put three in a package. I figured it was because a guy
like me might shoot off so strong that he'd tear through the first
one, so the other two were for safety purposes. I put all three of
them on.

"Once my dick had three layers of armor, I was ready. Unfortunately, when she took it in her hand, I lost control. So, there lay
my sperm safely in the end of three rubbers. I tried to apologize
to the girl, but she said it was no big deal, which didn't do a lot
to make me feel better.

"I saw her in church the next day and kept trying to apologize
to her. Maybe I overdid it because she finally told me to just
leave her alone, that she never wanted to see me again.

"I felt so bad that day that when the invitation was given I
went down the aisle and rededicated my life to God. I tell you,
Carl Henry, between mother and the church, I was one mixed
up mother fucker."

He knew Joe Bob was full of bullshit, but there was some truth
in his story.

That's all the church is good for, he thought, to mix up some
poor, dumb mother fucker. It's not God's fault, though. It's all
these stupid sonofabitches who claim to be Christians.

The singing ended and Barrilleaux began his sermon. Carl Henry
had to admit he was impressive. He made all the right motions
and said all the right things. He kept referring to *we* throughout
the sermon. Carl Henry supposed he was talking about himself
and God.

People are so damn pious, he thought.

Barrilleaux preached from some of the Apostle Paul's writings, stuff like *All have sinned and come short of the glory of God,* and *There is none righteous, no not one.* Carl Henry had heard it all before.

People think I'm cynical, he thought. Hell, Paul was more cynical than I am. Paul was right about one thing. People are just no damn good.

The sermon ended and Barrilleaux invited non-Christians to accept Christ and join the church. The congregation stood and sang the invitational hymn and a few souls moved down the aisle to join the church.

The standing, the singing, the invitation, the prayer . . . these were all things to be endured. Finally it was over.

Barrilleaux stationed himself in the foyer to greet the departing churchgoers. Carl Henry was among the last to leave.

"How are you, Tim?"

He watched the look of surprise on the preacher's face, then Barrilleaux flashed a plastic smile.

"Carl Henry Hayder. I knew you lived here, of course, but I sure didn't expect to see you today. How long has it been?"

"A few years," Carl Henry said.

"How's your family?"

"They're fine. How about yours?"

"Fine. I don't know whether you know, but we have a son."

You'd better believe I know, you stupid bastard, Carl Henry thought, but said, "Yes, I read it in the press release sent to the paper."

"Oh, here's Tommie Jean and Timmy now," he said. "Tommie, you remember Carl Henry Hayder, don't you?"

She had come up from his blind side, and as he turned their eyes met momentarily before she looked away.

"Hello, Tommie."

"Hello, Carl Henry. It's nice to see you."

She was a bit pudgy, and her cheeks were flushed by the unexpected encounter. She gave him the same plastic smile he had received from Barrilleaux.

They must teach it at the seminary, he thought.

"This must be Timmy," Carl Henry said, reaching down and shaking hands with a good-looking boy who seemed uncomfortable in a suit and tie.

"Mr. Hayder was in college with daddy and mommy," Barrilleaux said to the boy. "He owns the newspaper here."

Carl Henry thought the boy was too old to have his parents referred to as *mommy and daddy*.

"We're going on to the house, Tim," T. J. said nervously. "It's nice to see you again, Carl Henry."

"Nice to see you, Tommie."

"I'll be home in fifteen or twenty minutes," Barrilleaux said.

As she walked away, Carl Henry could not help but notice that T. J.'s hips had spread out considerably since he had last seen her. He tried to remember what she had been like in bed, but couldn't.

"Let us see you more often, Carl Henry," Barrilleaux said.

He hoped it would be the last time he saw the sonofabitch, but said, "I'll do that, Tim."

CHAPTER
THIRTY-SIX

Soaking in a tub of hot water gave him a nice feeling, and the cigar tasted good. Carl Henry seldom smoked, but for some unexplainable reason he had felt the need for a good after dinner cigar and a hot bath.

I must look pretty ridiculous, he thought, sitting here in the bathtub smoking a cigar and reading the newspaper, but what the hell . . . it feels good. People shouldn't worry so much about the way things look. They ought to concern themselves with the way things feel. Yvonne is always worrying about the way things look.

For instance, when she discovered he had gone to the First Baptist Church without her, she worried about what some of her friends might think, seeing him there alone.

"Hell, I didn't even know you had any friends who were Baptists," he said.

"Don't be silly," she countered. "There are lots of women in the clubs I belong to who are Baptists. Besides, I would like to have seen Tommie and Tim, too. And another thing, I thought you were feeling too rotten to go to church."

"I was when you brought it up," he lied, "but I got to feeling better and decided to wander over and see how much Tim had changed, or if he had."

"Well, I would like to have seen them myself," she restated. "Would you like to invite Tim and Tommie over for dinner some night?"

"No, I wouldn't."

"Why not?"

"A better question would be, why?"

"After all, we were in college together."

"We were in college with lots of people, but I don't want to invite them over either."

"Well, being pastor of the largest church in town, Tim is pretty important in this community."

"Not as important as me."

"Sometimes you're impossible."

"Most times," he agreed. "Where's C. H.?"

"He's out in the backyard."

"I promised to play a little football with him. Rescue me in an hour, will you?"

"Only if you'll play with me a little."

"That sounds like a pregnant idea."

"That's not funny."

After he played with C. H., he and Yvonne made love. Just thinking about how pleasurable it was excited him.

Mentally addressing his penis, he thought, down boy. I have to give Yvonne credit. She can always stir me up. She's an exciting woman and I'm a stupid sonofabitch for being unfaithful to her. Of course, she pisses me off sometimes, but hell . . . everybody pisses me off. She's still the best piece I've ever had.

Shit, the worse piece I ever had was wonderful. I guess I've been looking for that super piece just like the Knights of the Round Table searched for the Holy Grail. Hell of a thing to do, spend your life looking for a fucking cup.

T. J. sure has changed. It's a crying-assed shame when a good looking woman like that just lets herself go. I have to give Yvonne credit for taking better care of herself than damn near any woman I know.

God, it seems like a million years ago that I screwed T. J. She doesn't even seem like the same woman now. I guess we've all changed, and who's to say . . . maybe she changed for the better. I can't really say that about myself.

I wonder what kind of salary Tim makes dribbling out all that shit on Sunday. I'll have to remember to get someone at the bank to check on it.

I don't know how I feel about the boy, not much of anything I guess. It's really hard to think of him as my son. It's funny, but I sort of wanted Tim to know he was my kid, that while he was shafting me out of my position on the football team I was putting it to his old lady. Hell, that's childish. There's no reason he should know. T. J. knows, and that's good enough. It sure wouldn't do the kid any good to know, and it wouldn't do C. H. and little Vivian any good either. It's best to let sleeping dogs lie.

But congratulations on a fine son, Tim Barrilleaux, courtesy of old Carl Henry Hayder.

CHAPTER THIRTY-SEVEN

CARL HENRY often went through seiges of melancholy, often thinking about the past and wondering about the rightness of some of his decisions. During these periods he often wished for a closer relationship with his father, one similar to that he enjoyed with his grandfather. But he angrily had to admit to himself that it was not meant to be, that his father's only close relationship was with the bottle.

He had often been tempted to ask his father about the woman from Virginia, but his grandfather had told him to let well enough alone. That didn't keep him from wondering about her, though. After all, he had a sister out there somewhere he had never seen, if the woman had told the truth.

Well, he thought, C. H. and Vivian have a brother they'll never know anything about if I have anything to do with it. It's different with me, though. My little affair didn't ruin everything.

There had been some good times with his father, of course,

before the booze started controlling his life. But even back when they had fished and hunted together, it was not the same as with his grandfather. He knew even then his father was weak, that his mother was strong.

Over the years, his father had grown increasingly weaker, not physically but mentally. He now felt absolutely no common bond with the man, even considered him an embarrassment to the family. He thought it might be far better for all concerned if he just died.

How much different grandad is than my own father, Carl Henry thought. He's so strong. Even though he's more than ninety years old, he's still full of life. He's disgusted with dad, too. The one thing the old man can't stand is weakness, especially on the part of a Hayder.

He appreciated the fact that Henry had taken C. H. under his wing, that he was now teaching him many of the things he had taught him when a boy.

C. H. is going to have to be strong, he thought, because he's the last of the Hayders. Maybe Yvonne and I should have another kid or two, just to make sure there's someone to carry on.

On these melancholy trips, Carl Henry and C. H. would often go swimming with the old man. He still swam every day in the creek by the old homeplace. They would also go fishing, and during these nostalgic times he would recall the first deer he had killed. He remembered it so vividly he often felt the same nausea he experienced then when field dressing the animal.

Life is so fleeting, he thought. I thought my days as kid would never end, that I'd never grow up and be a man. It's funny. You spend part of your life wanting to grow up, the other part longing for the freedom of youth. I guess everyone would like the chance to relive life again. I don't guess a man's ever satisfied with where he is, or with what he's got.

CHAPTER THIRTY-EIGHT

CARL HENRY met Mary Lou Jones when at his parents home. She was Anise Marie's granddaughter, the youngest of Edward's three daughters.

It seemed to Carl Henry that Anise Marie was constantly visiting his parents, which annoyed him to no end. It was like she was always trying to establish herself as his grandmother's replacement. The only thing about Anise Marie that pleased him was that his grandfather had never married her.

In fact, it was very difficult for him to understand how the old man could put up with her bullshit. She paraded around as though she owned the town, just like she was a Hayder.

The old man had asked Carl Henry to make sure Anise Marie was provided for after his death. It was the only request his grandfather had ever made of him that he didn't plan to fulfill.

Fuck her, he thought.

"Carl Henry, I want you to meet my granddaughter, Mary Lou."

He rose from a semi-prone position on the couch and gave a casual salute with his right hand. He had been watching television.

"I was wondering if you'd mind telling Mary Lou about journalism," she continued. "I told her you knew all about it."

Goddamn, he thought, the old bitch can make some of the most assinine requests.

"Anything specific, or do you want me to take about ten seconds and tell her everything I know?" he quipped. Like Henry, he was always sarcastic with her, but it didn't do any good. She was too dense to understand sarcasm.

He could see, however, that the girl read him loud and clear, and that she was uncomfortable. "Have a seat, Mary Lou, and I'll try to answer any questions you might have, but I warn you the only expert status I have has been bestowed on me by your grandmother."

"I really don't want to disturb you from watching television," she said.

She was a slightly built girl, with silky-looking blonde hair that touched her shoulders. Her clothes were not revealing, but he could tell that she had a beautiful body. Pretty legs, firm tits.

I'd say she wears about a C-cup bra, he thought. If the gossip around town is correct and Edward is really grandad's son, then Mary Lou is my cousin. She's damn sure the best looking cousin I've got.

"Well, Mary Lou, ordinarily I'd be pissed if someone interrupted my television watching, but I've probably seen this Tarzan movie twelve times, and it has ended the same way every time. There's about a hundred percent chance it's going to end the same way again. But there's always the chance of a different ending with a beautiful young woman, so have a seat."

"You're very flattering," she said, taking a chair facing the couch.

"She is pretty, isn't she?" Anise Marie said.

He considered it one of her more inane comments and said, "She certainly is," thinking, the remarkable thing is that she's related to you, bitch.

"Carl Henry's a lot like his grandfather," Anise Marie said. "He appreciates beautiful women."

You saggy-titted old bitch, he thought, always bringing the old man up in every conversation. Have you told your granddaughter that he's fucking you, that he's her grandfather, too?

He mentally pictured a bulldozer running over Anise Marie, her mouth still going full force when the gleaming silver blade covered her up.

He dismissed her with, "Mom and dad are in the kitchen having coffee, Anise Marie. Why don't you join them?"

"Well, you two talk and I'll go visit with Carl and Vivian," she said.

When she left Mary Lou said, "She talks a lot."

"Yeah, she does," he agreed. "What did you need to talk to me about?"

"Nothing really. I just happened to mention that I work for the school newspaper and she insisted that I talk to you. She called your mother earlier and found out that you were here."

"That figures. Where are you going to school?"

"Northeast State."

"And majoring in journalism."

"Yes, with a minor in sociology."

"I guess that's a good combination if a person is crazy enough to be a journalist. Are you planning to work for a newspaper?"

"I don't know yet. I'm sort of thinking about broadcast journalism or public relations."

"The money is better in either of those fields, but I'm sort of prejudiced toward the printed word."

"Listen," she said, apologetically, "I really don't want to take up your time."

"You're not," he assured. "Have you ever tried to find something to do in Bethel? It's hell, and a real live person to talk to is a big improvement over television reruns."

"God, don't I know it. Back before I started to college my parents dragged me down here at least once a month. Daddy is such a momma's boy."

"You might offend me talking like that," he teased. "For all you know, I might be a momma's boy."

"I know enough about you to know you're not anybody's boy."

"I wouldn't touch that statement with a ten-foot pole."

"Well, grandmother does talk about you an awful lot. I've been hearing things about you since I was a little girl."

"You're making me feel old," he said.

"Sorry."

"Don't be. I probably am old in your estimation."

"You're just a little over thirty."

"That's right, so that makes me untrustworthy with young girls."

"I'll bet you are, too, but not because you're over thirty. I have a feeling you've been untrustworthy in that respect for a long time."

"Now what do you mean by that?"

"I'm sure you know, just as I'm sure every woman who meets you would agree with me."

"What can I say. Might I inquire as to your age?"

"I'm a very robust twenty-one."

"I'll just bet you are."

They both enjoyed the banter, and he was very much aware there was a magic between them. They talked for more than an hour. He was sorry when Anise Marie came back into the room and announced to Mary Lou that it was time to go.

Carl Henry met Mary Lou in late spring, and he didn't see her again until the first week in June. The June meeting was not accidental.

A few days after their initial conversation, he received a letter from Mary Lou. It came to him at the newspaper office and was delivered to his desk by the old man who worked as mail clerk and did cleanup work in the back shop.

"This one has the smell of perfume about it," the old man said, grinning.

He wished the old man would have his teeth cleaned.

"Well, Charlie, these bill collectors are getting trickier by the day," he said.

He leaned back in the chair and opened the envelope, noting that it had a return address. Basically, it was just a note of thanks. However, the last sentence expressed the hope that they would have the opportunity to talk again soon.

He received her letter in the morning and, while drinking a

cup of coffee that afternoon, decided to reply. His initial letter was like hers, cautious.

It was a beginning. Her letters began to come frequently, two or three a week, and he responded. There was more unsaid than said in every letter. The letter he enjoyed most was the one where she said she planned to spend part of the summer with her grandmother, that she would be in Bethel the first week in June.

Carl Henry wasn't sure why he was pursuing the situation with Mary Lou, nor could he be sure why she seemed so interested in him. He figured he would follow up on it though, because he always played the cards dealt to him. He never really knew why. Maybe it was because his relationship with Yvonne fluctuated so much.

One week he would feel his relationship with Yvonne had deteriorated to the point where it could never be repaired, and the next week he might feel an intense and abiding love for her. He was aware his feelings for Yvonne fluctuated on the basis of his relationships with other women, and on whether he had close contact with his children. When he felt especially close to his children, that's when he most detested his relationships with other women. That's when he wanted to hold Yvonne close, that's when he wanted to love only her.

He had begun to feel that closeness to Yvonne when the letter came from Mary Lou. The letter reminded him of the afternoon they shared together, the closeness they had begun to feel before Anise Marie took her away. He had thought it would be the end of it until the letter came.

Then he began to wonder how Mary Lou would be in bed, whether she had ever been to bed with anyone.

Someone's probably had her, he thought. Cherries are hard to come by nowadays, and that's really a shame, too.

He tried to remember how many virgins he had made.

Yvonne and Gloria, he thought, and some other chick when I was a freshman in college. I can't remember her name. I could have been shutout, though.

CHAPTER
THIRTY-NINE

L ET'S DUCK in here," Carl Henry said, taking Mary Lou by the hand and breaking into a trot toward the barn. The rain had just started, one of those summer thunderstorms that come up suddenly, without warning. By the time they were inside, the rain was coming down in sheets.

"Whew, I bet my hair is a mess," she said.

He was still holding her right hand with his left, and with his right hand he stroked her hair and said, "Hardly a drop on your pretty little head."

"I feel awfully damp."

"Cold?"

"A little." A clap of thunder shook the barn, causing her to shudder and continue, "Well, our little Sunday stroll turned into a fiasco."

"I don't know about that," he said. "I think it's kind of nice here."

273

"Whose barn is this?"

"It's one of grandad's."

The barn was still partially filled with winter hay, and the rain accentuated its sweet smell. The stacatto beat of raindrops on the tin roof lent a feeling of vitality to the building's semi-darkness.

He had called Anise Marie's house that Sunday morning, at a time when he knew she would be in church. Mary Lou had answered the phone and said, "I'm so glad you called. I wanted to see you yesterday, but there was no way without being obvious."

"Yeah, I know. How does it look for today?"

"Good, I think. I'm pretty sure grandmother plans to visit your parents house this afternoon."

"Great. Do you know where Lewis Road crosses Ayish Creek?"

"Yes."

"We could meet there at two o'clock."

"I'm really a little scared, Carl Henry. This is a pretty small town and someone might see us."

"Who gives a damn?" then as an afterthought added, "I give a damn, of course, and I'm sure you do. I can understand your not wanting to be seen with me. Maybe you should just come over to my parents house with your grandmother."

"I would rather see you without a lot of people around."

"There's not much chance of that there, and anything we do other than sit in the living room could be misinterpreted."

"Maybe we ought to risk meeting at the creek."

"That's up to you."

"Okay, let's do it, but would you mind getting there a little early? That's a lonely road and I would be afraid to wait there by myself."

"I'll be early."

He was, about fifteen minutes before she arrived. And now they were in the barn. They had been walking down a dirt road when the storm came up.

"Well, here we are," she said. "After two months and God knows how many letters, we're together again. Do you know why, Carl Henry?"

"I don't guess I do, Mary Lou. Didn't you want to see me?"

She shrugged her shoulders and said, "Yes, but I really don't know why. I just wanted to see you."

"Well, I wanted to see you, too."

"I guess I'm just a little scared."

"Why?"

"I can't really explain it. I just have these feelings for you that I don't understand."

"What sort of feelings?"

Her voice registered resignation as she said, "I don't know, but I do know they're wrong because you're married."

"Do you think I'd be here if I didn't have strong feelings for you?" He was still holding her hand. "The first day we talked at my folks house I knew there was a kind of magic between us."

"I knew it, too."

"Then I don't think there's anything to be afraid of," he said.

"I do," she countered. "I don't want to get hung up on someone who's married."

"Sometimes people don't really have a choice as to who they care for. I know I would prefer to care only for my wife, but I don't. I don't think I've ever really cared for her."

"Carl Henry, please don't feed me any phony lines. I don't need that."

"Look, baby, I don't have to feed you any phony lines. I'm past that. You don't know me very well or you'd know I wouldn't play games with you about something like this."

"This is all so hopeless. This whole conversation is so . . ."

He interrupted the sentence by pulling her body against his and kissing her tenderly. She wanted to protest, but she wanted to respond even more. There was an awkwardness at first, the kind of awkwardness that exists between two people who don't know what to expect of each other.

"This is wrong," she said, pulling her mouth away from his.

"No, it's not," he whispered.

He found her lips again and they kissed for a long time, holding each other tightly while the storm intensified. They were soon

lying on a mattress of dry hay, smelling its aroma, kissing passionately. The rain pounded the tin roof unmercifully, but they were
oblivious to it.

He tore her panties from her, then removed his pants. Then
he was on top of her, feeling a fiery heat surging through him
when he penetrated her. They moved in unison then, the ecstacy
expressed with groans of pleasure.

After they had finished their lovemaking, they lay quietly holding each other, listening to the music of the rain.

Carl Henry broke the silence with, "Was this your first time?"

Her answer disturbed him because it was, "No, I was engaged
to a boy last year, and we made love several times before breaking
up."

He felt cheated, but without emotion asked, "Why did you
break up?"

"Does it matter?"

"No, I was just curious."

"If you must know, we would have been disasters to each other.
I didn't love him and he didn't love me. Getting married seemed
to be the right thing to do at the time, but I realized it would
have been a marriage of convenience. The closer it came to time
for the wedding, the more I came to realize that it would never
work."

"Well, maybe you're just more perceptive than most people.
Most people would have gone ahead and gotten married, maybe
gotten a divorce later. It's tough to admit you're wrong."

"It sure is," she laughed. "My mother was really excited about
the wedding, and now she's afraid I'm going to be an old maid."

"I doubt that's even a remote possibility."

"Well, I'll tell you one thing," she said, emphatically, "I'm not
going to settle for second best. I'd rather be an old maid than do
that."

"I can identify with that."

"You can," she said with a tinge of sarcasm. "I thought you
did settle for second best."

"You mean with Yvonne?"

"Yes."

There was resignation in his voice as he said, "I guess I did. It's pretty easy to make a mistake when you're young."

How can I call it a mistake, he thought, when I've got two fine children?

He often felt sadness after making love to a woman other than Yvonne.

"It's hard for me to believe that we made love on just our second meeting," she said. "I still can't believe it. You affect me in some ways I just don't understand."

"Time doesn't have a lot to do with it when two people care for each other."

"That's true, but I'm not at all sure about my feelings toward you, and I don't believe in so short a time you can honestly know your feelings toward me."

"I know I care about you."

"But do you love me?"

Normally, he might have told her he loved her, but he didn't want to expose himself in this relationship. He didn't want to express love first, to be the vulnerable one.

"What's love?" he asked. "I'm not at all sure I know what love is."

"You don't make it very easy. I guess I suspected I was in love with you the first time we met."

"And now?"

"I'm almost sure, but you don't have to worry about it. I'm not going to spread it around."

Pulling her close he said, "I'm sure not worried about it."

"You should be. You have a wife and two children."

"My life with her has been over for a long time, and kids are resilient. Besides, with the kind of money the Hayders can provide, they'll be well cared for. I care for you, Mary Lou, and I want you."

It was all so crazy. He was startled by his own words because they sounded so true.

"You say that now, but . . . ."

"Hush," he interrupted. "Sometimes people spend too much time talking."

He pulled her close and began kissing her, but she pulled away and said, "And sometimes people don't talk enough. Maybe if I had spent more time talking and less time feeling, I wouldn't be in this mess now."

"Honey, this is the nicest mess I can imagine."

"Yeah, for you it probably is."

Her act was beginning to piss him off.

Why are they all like this? he thought. They always act as though they are forced into fucking.

He had hoped she would be above all the bullshit, that she would just simply admit she craved him as much as he craved her.

"I take it you think this was all a mistake," he said. "I guess it was, but there's not much we can do about rectifying it at this point."

With the proper amount of hurt in her voice she said, "That's a fine thing to say after we've already made love."

"I guess it was a piss poor thing to say," he admitted.

But goddammit, he thought, it's not like I'd gotten a cherry. She's been fucked before.

"I'm just being a bitch," she said. "Things just happened so quickly between us. I guess I really haven't gotten my bearings where you're concerned."

"That's understandable."

"It's just very important to me that you don't think I'm the kind of woman who sleeps with just any man who comes along."

"I don't think that at all," he said. "I think you're very special, and I don't think you would have made love to me if you didn't care a great deal about me."

"You're right about that. Even though we haven't known each other that long, from the first time I saw you I just couldn't get you out of my mind. I can't explain why."

"You boggled my mind, too."

That's the way it was between them on that Sunday in June.

For Carl Henry, being with Mary Lou was beautiful, but being apart from her was miserable. He had begun to think he had discovered real love, something he deluded himself into thinking he had been searching for all his life.

That summer they spent every possible moment together. They made love on the front seat of his car, on a blanket beside Ouachita Creek, in the barn where they first had each other, and in various motel rooms throughout the area. The barn was by far their sentimental choice for lovemaking, but as the summer wore on it became unbearably hot.

Yvonne did not notice any particular change in her husband that summer. She had no quarrel with their sex life. Carl Henry was always ready to make love to her. In fact, he wanted to make love with a great deal more regularity than she did, which had been the case since early in their marriage.

Her only real complaint about their lovemaking was that he was not verbally tender enough prior to intercourse, nor was he interested in much foreplay. That really didn't seem strange, however, because his aggressiveness had always overruled his expressiveness.

He was, that summer, showing an inordinate amount of interest in business. It seemed he was always going on a business trip, but that didn't bother her either. She had a lot of club work to keep her busy, and when Carl Henry was around the house for long periods of time, he could be very demanding.

While Yvonne labored with various club duties, Carl Henry and Mary Lou were busy making love in motel rooms from just a few miles west of Bethel all the way to Oklahoma City and Tulsa. They rarely stayed in the same motel.

Mary Lou's primary complaint with Carl Henry was that he watched too much television. They would make love and he would then, almost immediately, turn on the television set. She spent considerable time trying to distract him from watching baseball games.

Summer and fall gave way to winter, and by then Yvonne was becoming a bit concerned about Carl Henry's absence from home. He was spending very little time with the children, and this became a source of contention.

It was not that Carl Henry did not care for his children, but

rather a matter of his desire for Mary Lou intensifying to such
an extent he was reacting without reason, much like a male dog
following a bitch in heat. Caution had given way to lust.

Mary Lou spent that Christmas with her grandmother. She met
Carl Henry at the barn early on Christmas Eve and, though it
was cold, they stayed there together past midnight. He had
brought two bottles of good wine, so they drank, made love and
talked. It was the first time he had talked seriously about leaving
Yvonne so he could marry Mary Lou.

She wasn't sure whether to believe him, but she wanted to
. . . desperately. She hoped it wasn't just the wine talking.

Leaving Yvonne was on his mind when he crawled into bed
beside her about one o'clock Christmas morning. There was much
planning to do, and he would have to talk to the old man. That
bothered him most, wondering how his grandfather would react.

Yvonne stirred from her slumber and said, "Have you been
out celebrating with the boys?"

"Yeah."

"That's nice," she responded, then went back to sleep.

At first he was grateful that she didn't want to make love, but
then, the fact that she didn't, made him angry. He was tired,
though, so he went to sleep.

All Christmas Day he thought about discussing a divorce with
Yvonne, but the timing was all wrong. She was so happy. She
was always that way at Christmas. He decided not to ruin Christmas for Yvonne and the children. He would talk to her about it
after the holidays.

He saw Mary Lou Christmas night. She didn't mention the
divorce. They just made love. It was like she also didn't want
any unpleasantness during the Christmas season. It was too happy
a time.

It was a different story after the holidays.

Carl Henry really intended to confront Yvonne about the possibility of a divorce, but he kept putting it off. Mary Lou became
increasingly agitated with his explanation about the timing being
all wrong.

Carl Henry's reluctance was not from lack of courage. He possessed an abundance of that nebulous substance. It was merely a matter of him having second thoughts. There was also Henry with whom he would have to contend.

A few months earlier, he was sure that he couldn't live without Mary Lou. He now realized such thoughts were foolish, the mental assessment of a child. He didn't want to give Mary Lou up, but neither did he want to lose Yvonne. As it was, he had both. Why change things?

By late April he was meeting Mary Lou less frequently. Their love affair experienced a brief revival in May, but by then they both knew it was doomed. She suggested they call it off, knowing he would be relieved. She loved him too much to make him unhappy.

At the time, she didn't know she was pregnant. When she found out, she didn't bother to contact him. She didn't want him that way.

CHAPTER
FORTY

EDWARD JONES was a man who always accepted life as it came, believing if a man placed his trust in the Almighty he would be able to cope with any adversity that came his way. For that reason, he felt a special affinity for Job, often likening himself to that ancient Biblical character.

While in Bethel High School, Edward had done nothing to distinguish himself, though he did make excellent grades. Because he was shy, it was difficult for him to relate to other students, equally difficult for them to relate to him.

He never dated in high school, but often fantasized about being intimate with a number of the girls in his class. He curbed his desire by masturbating, usually two or three times a week. He always felt guilty about it, always prayed for God's forgiveness.

Edward figured masturbation was a sin, but considered it a lesser sin than sex out of wedlock.

Anise Marie had forbid Edward's participation in high school sports, though he probably wouldn't have participated anyway. It was not a matter of physical stature. He was very muscular, very strong, built along the lines of Henry Hayder.

Several girls in high school had wanted to date him, not merely because he was handsome, but also because they were intrigued by his shyness. Edward sensed their interest in him, but at the time he was too shy to take advantage of it.

His college life followed much the same pattern. He majored in business and didn't date until his senior year. He might not have dated then if Marilyn had not been so aggressive. She was the one who pushed the relationship.

A week after graduating from college, Edward took a job with an oil company and, a month later, married Marilyn. He was sure she was a virgin, and proud he was presenting himself to her as a virgin, too.

The job and the marriage stood the test of time. Though the company did not promote him as rapidly as it might have promoted a more aggressive employee, he stayed. The benefits were good, the salary increases regular.

And his marriage had been smooth. He had never even had a desire to be unfaithful to Marilyn.

Edward was still a fairly handsome man, though the once firm midrift had given way to a slight pauch, and the once thick black hair was now gray and thin. But life was good. He had the job, modest house, three-year-old car, three lovely daughters and a wife who loved him.

His social life consisted of going to church three times a week, and an occasional dinner out with Marilyn. His contentment multiplied when his daughters came to visit, though it was offset somewhat by their spouses and children. He was tolerant of his sons-in-law, though he felt they were not serious enough about their work. He liked his grandchildren, but they made him nervous.

Since their two older daughters primary interests were in their own families, he found himself increasingly reliant on Mary Lou's love for him. When she visited, they took long walks together. She did most of the talking, he listened.

So, when Marilyn told him that Mary Lou was pregnant, he

felt as though the breath had been knocked from his body and
would never return. He tried to be strong for his tearful wife,
but his shoulders sagged and millions of unshed tears waterlogged
his body.

Marilyn had visited Mary Lou, had found some letters, knew
the father of the unborn child was Carl Henry Hayder. That knowledge hurt Edward even more. He knew the stories about his
mother and Henry Hayder, but he never believed them. Even
now, with the old man in his nineties, he was distressed about
the amount of time his mother spent with Henry Hayder.

Edward did what he always did when adversity came. He
prayed. And in the course of his praying, he came to believe
that God had given him a direction and a solution to the problem.

That night he drove to Bethel.

CHAPTER FORTY-ONE

CARL HENRY was dreaming, about night falling on a parched land, about roaches coming from their hiding places in the fields and from the cracks and crevices of houses. He tried to stop them, but couldn't. They came to rule the night, doing what they have done for thousands of years, eating and copulating, copulating and eating, doing what is their entire reason for being.

He dreamed of ageless females laying thousands of eggs, resulting in millions more roaches coming forth to rule the night, eating and copulating, copulating and eating. The process was never-ending.

Then he dreamed about stomping the roaches, crushing them beneath his shoes, worrying about their filth seeping through the soles. But no sooner had he killed the roaches than the flies came, eating and copulating, copulating and eating. He swatted at them, smashed them, but there was no way to kill them all.

He awoke in a sweat thinking, most people are like flies and roaches, no purpose except eating and fucking. They ought to be killed.

Shit, he thought, if there's such a thing as reincarnation, I might even come back as a roach.

CHAPTER
FORTY-TWO

IT WAS early afternoon and rays from the August sun scalded the land. Carl Henry was lying on a couch in his parents den, watching the *Game of the Week*, oblivious to the outside heat. The drone of the air-conditioner competed with the sound emanating from the television set.

He was sort of semi-conscious because it was such a boring game. The Dodgers were leading the Pirates by seven, and the players on both teams seemed anxious for an end to their afternoon.

Carl Henry had downed several drinks during the course of the afternoon, mostly scotch and water. A half-empty glass was setting on the floor at the end of the couch, adjacent to the pillow where his head was positioned.

He heard the car screech to a stop in front of the house, but was too groggy to check on the identity of the driver. He figured his mother could do that.

It wasn't until he heard the footsteps, the front door opening, that he sat up on the couch. Seconds later he was looking at Edward Jones standing in the doorway of the den. The man was trembling, pointing a shotgun at him.

There wasn't time to be afraid. Carl Henry stood up and raised his hands in a futile protest, but Edward pulled the trigger anyway.

It was like a dream, but then the shot hit him in the chest like a sledgehammer and he felt himself being pushed backward by an uncontrollable force. An attempted protest lodged in his throat, and great weakness enveloped his entire body. He was falling, but it was as though he was falling in slow motion. It seemed as though he would never hit the floor, and he wanted to because he needed it for support. All the while he was looking at the big red splotch on the front of his shirt and, through glazed eyes, he could see Edward dropping the shotgun and disappearing from sight.

Run, you sonofabitch, run, he thought. Oh, shit.

His insides were on fire. He had never known such intense heat. But then, just as suddenly there was coldness. He was in the creek, swimming with his grandfather. The clear, cold water felt good.

He started swimming across the deepest part of the creek and the weakness came back again. He began to sink, into the black and the cold.

Then the fire came back, its flames licking at his chest, burning him. Through half-closed eyes he could see his mother's face, could see the tears streaming down her cheeks, and he realized his head was in her lap. Then the fire began to flicker and die, and he closed his eyes to sleep.

CHAPTER
FORTY-THREE

Y VONNE ARRIVED at the Hayder house just ahead of the ambu-
lance. When she walked into the den she saw Vivian sitting in
the floor, Carl Henry's head in her lap. Carl was sitting on the
couch, a stunned expression on his face, a cigarette dangling from
his mouth.

The blood on the floor and on Carl Henry's body nauseated
Yvonne almost to the point of vomiting through her tears. She
knew her husband was dead, and that knowledge drained all the
strength from her body.

"Why, Yvonne, why?" Vivian cried.

As Yvonne came closer to the body a roach seemingly came
from beneath it. She stepped on it.